I0773497

ANXIOUS TO WED

A Novel

FANNELI ROBLES

Oak Seed Publishing LLC
Newport Beach, California

Oak Seed Publishing LLC
PO Box 323
Tustin, CA 92781

ISBN 979-8-98758-863-5 (paperback)
ISBN 979-8-98758-867-3 (e-book)

Printed in the United States of America.

CONTENTS

HELP! I'VE CALLED AND I CAN'T HANG UP

've wanted to get married for as long as I can remember. As a kid, I couldn't wait to grow up, have a big wedding, and spend the rest of my life playing house. I wore down the plastic heels of my dress-up bridal shoes faster than I could outgrow them. At thirty-three years and two months old, I can say with some confidence that I am officially, if reluctantly, a grown-up. I have a responsible career as an insurance agent and an apartment in Costa Mesa, the "nice" part.

I drop my purse and keys on the kitchen counter, then slump onto the love seat in the living room. It's snug. The living room, dining room, and kitchen all blend into a tight "open floor plan." There's not enough room for a full-length sofa. Just the love seat and a single leather chair beside it. I squeeze my eyes shut and let out a breath, short and loud. The unfamiliar sound of it makes my eyes shoot open. I scan the room expectantly, but there's no one else there. I close my eyes again. Then place my hand over my chest. Feeling the quick thump of my heart against my palm. *Just breathe.* I let out another noisy breath. Then slowly open my eyes and look down at the neat stack of magazines on the coffee table. My shoulders sag, and the seams of my sleeveless dress dig into my underarms.

The stack, now covered with a thin layer of dust, showed up, unannounced, over a week ago and has silently tortured me since. *Fine, you win.* I reach for the top magazine and flip it open. A colorful image of a nouveau-red-dress-wearing bride strolling through a floral wonderland. My heart thuds. Flip. The page sticks to my palm. *It's stuffy in here.* The seams against my underarms feel damp. I spring up too fast, and the room spins slightly as I walk toward the thermostat.

I linger in front of the small gray screen until there's a loud whoosh from the air-conditioning vent, then resume my position on the love seat. I pick the magazine up again and stare at the happy couple holding hands on the cover without opening it. I feel my breath accelerate to a staccato, trying to match the pace of my now-racing heart. *Stop.* I set the magazine on the coffee table, happy couple facedown, to focus on inhaling. I close my eyes. *Take a deep breath.* But my lungs refuse to expand fully. *Just breathe.*

I need to leave. *If I go now, I can still make it in time.* Having failed to learn, I pop up again and feel the blood drain from my head. Then stagger through the living room to the bedroom closet in a woozy rush. Balancing myself against the closet shelves, I slough off my dress and let it fall in a pool at my feet. Then kick it aside into a wrinkled black heap. Rows of color-sorted clothing hang on each side of the closet. Its drawers filled with freshly folded sweaters and shirts, its shelves filled with purses. It smells like fabric softener and leather.

I grab a T-shirt from a drawer. Even light-headed I can't ignore the smell of sweat as I tug the shirt over my head. I stink. Not the way I smell after an hour at the gym but the way I had stunk after a final exam in college or a job interview. *Stress sweats.* I scrunch up my nose, then pull on a pair of jeans. I swipe on a fresh coat of deodorant as a muffled ring comes from inside my purse on the counter. I set down the stick of deodorant and don't bother to cap it. Then grab the phone just before the call goes to voice mail.

"Hey, Mom," I breathe into the phone as I tuck my hair behind my ear. I catch another whiff of sweat and grimace.

"Hi, Ruthie. Are you OK?"

"I'm fine." I pace back to the bedroom to reapply deodorant. "I'm running late for Bible study, though."

"Do you want to call me back after?"

"Well, actually, I wanted to ask you about something."

"What is it? What's wrong?" she asks, her voice shrill.

"Nothing." I sigh. "It's just . . . I've been doing this weird breathing thing lately. Do you think it's possible to develop asthma as an adult?"

"I don't know. I guess it's possible. I can call Doctor P to ask for you. I was just on the phone with him. How long has this been going on for? I wish you would have told me about it sooner. I would have asked him about it." Her words come out rushed.

"It's not a big deal, Mom. You know what? Never mind. Don't call Doctor Peterson. I'll call you later."

"No, it's fine. I'll call Doctor P and call you back."

"All right, but if I don't answer, it's because I'm in church, OK? I gotta go. Love you, Mom. Bye."

"Love you too! I'll call you back. Bye."

The phone beeps three times, signaling the call's end. I cap the deodorant, toss it in my purse, then rush out the door. I lock it. Then briefly consider running down the stairs. But the tightness in my chest makes me turn toward the elevator. The hallway is long. It smells old, like too many coats of paint and damp carpet, despite a recent remodeling. The elevator doors are open when I approach. I step inside and smack the button. By the time I reach the parking garage, I'm gasping. I stumble out of the elevator and watch my feet as I walk hurriedly to my car. *Am I OK to drive?* I shake my head and start the engine.

The freeway is a sea of red lights. I ease my foot off the brake and inch forward before pressing the brake again and smacking the wheel. I slap my hands against it over and over until my palms ache. *Idiot. Idiot. Idiot. What was I thinking? I should have taken the toll road.* I let out a breath I didn't realize I was holding. I'm light-headed. *Is it hot in here?*

I press the Down button to lower the temperature repeatedly, then finally press the AC button when I realize it's not on. Air blows out loudly, stinging my eyes, which have gone dry. *Breathe. Breathe. Breathe. It's fine, Ruthie. Keep it together.* I focus on the air blowing across my face. Trying to drown out my thoughts with the forceful whirring.

"Call from Mom," the disembodied voice of my car announces.

My shoulders jolt back, and I sit up straight. *How long was that?* I wrinkle my nose and look around for freeway signs. Three more miles to my exit. The car repeats, "Call from Mom." I press a button on my steering wheel to ignore the call. My shoulders sag, and I sigh. "Call from Mom." My grip tightens on the wheel, and my teeth lock together. "Call from Mom." *Shut up!* "Call from Mom."

I let out a groan, then force myself to press the Answer button on my steering wheel. "Mom. It's not a good time."

"What's wrong?" Her voice is strained, panicky.

"I don't feel good."

"What? Are you driving? Where are you? I have Doctor P on the line. Hold on!" she rapid-fires.

"Mom, I have to go. I don't feel good. I need to pull over."

"Ruthie, what's wrong? This is Doctor P. Tell me what you're feeling."

"I can't do this. I have to go." My voice cracks.

"Don't hang up," he says. "We'll be here with you. Just tell us what's wrong."

My shirt sticks to my skin as my chest heaves. "I can't! I have to call 911!" I press the End Call button.

Everything is going numb. My head feels cloudy. "Stop honking!" I scream for no one to hear. Cars whir past me, speeding blurrily ahead, but I can't focus. "Move!" I shout as I honk back at the cars around me. My hands shake as I reach for my turn signal. "Let me get over." My voice comes out ragged and desperate.

"Call from Mom" repeats in the background, but I'm disconnected from it now. It only vaguely registers as the pounding of my chest echoes in my head.

Am I dying? I feel my eyes widen. *Oh my God, I'm having a heart attack.* I fight to swallow the burning stomach acid that has rushed into my throat. *I'm going to die in my car. Alone.* My arms tingle with every failed attempt to move my hands, which have frozen into claws on the steering wheel. The car bumps along as little rocks kick up against it from the freeway shoulder. I wrench my warped fingers off the wheel to grab for my phone. I try to straighten my fingers, but they're stuck, still locked into misshapen claws. I stuff my disfigured hand into my purse but can't pick up the phone. I'm suddenly suffocating. It feels like I'm drowning.

I'm panting. My lungs won't expand. *I can't breathe.* Everything is tingling, needles pricking my hands, my arms, my legs. The blood rushes from my head. Finally, I think to use the Bluetooth. I push the button with the side of my hand and mutter, "Call 911." I want to shout as tears run down my face. I feel out of control of my own body. As if I were possessed, trapped inside a too-hot meat suit.

"Calling . . . 911," the robotic voice confirms.

I press my head back into the headrest to slow its spinning.

"911. What's your emergency?" answers a calm female operator.

"Help! Something is wrong with me. I just pulled over on the freeway, and I can't breathe, my legs are numb, and my fingers are locked up. I don't want to die here." My voice is hoarse as though I've been screaming.

"Ma'am, I need you to remain calm. Take a deep breath. Can you tell me your precise location?"

I shake my head and look around. The force of cars speeding by makes my seat tremble. "I don't know!" I shout, sobbing. "I just merged from the 405 freeway. I'm in a gray Lexus parked in the shoulder." My nose runs along with my tears. I'm sweating. I swipe at my face. Watery black mascara smears across the back of my hand.

"Stay calm, and remain in the vehicle. I will stay on the phone with you until the paramedics arrive."

"Thank you," I choke out just before another loud sob rises from my gut. I can't hold it in. My arms prickle with goose bumps. I'm hot and cold. *I don't want to die.* The operator drones on, but I can't comprehend anything she's saying now. It's all running together. It feels like I dunked my head in a bucket of ice water. It's so cold that it burns. Tears continue to roll down my face. I want to wipe them away, to swipe at the hair stuck to my cheeks and forehead, but my hands are no longer functional.

I feel myself spiraling down. *There's not enough air.* I'm drowning. Down. Down. Down. Deeper and deeper. Everything is white noise.

A tap on my window makes me jump and finally slows the spinning. I don't know how long I sat waiting. When a face appears behind the glass, the world slowly comes to a stop. I blink, then touch the button to roll down the window.

"Ma'am, I'm Stan with the Orange County Fire Department. What is your name?"

"I'm so sorry. I'm so embarrassed. I don't know what happened. Suddenly I couldn't breathe, and I lost feeling in my legs, but I think

I'm OK now." The words sputter out hurriedly like the first breaths after a resuscitation.

"Ma'am, what is your name?" he repeats, with a smile I'm sure is meant to reassure me.

Feeling pathetic, I answer, "Ruthie."

"All right, Ruthie. I'm going to take your blood pressure and ask you a few questions. May I open your car door?"

I nod softly, then unlock the door for him to open it. He takes my arm and dutifully wraps a black cuff around it. As the cuff tightens its grip, I drop my head against the headrest, its weight too much for my neck to bear. I hear the operator mutter something in the background, and the call disconnects. It feels as though I haven't slept in days. I nod absently as he talks, focusing on the feel of my fingers and hands as the tingling wanes and normalcy slowly seeps back in.

"Would you like to go to the hospital for a doctor's opinion?" he asks, pointing to the ambulance parked behind me, silhouetted by an enormous red fire truck.

I squint as the lights flash, then realize what he's asking. "Huh? No! I don't want to go in an ambulance." I sit up straight. "I don't want to go to the hospital. No, I'm fine. Wait. . . . Unless you think something is wrong with me?" My breath catches again. "Oh my God, something *is* wrong with me!"

He barks out a loud, genuine-sounding laugh as if to dismiss my worry. "You'll be fine. You don't have to go to the hospital if you don't want to. But it might be a good idea considering you had a panic attack." His thick mustache curls back against wrinkly tan skin, revealing a gentle, pearly smile. This time his smile does reassure me.

I try my best to smile back but feel my lips twist into a grimace instead. I shake my head, relieved but irritated. "Are you serious?" I let out a snort. "Like a 'take a chill pill, don't have a panic attack' panic attack?

People don't have panic attacks in real life!" I feel like I'm thirteen again, embarrassed and insecure.

"They do. And you did. It sounds like this is your first?" His brows lift, and I pinch my lips shut. "I'm going to strongly recommend that you talk to your doctor to discuss possible triggers. I'm no medical expert, but I know it can't be safe driving around in the state you're in."

I cross my arms and search my mind for a snarky reply. But the lingering tingle in my fingertips makes me frown instead. Finally, I nod. "Yeah. You're probably right."

He nods back in response, his expression soft and patient, as if I really were a thirteen-year-old girl. Lost and confused. "In any case, I'm going to need you to move out of the driver's seat and into the passenger side."

"What? Why?" My voice is whiney and strained.

"Because it's unsafe for you to drive. I'm going to drive your car to a parking lot at the next exit. I'm going to have the boys follow us. Now get into the passenger seat, and buckle in. I'll be right back." He walks away in the direction of the parked fire truck and ambulance.

I climb over the center console into the passenger seat and buckle the seat belt. I look down and blink hard, but it's as though I'm outside myself watching everything happen to me. I hardly notice when Stan returns to the driver's side and sits beside me. He adjusts the seat and rearview mirror. The trip is brief and silent aside from my occasional sniffle. When we turn into a Vons shopping center, he parks my car at the rear of the lot, and I thank him profusely.

After I assure him I won't drive, he smiles and shakes my hand goodbye before stepping out, shutting the door gently behind him, and jogging to the idling fire truck. I watch the huge red vehicle navigate slowly out of the parking lot and roll away. No lights. No sirens. The emergency is over. Still woozy, I remain in the passenger seat and wait until the tears subside before hesitantly dialing Mom's number.

"Is everything OK?" she says. "I got in my car as soon as you hung up. Where are you?"

"I'm in a parking lot somewhere in Irvine. I'll send you my location. How long until you get here?"

"I'll be there in twenty minutes. Stay in your car. I'll call Tom. See you soon."

Tom. I didn't even think to call him. I remind myself to breathe as I twist the diamond ring round and round on my finger. I met Tom on a Taco Tuesday at a dive bar near my old apartment. He was there alone wearing a black sweatshirt with the hood pulled over his wispy auburn hair. I backed into him while dancing and bumped the drink out of his hand. "Watch where you're going!" he shouted as I turned to face him. Then he stopped and said, "Has anyone ever told you your smile is too big for your face?" I shrugged and bought him another drink.

I watch as his car drives up behind mine, then pulls into the empty stall beside me. I don't move. Just sit watching. I'm sweaty. I feel my hair matted against my scalp. I know I stink. And I can feel my makeup, heavy and oily on my face. The black streaks across the backs of my hands warn of what my face must look like. I finally flip down the visor and stare at my reflection in the tiny mirror. I wipe at my face, but it's no use. I flip the visor back up when I see his figure approach my window.

The shiny black buttons of his suit jacket gleam in the sun. His garnet tie dangles at eye level, and the thought of yanking it crosses my mind. *He'll be annoyed that he didn't have time to change out of his work clothes.* I stare at his torso in the window. When he steps back and lowers his face to the glass, I reluctantly roll it down.

"Hey." I frown.

"What's going on? Your mom called me and sent me your location." His voice is soft, but I can see the irritation in his eyes.

I force myself to lower my shoulders, feeling tension radiate off me in waves, though I'm trying to look "normal." *Does he feel it?* He stares at me, wordlessly, through the open window. His eyes narrow, and he opens his mouth as if to speak before shutting it and shaking his head slightly. *He looks disappointed.* I look down at the darkened sweat patches on my jeans and rub my damp palms over my thighs to dry them. My hands still shaky, I tuck them under my legs to conceal them from his searching gaze.

"What's wrong with you?" His tone is flat.

Is he concerned or angry with me? "I don't know," I say. "The paramedic said I had a panic attack."

"OK?" His voice trails off and his brows lift.

I shrug.

The slam of a car door makes my posture go straight. "Are you OK?" Mom shouts as she walks toward my car. I hear the worry in her voice before I can see her. "What happened?" Mom asks as she barrels over to my window, nearly shoving Tom over. Her face is panic stricken despite the Botox. The creases in her brow are new. She looks older than she should. She puts both hands on the door and exhales loudly.

"I'm sorry, Mom."

"I'm just so glad you're OK." She pinches her lips together. Her eyes look watery.

"I'm fine, Mom."

I'm suddenly grateful for the car door dividing us as I imagine her squeezing me like an overloved stuffed animal. Tom mutters something to himself, then lowers his face to the window beside me. "Why don't we get you something to eat?" He gives a thin smile. "You'll feel better if you eat something."

"No, no, let's just go," I say. "I'm not hungry. I want to go home. I want to lie down."

"Tom's right, Ruthie. You should eat. You can lie down in Tom's car when he drives you home after."

The thought of being trapped in the car with Tom during rush-hour traffic makes me push open the car door. He places his hand on the small of my back as we walk across the parking lot to a dumpy-looking burger joint. My shirt is damp. *Does he feel me sweating?* His touch is more insistent than gentle as he steers me to a booth in the back of the restaurant. I swallow against the sharp smell of grease and sit down. Mom goes to the counter to order. *She doesn't know what I want.* I open my mouth to object, then close it. *It doesn't matter.*

I watch her stare at the menu above her. Her hand to her face as she thinks. The employee looks as greasy as it smells in here. A bored, vacant expression on his face. He pokes at the register as she orders. She slides her card and finally walks back toward our table. I expect her to sit down beside me, but instead she sits down next to Tom.

I look down at the table, but it's no use. I can feel their eyes on me. *They're waiting for me to say something.* I pick at my thumb cuticle until Mom raises a brow, watching me. Then I stuff my hands under my legs to keep from fidgeting. I shift in my seat. Then force a cough to break the silence. I keep my eyes on the table. "RA + FR" is crudely carved into the laminate. I think of scratching it out with my keys, slap my hand over it, and finally speak.

"I don't know what happened." I pause, still hoping they'll leave me alone or disappear somehow. I force my mouth open when they fail to vanish. "I just. I. I just couldn't breathe suddenly. It was weird." I reach up to the back of my neck and scratch at the hairline. "And then my legs went numb. The paramedic—he thinks it was a panic attack. Like, yeah right. What do I have to panic about?" I try to laugh, but the strained noise that comes out makes Mom's eyes widen.

With her head tilted, she looks like a worried border collie. I wish I fell down a well. "That sounds very serious. You could have gotten in an accident, Ruthie." Her eyes narrow, and I feel myself shrink into the seat. "Doctor P had an opening Friday. I made you an appointment."

I nod as the bored-looking employee drops our tray of food on the table, grabs the plastic order number, and walks away. Mom hands me a box of chicken strips slick with frying oil and nods back at me. As if to say, *Go on. Eat it.* I open the box, take a strip out, bite it, and chew slowly. Then stretch my arm across the table and lay my head on it. Holding up the chicken strip like I'm playing heads up, seven up with it.

They eat slowly, quietly, observing me, as if through mirrored glass. I take one more bite and nod when Tom finally offers to wrap up the rest of my food. Leftovers in one hand, he offers me the other to help me out of the booth. It takes me faking energy I don't have to convince them I can drive.

Once they are both in their cars, I take a deep breath and start my engine. The road stretches ahead. I press the gas. Then the brake. Then the gas again. Slowing down and speeding up in traffic until I reach my exit. By the time I pull through the gates of my apartment complex, I've forgotten the drive altogether. Only Tom's car tailgating behind me is a reminder.

Inside the apartment it's cold. I had left the AC running. I walk into the bedroom closet and shut the door behind me. I flip on the light and let out a breath. *I'm doing it again.* I bite my lip. *I'm breathing weird.* I put my hand on my chest and focus on my breath. I want to force myself to be "OK," to breathe "normally." I close my eyes and drop my purse on the floor.

"What'd you do?" Tom calls from the living room. When I don't respond, he lets out an irritated-sounding grunt. Then it's silent. I pick up my purse and the black dress I kicked aside earlier and put them away. I press my back as quietly as I can against the door and slide my body down to sit on the carpet. *What's wrong with me?* I look down at my engagement ring and straighten it on my finger. It glitters in the soft light of the closet. I pull it up to my knuckle, then push it back down. Wiggling it over and over until finally I pull it off and clutch it in my fist. My heart quickens.

The sound of footsteps in the bedroom makes me sit up straight. I put the ring back on and stand. He doesn't knock. Through the door he asks, "Everything OK in there?" A beat later, he says, "I heard you drop something."

"It—" I choke out, then clear my throat. "It was just my purse." I open the door. "Sorry, I was just straightening up in here." I tuck a loose lock of hair away from my face and look up at him. He looks worried. The wrinkles in his forehead seem deeper. His thin lips pursed into a frown. His eyes hooded and tired. I want to press myself against him and tell him everything is OK. Instead, I look down. His dress shirt is unbuttoned now. He has taken off his tie.

"Talk to me," he says, and backs toward the bed.

"I don't know what to say."

"Say something. . . . Anything." He sits down and stares at me.

"I'm really tired."

"I'm tired too." He runs his hand through his hair. Wet looking from his gel but no longer coiffed neatly, it falls stringy against his scalp. "I rushed out to find you after your mom called. Why didn't you call *me*?"

"I don't know. I was talking to my mom when it happened." I shrug and feel my back ache between my shoulders.

"What's wrong? Should I be worried?" His brows draw together.

"I don't know. I keep feeling like I can't breathe. And today I felt like I was dying. It couldn't have been a panic attack. I'm scared that I don't know what's wrong." I slump onto the bed beside him.

"What do you want to do? Do you want to go to the emergency room?"

"No." I sigh loudly. "I don't want to go. . . . I don't know. I don't know what I want."

"Well, what am I supposed to do?" He throws his hands up.

"I don't know. I don't want you to do anything." The sobs rise again, and I can't force them back down. I drop my face into my hands. He sighs, then strokes my back.

His touch startles me. "Stop it!"

"Stop what?" he says, confused.

"Stop *touching* me!"

"What? Am I hurting you? I'm sorry." He shrinks back.

"No. I'm sorry. I just . . . I don't know. I . . . I need a break!"

"OK, I won't touch you. I was just trying to help," he mutters, then groans. "I hate it when you get dramatic like this."

"Like what?" I furrow my brow, narrowing my eyes. "This has literally never happened before."

"You're right. The 'panic attack' is new, but your meltdowns are old, Ruthie, and I'm getting really tired of it. I don't know what you have to be so stressed about. Your life is a cream puff. Give me a break." He stands.

"Screw you, Tom."

"Screw me? Screw you! You're such a drama queen." He shakes his head and rolls his shoulders. "What? Are you stressed about wedding planning? Shouldn't you be done by now? You've only had six years to prepare."

I swallow hard and pinch my lips shut.

"Like you haven't been planning this whole time. I know about your Pinterest full of wedding crap. You've been talking about marriage since the third date."

I close my eyes and lower my head. "I need more time."

"It's a two-year engagement. We're still over a year out." He lets out an exasperated laugh. "We just bought those cards with the date. Nine, sixteen, seventeen. Remember? You picked the date." He sighs loudly, then slouches beside me. "I'm sorry. OK. You need *more* time." He strokes my lower back.

I scoot away from him, feeling tension in my neck and shoulders.

"Fine." He gets up.

He walks to the bathroom, cursing under his breath. He slams the door so hard it makes me shudder. When I hear the rush of water from the shower, my shoulders finally drop. My whole body sags limply as though all the tension holding it upright has released. I flop over on the bed and pull the covers up over my face. Squeezing my eyes shut. *Go to sleep. Everything is fine. Just go to sleep.*

I pull down the covers to look at the time. I haven't washed my face or brushed my teeth. But I'm tired. The room is dark now. The only light is from the red glow of the alarm clock and the light that seeps out under the bathroom door.

I watch the minutes slowly change the red numbers on the clock until the shower knob squeaks. I tug the covers back up and feel my body brace as I close my eyes and roll over. Barely breathing as the bathroom door slowly creaks open. Heat and steam fill the bedroom. I keep my lids squeezed shut and listen as he rustles in the closet and loudly clears his throat. *Roll over. Say something.* I breathe. He clears his throat again. The sound is dry and forced. I don't move.

I hear the click of the light switch, then feel a tug at the cover as he gets into bed beside me. I feel his eyes on me but don't flinch. I imagine us dueling. With my back to him, I'm ready to lose. Finally, he lets out a sigh, then I feel him roll away. *He's tired too.*

2.

THERE'S NO "I" IN "DENIAL"

I arrive late to work and park my car in a tight stall at the rear of the lot that everyone avoids. Inside my office, I stuff my purse into a small cabinet under the desk, then shake the mouse, startling the monitor to life. Forty-seven unread emails. I click on the first subject and pretend to read, then look out my doorway. Nothing. I look at the time on the bottom of the screen. Nearly an hour late. *No one cares.* My head drops and I press my fingertips against the sides of my head. I've seen actors massage their temples in commercials and movies as if to relieve pressure. It doesn't work for me.

My head pounds softly. A muted headache left over from yesterday. My eyes are dry, swollen, and puffy. *I should have worn glasses.* I'm going to have to peel the contacts off my corneas when I get home. My teeth grit at the thought. An email alert chimes, and I blink hard, then reopen the email I pretended to read. I type a generic response, then add a signature.

Best,

Ruthie

Smart State Insurance

Best what? Best regards, best wishes, best intentions? I never really thought about it before. Other people sign their email "Best," so I followed suit. *It doesn't really matter. I'm one tiny person in one small office of one giant corporation.* I open the next email and repeat. The crappy part is I like what I do. I like insurance. I like my tiny office. But apathy is contagious, and I caught it from my coworkers.

Tammy knocks on the frame of my open door, and I look up. I heard her coming before she knocked. The sound of her kitten heels catching on the matted carpet as she sashays around the office gives her away.

"Did you pack your sad little salad?" she asks, brows drawn together in an expression of mock pity as she pouts.

"Yeah," I lie and tap on the cabinet beneath my desk where I usually store my "sad little" lunch pail.

"Why don't you cheat today? It looks like *you* need it." She folds her arms across her chest as if to say, *I won't take no for an answer.*

"I can't. I have to run an errand on my break. I'm just going to eat lunch at my desk today." I frown.

"All right, suit yourself. If you change your mind, I'm leaving at one." She turns and leaves, tossing her waist-length kinky blond hair behind her for effect.

The errand is a blood draw, which Dr. Peterson ordered. I hate getting my blood drawn, almost as much as I hate eating salad alone at my desk. When I return from "lunch," I take a newly emptied spot in the parking lot.

The office is cleared out. Cubicles abandoned. A phone rings softly from a vacant desk. I knock on Martha's shut door. A shiny gold plate displays her name and title in a bold, important-looking font. I hear what sounds like paper crumpling, then, "Come in."

She smiles broadly, pushes a Ballard Designs catalog away, and motions for me to sit down. I shake my head slightly and shift my weight. Still standing in the doorway, I stare at the paper fast-food bag in her wastebasket.

Finally, I ask, "How was your lunch?"

"Fine," she says and smiles patiently, her expression soft and motherly, though she doesn't have children and never married. On her desk, where you'd expect a family photo, is a hinged gold frame with photos of her two cats, Jean-Jacque and Jean-Luc. My lip curls as I look at their shiny black coats. *She treats them like babies.*

"Good. Um, I just wanted to come by and ask if it was OK for me to take a personal day tomorrow? I've got a doctor's appointment in Fullerton. . . . And since there is so much traffic in both directions, I thought I should ask for a day of PTO. Is that OK?"

"Sure. Is it for that eye infection you've got?" Martha narrows her eyes as though studying me, then widens them again. "Take all the time you need. Let me know if you need Monday too."

She knows. "Thank you, Martha. I really appreciate it." The words rush out of me, and it feels like I might cry. I turn and face the door to hide the flush I feel stretch across my face, then quickly shut it behind me as I scurry out.

"Sure, don't mention it," she calls out, muffled.

With both hands on the steering wheel, I stare straight ahead and focus on my breathing. *I'm OK. Everything is OK.* An advertisement for car insurance drones softly in the background. As I pull into the parking garage of my apartment complex, I exhale deeply and release the white-knuckled grip I had on the steering wheel. My hands are achy and tense. I park and flex my fingers. Then shake my head as if shaking off a bad dream.

Home, I unlock the door and push it open slowly. I peer in, then flip on the light and flinch. Needlessly expectant. *Everything is fine.* Tom won't be home for another hour. I set my purse on the counter, ignoring the crusty oatmeal bowl, coffee mug, and banana peel he left in the sink for me to clean up. I slump on the love seat. Flip on the television and wince as the shouting of an angry sports commentator fills the room. I fumble with the remote, changing channels, then finally turn the television off and stare at my black reflection. Beneath the TV a thin shelf smugly displays photos of us smiling and embracing in matchy-matchy picture frames.

When I first moved in, the frames were filled with photos of me and my girlfriends. A picture of Courtney and me in Cabo. A group photo of me and my five best friends in matching onesie pajamas for a bar crawl on my twenty-second birthday. A Mickey Mouse frame with a photo of Sam and me hugging in front of Cinderella's castle. Slowly over the years, every picture was replaced. I have a silver "She Said Yes" frame hidden in an old shoebox in our closet. I bought it at HomeGoods four years ago when I thought he might propose. It still has the price tag on it.

Tom moved in so slowly, I didn't realize it was happening at first. It started with a couple of left-behind T-shirts. Then a toothbrush and changes of clothes. Finally, his retainer and bottle of Propecia. "Babe, you're out of toilet paper," he'd announced as he plopped on the bed beside me and continued scrolling through his ESPN app. It was what I wanted. *Right? I wanted him to move in.*

He didn't start helping with the rent until long after his mail started showing up. He asked me for stamps with his face in the open fridge. When he peeled the lid off my last low-fat vanilla yogurt, I finally snapped. "Tom, you have a key, come and go as you please, and help yourself to everything in my apartment. You live here. Either help with the bills or move out."

Since I added his name to the lease, the rent has increased every renewal. Whenever I've thought about breaking up, I've worried about losing my apartment.

He'll be home soon. I force myself off the sofa and change out of the dress I wore to work and into sweats to start making dinner. Inside the fridge the shelves are bare. I was supposed to go to the grocery store Sunday, but I had a migraine. I check the date on a wedge of cheese, then toss it. Pizza sounds good right about now. As I unlock my phone screen to call in an order, an alert reads, "New message from Tom."

"Not coming home tonight. I'll be at my parents if you need anything."

"What do you mean you're not coming home?" I type, staring at the ellipsis on the left side of the screen.

"You said you needed a break." Another ellipsis. "So, I'm giving it to you."

I squint at the message until the meaning seeps into my brain. My thumb's positioned over the keyboard. I bite at the inside of my cheek and tap my nail against the screen. Then set the phone facedown on the counter. I run the tap and fill the oatmeal bowl, watching the water overflow and bits of oats circle the drain. Then I grab an old bottle of vodka from the freezer and finally dial the pizzeria.

* * *

My eyes are dry. Blinking feels like rubbing fine-grain sandpaper against my corneas. I forgot to take my contacts out last night. I groan as I realize the muted headache from yesterday is now a pounding migraine. My brain throbs against my skull in rhythm with my heartbeat. I don't remember the last time I woke up with a hangover. It's been years. I throw the covers off, and my hand slaps against the half-empty pizza box on his side of the bed. I choke down a sob.

I take two more Excedrin when I park in front of Mom's office building. I took two this morning after I peeled my lenses off, but my head still hurts. My eyelids are swollen, the lashes swallowed up like a thin patty between two fat hamburger buns. I can't even hide behind sunglasses, since contacts are out of the question. It doesn't matter. Just the fact that I'm wearing glasses will raise a flag for Mom. She'll know I've been crying. I take a deep breath and get out of my car.

It's too bright outside. Hangover weighing on me, I drag my body to the glass doors of the lobby. Every muscle aches. I'm exhausted despite sleeping in. Inside, the industrial-strength fluorescent lights make me want to turn around and go back home. But I force myself to wait for an elevator. Her office is on the second floor. I usually take the stairs, but taking that many steps feels impossible today.

Her suite, mercifully, has softer lighting. Generic jazz plays softly in the background, audible under the sounds of keyboards clacking and chatter. It smells like someone is burning a candle—floral and saccharin. I have to choke back my urge to gag. I skipped breakfast. Tom ate the last of the oatmeal, and I couldn't bring myself to eat anything else lingering in the cabinet.

I stand by the door waiting for the receptionist to finish her call. I've met her a handful of times, but I can never remember her name. It makes me feel like garbage every time she greets me. She looks up from her screen and presses a hand against her headset. I watch as her expression changes from the furrowed brow of mild irritation to the broad smile of recognition when she sees me. *Crap.*

"Ruthie!" Mom practically bursts into the reception area. "How *are* you?"

"Um . . . good," I mutter.

"Patty, you remember Ruthie. This is my daughter." Mom beams.

Patty nods, smiling. Before Patty can say anything, Mom looks at me and says, "Let's go relax in my office, and we'll get ready to head out for your appointment soon."

I force a tight-lipped half smile and nod at Patty before following Mom down the hall. She walks fast, but I don't bother to try and keep pace. She seems to be always in a hurry. Always busy. She pushes open the door to her office and holds it, waiting for me. Inside, I sit down on the sofa instead of the guest chair at her desk. I watch as she sits in her executive chair. The enormity of it would dwarf any other woman her size. But her presence seems to fill up the room. She smiles cautiously. Eyeing me.

"So, what's going on, kiddo? How are you feeling?" she asks.

"Fine."

Her gaze steady, she doesn't flinch. *She should have been a hostage negotiator.* I clear my throat. "I'm OK. I'm a little nervous about my lab results. I hope everything is all right." I pause. "I guess I'm glad to be seeing a doctor." I force an awkward smile. My sweaty palms feel hot on the legs of my jeans.

"Well, I'm glad too." She presses her lips together.

My smile melts into a grimace as tears wet my eyes. I shove my fingers under the rim of my glasses and wipe at my puffy lids. A moment later I feel her next to me. She pats my shoulder and holds up a tissue.

"It's going to be OK." She squeezes my shoulder gently. "Do you want to talk about it?"

"No." I sniffle and let out a strained chuckle. "But I'm happy you're driving."

Dr. Peterson's office is closed from noon until one for lunch, but since he's a client of Mom's, we are granted early entry. The sparse waiting room is quiet except for a muted conversation coming from a room somewhere beyond the reception desk. Mom, lips pursed in concentration, fills out my medical and insurance forms. It's been well over a decade since she last escorted me to a doctor's office, but it's comforting having her with me. The office is cold. Colder than usual for a doctor's office. But I can't rub my arms. If I do, Mom will insist on giving me her jacket. After a few more silent minutes, a heavyset older nurse calls my name. I take my time rising to my feet.

"Do you want me to come with you?" Mom asks.

I shake my head. "I'll come get you if I need you. Thanks, Mom."

I avoid looking at the numbers on the machine when the nurse takes my blood pressure. My weight has dipped a few pounds despite the pizza last night. Not eating much lately is catching up to me. She leaves and I pinch the bridge of my nose to stop from sneezing at the odor of disinfectant that hangs thick in the room. When the urge passes, I remind myself to breathe. I close my eyes. *In through the nose. Out through the mouth.* A knock on the door startles me, and I watch wide eyed as it opens.

"Ruthie!" Dr. Peterson's voice fills the sterile room. He smiles brightly, his teeth nearly the same hue as the pristine lab coat he's wearing. "How're you doing?" he asks warmly as he grabs my file from the door.

I press my lips together in a half-hearted smile and nod. He nods back, then shuts the door and puts on his reading glasses. He says, "All right, well, let's have a look at your blood work then."

I shift and the paper under me crinkles loudly. *Should I have sat in the regular chair instead?* I pick at the cuticle on my thumb and bite at my lip. I could easily bite off the hangnail I've made. *Don't do it.*

"Mmmm-hmm, mmm-hmm," he hums to himself, reading, as he takes a seat atop the exam stool and rolls toward me.

I stare at him, trying to glean some insight from the "mmm-hmms" with no success. His wrinkle-free dark face reveals nothing. He doesn't so much as lift a brow as he reviews my chart documents. My heart starts racing. *What is it? What's wrong with me?* I look down at my hands just as a crimson bead forms beside my thumbnail. *Crap.* I put my thumb in my mouth to stop the bleeding.

I hide my hand behind my back and ask, "Could I have a tissue?"

"Hmm?" He looks up, his brows scrunched together, agitated by the interruption. I force a smile, and slowly his brows smooth, my request seeming to register. He smiles back and grabs the tissue box behind him and offers it to me.

"Thank you," I manage. Then pull out a tissue and quickly press it to my bleeding thumb.

"Mm-hmm," he says, eyeing the wadded-up tissue in my hand.

I feel my face flush. Sheepishly, I say, "I pulled a hangnail."

He takes off his glasses, runs his hand over his smooth shaved head, and smiles at me. "So, tell me what's going on."

"What do you mean? Like, what are my symptoms?"

"Sure."

"Well, I've been having a lot of difficulty breathing lately. It happens mostly when I'm in the car . . . and sometimes in the shower. And lately, it's been happening before bed. I can't sleep. I catch myself holding my breath, and by the time I realize it, I have a hard time breathing properly again." I pause to search his face, but his expression is unchanged. I hesitate. "Did I develop asthma as an adult? Or do you think it's something more serious, maybe something to do with my lungs?"

"Mmmm-hmm. Yeah. It's possible to develop asthma as an adult. That's not a problem for you, though." Dr. Peterson then looks at me, really looks at me. He squints and furrows his brow as he examines my face. Finally, he shakes his head and asks again, "Ruthie, what's going on?"

I feel my face grow hot. My ears burning. *What did Mom tell him?* Tingling creeps into my fingertips. It's suddenly too hot in here. I open my mouth to tell him everything is fine and apologize for wasting his time. Then shut it and press my hands against the examination table.

He says, "Ruthie, I can't help you if you don't tell me what's bothering you."

"Nothing is bothering me. I'm fine." I scoot forward and push myself off the cushioned table. The bloodied tissue falls from my hand. The torn flesh is bleeding more than it should. *It was just a hangnail.* "Can I have another tissue?"

He passes me the box. I pull out a few tissues and sit back down.

My stomach flutters. It feels like I got called on to answer a question in class when I didn't raise my hand. I don't know the right answer. I grip the examination table beneath me, tearing the paper with my moistened palms. I feel like I'm going to be sick. I open my mouth, and the words just fall out. "I can't do it anymore. The more I think about it—the more I think about our wedding—the worse I feel. I know I should be *so* happy, but I'm not. I don't know what's wrong with me. I want to get married. I really do." My eyes water, stinging my swollen eyelids. "I don't know what's wrong with me," I repeat.

I feel winded. I'm struggling to inhale as deeply as I need to. *I'm doing it again. I'm holding my breath.* I wipe my face with the sleeves of my shirt. Then feverishly rub my palms against my thighs, my shirt clinging to my dampened underarms.

"And you're having difficulty breathing now?" he asks, knowingly.

Feeling defeated, I nod.

"Lately, when you find yourself short of breath, is it because you're thinking about your engagement? Or are other thoughts bothering you?"

I bite down hard on my lip. "I guess it's mainly the engagement," I say, shrugging.

"Mmm-hmm." He sets down my file. "Well, your blood work came back normal." He clasps his hands. "So, now, based on the symptoms you described and what you're telling me about the engagement troubling you, it sounds to me like you might be suffering from anxiety." He pauses and fits his knee through his clasped hands. Waiting for my response. He looks fatherly, as though he's just given a lecture on an important lesson.

I drop my face to my hands. I feel embarrassed. Like I've failed somehow. *He's going to tell Mom.*

"It's all right, Ruthie." He sits up straight. "It's not terminal." He lets out a strained chuckle. "I'm going to write you a prescription." He puts his reading glasses back on and pulls the script pad from his coat pocket.

"But . . . if my chart looks good, why do I need a prescription?"

"It's in case you feel yourself unable to breathe and start experiencing panic symptoms again. Your chart looks normal, but your symptoms tell me you need a little help, and that's OK. The prescription is for you to take only as needed, all right?"

I frown but nod.

"How did it go? Did Doctor P answer all your questions?" Mom asks as we climb into her SUV.

"Yeah. He's great, Mom." I buckle my seat belt, then clutch my left arm as if to hold myself together.

"Do you want to talk about it over lunch?"

"No. Thanks. I'm not really hungry," I mumble out the car window.

"Well, why don't you come over? Do you have any plans? We can watch a movie together. I'll order food later."

I shrug. I don't have any energy left to fight off her advances. "OK."

"OK?" Mom gasps. "Call the newspaper. She said yes!"

I hear a laugh escape me and put my hand over my face.

She says, "I just have to wrap up at the office, and I'll come right back."

We don't talk the rest of the drive. She parks illegally in front of her condo building and puts on the hazard lights. I follow her upstairs, and she unlocks the door for me.

"I'll be home soon. Help yourself to anything. I love you," she calls out as she power-walks down the stairs.

"OK," I mumble to myself as I walk into the entryway and set my purse down on her counter. It's clean. No dishes in her sink. The condo smells like a Glade plug-in. I groan. *Of course, it's clean. She lives alone.* I open her fridge. It's filled with Diet Coke and little cans of Perrier. I open the fridge's snack drawer and pull out a wedge of Cotswold. I check the date. *Still good.* Inside the pantry she has three boxes of the fancy crackers I like. I pull out the opened box and grab a plate, eyeing the wineglasses in the cabinet. I check the time on my phone. Quarter after 2:00 p.m. *Screw it.* I pour myself a glass from an uncorked bottle of chardonnay I found in the fridge and sit down at the counter.

By the time Mom gets home, I'm on my second glass of wine, and I've finished the wedge of cheese. She sets her purse down next to mine. Then pulls the bottle of chardonnay from the fridge and pours the rest of it into a glass. She takes a long drink and smiles at me.

She says, "It's good, right? I've got another bottle in the veggie drawer." She winks.

"I ate all your cheese."

"That's all right. I have more cheese too."

I groan and put my head down on the counter. "My cheese was expired."

"OK?" she says tentatively, voice full of concern. She sets her glass down. "Are you feeling OK?"

"No." I look up and rest my cheek on my fist. "There's always dishes in my sink. And if I don't go to the grocery store, then we don't have food. And I always have to do the cooking and the cleaning and the planning and the shopping. And he eats *all* the food." I sit up. "I buy extra of my favorite snacks, and he still eats everything!" I slap my hand on the counter. "If I don't make food for him, he won't eat. He's like a child. If I go out, I have to bring him home food. He's probably home and hungry right now. Ugh. Can't he just order a pizza?" I sip the last of my wine and hold out my glass.

"Maybe you should slow down on the wine. I'll order some food, and you can have another glass with dinner," she says.

My eyes water and I take off my glasses. "OK." I set my head back down.

She sits down on the stool beside me and pats my back. "Do you want a glass of water?"

"Yes."

"Do you want to talk about it?"

"No."

"Do you want to move in?"

I look up, and tears run down my face. "Yes."

"OK." She nods slowly. "OK." She tucks a hair behind my ear.

3.

SLIDE TO THE RIGHT, EVERYBODY PACK YOUR BAGS

"Tom, I'm back," I call out from the entryway, my voice strained. "Tom?"

I set my keys and purse on the kitchen counter. No response. It smells like overcooked Hot Pockets, greasy and burnt. *He exploded something in the microwave again.* I'll have to clean it later. I flip on the kitchen light, then approach the shut bedroom door. I take a deep breath then force myself to knock.

"Tom, I'm sorry for not calling last night." I tuck my hair behind my ear, then press it to the door. "Tom?" I press the handle. The door is locked. "This is ridiculous. What are you doing?"

The lock pops, and the door swings open wide.

"You're right. This *is* ridiculous." He takes a slow, deliberate step forward.

I step back.

"You know what else is ridiculous?" His lips curl. "Waiting all night for my fiancée to come home. Worrying and feeling pathetic because she hasn't called. That's ridiculous. What is going on with you, Ruthie?"

I back into the love seat and sit on the arm. "I don't know."

"I'm tired of 'I don't know.' I'm tired of playing games. We're too old for that. Are you cheating on me?"

"No!" I feel my face tighten as it reddens.

"What is it then?" He stands over me, arms outstretched.

"I don't—"

"What is it?" he interrupts.

"I don't want to marry you!"

His body jerks back as though shoved in the chest. My fists squeeze, my nails biting into my palms as pounding starts up in my ears.

"Are you joking?" He steps toward me again and wipes his brow.

"I'm sorry."

"You're sorry? You're telling me you don't want to marry me, and you're *sorry*?"

"I'm sorry," I repeat, shaking my head to fight back the tears. "I don't know what else to say."

"Why not?"

"I . . ."

"Don't say you don't know. Why don't you want to marry me? Huh? How much longer were you going to wait?"

I shake my head again, tears running down my face.

"Were you waiting for our wedding day? The day after? *When* were you going to tell me?"

"I don't know!"

"I don't need this. *You* wanted to marry me. I asked because I thought *you* wanted it."

He straightens his posture and runs his hand through his hair. Then grabs his keys off the kitchen counter and heads for the door.

"Where are you going?" I ask.

"I don't know."

The door slams and I let out a scream. With one sweeping motion, I push everything off the coffee table. A glass vase full of musty potpourri falls to the floor scattering decayed petals and leaves all over the carpet among the splayed magazines. From the kitchen I grab the trash can, and I drop to my knees to clean up. The spicy aroma of the petals clashes with the odor emanating from a crushed pizza box stuffed into the bin. *He ate my leftover pizza.* I throw away handfuls of potpourri, then the magazines, and finally the framed pictures from the shelf. I tie up the bag and throw it down the trash shoot.

When fresh tears sting my eyes, I slap myself. *Stop it.* I grab my purse and keys off the counter and, without a second thought, rush out of the apartment. My cheeks are wet as I push the red emergency bar to open the door to the stairway and run down three flights of concrete stairs. By the time I reach my car, I'm winded and collapse into the driver's seat, panting. I can't breathe with the hammering inside my chest. I push back the sweaty strands of hair that cling to my temples and neck, then wipe the runny mascara stains under my eyes before starting the engine. The air-conditioning blasts me in the face, stinging my cheek where I slapped it. *Idiot.* I rustle through my purse, rummaging through lipsticks and tampons until I find the small white slip of paper crumpled at the bottom. I smooth it out on the steering wheel, pressing it flat until I accidentally honk the horn. My shoulders jump to my ears, lowering only once I realize the coast is clear. I smile at the prescription. *Good as new.* I shift into reverse.

The fluorescent lights of the Rite Aid force me to squint, and I regret having left my sunglasses in the car. I cross my arms over my chest and power walk to the pharmacy counter.

"Do you have, uh, any question about your prescription?"

"No." I shake my head. "Wait. Yes. My doctor said to take it as needed. What does that mean exactly?"

She looks down at the bottle, holding the label up for me to see, and starts explaining. Her accent is thick, and the words seem to clump together. When she stops talking, she looks up at me, and I realize I didn't understand anything she said. I scratch my head and pull my hair back behind my ear as if uncovering it will help me hear better.

"I'm sorry. Could you please repeat that?"

Visibly irritated, she says, "OK," then clears her throat. She speaks slowly as if I'm a moron. "It means if you have a symptom of anxiety like, uh, worry or insomnia or like sweating, you take one pill."

"One pill?" I hold up my pointer finger. *I feel like a moron.*

"One. Don't take while driving or with, uh, alcohol."

"Well, there goes my weekend plans." I laugh uncomfortably.

She narrows her eyes and points to the signature pad. "Sign here please."

I buy a bottle of wine, a bag of Oreos, and a Cherry Coke. In the car I rip open the bag of Oreos and put a whole cookie in my mouth. I haven't had an Oreo in years, but I know better. I twist the next cookie apart, scrape the filling off with my front teeth, and resandwich the two black wafers together. I pry off the vial cap next and swallow a tiny white pill with a mouthful of Cherry Coke. I eat the bare wafers, then take a second pill.

Seventy-eight dollars later, I return home with a trunk full of packing supplies. After I've unloaded, I slam the lid shut, then pause. *How am I going to get all this crap upstairs?* I grip the flattened boxes under my arms, the tips of my fingers reaching just far enough.

When the elevator doors open on the third floor, my arms can no longer bear the weight. Crouched over the boxes, I drag them down the hall, pacing backward, periodically checking over my shoulder. I trip only once. Inside my apartment, I shove the boxes into the entryway and shrink against the door, groaning as my sweaty shirt lubricates the slide down to the entry mat. I sit until my wheezing ceases and shirt dries, sticking uncomfortably against my salty skin. I pinch the fabric and air it out, then finally turn on the AC.

I cut the plastic binding off the boxes and let them fall to the floor with a thud. I fold and tape the first box into shape, then another one and another. Fueled by the Coke's caffeine and sugary Oreos, I mindlessly assemble boxes while zonked on Xanax. When the last box is folded, I lie down on the floor of the entryway. The wood-style laminate is hard and unforgiving beneath me. Somehow bits of potpourri managed to make their way from the living room to the entryway. *Ugh, I need to vacuum.*

I sit up just as ringing starts inside my purse. I groan and stretch as I stand, then hobble over to the counter.

"Hey, Sam," I mutter into the phone.

"Hey. . . . What's wrong with you? You sound like death," Sam responds, startled.

"I'm fine. It's nothing."

"I don't know why you think you can lie to me. I'm giving you a thirty-minute notice: I'm going to put on pants and head over there. Scratch that. Make it forty minutes. I gotta pick up a bottle of wine."

"No, Sam. Seriously, no!"

"Byyyeeee!" she singsongs.

Crap. I grab a box and take it into my room, then come back and grab two more. I pick them up two at a time and stack them all in the bedroom, then shut the door. I run to the bathroom, tie my hair into a messy bun, and put on fresh clothes. *There. It's like nothing happened*, I lie to myself and smile at the mirror until I notice black bits of cookie lodged between my front teeth.

I finish brushing my teeth just as a familiar shave-and-a-haircut knock raps at the door. I smile once more at my reflection, this time leaving the grin plastered across my face. It's been over two weeks since I last saw her. I knock back "two bits" reflexively before opening the door. She has a bottle of wine in one hand and a plastic bag of food in the other.

I find myself saying, "I'm actually so glad to see you."

She puts the wine and food down on the counter so she can throw her arms around me in a tight, sisterlike hug. I choke back the lump in my throat and pull away from her embrace.

"No. No, stop." I let out a nervous laugh as my eyes water.

"Do you want me to open the wine?"

I nod, pouting.

She opens the utensil drawer, grabs the corkscrew, and in a single fluid twist, pulls the cork out. I hand her the wineglasses and she pours generously.

"Oreos?" she asks, picking up the half-eaten bag off the counter.

I pause mid-sip to nod, then continue drinking.

"This is serious. When was the last time you bought Oreos?"

I bite my lip.

She shakes her head and takes a long drink. "When your dad died," she whispers into her glass.

"Probably." I force a close-lipped smile.

"What? Are these like your sad cookies?" She chuckles nervously, pulling one out.

"No. I just rarely buy cookies."

"Yeah. You only buy them when you're sad."

I shrug.

"So, what is it?" She puts her licked-bare wafers together and takes a bite. "Mm, these are really good with wine."

"Don't dunk 'em, though. It's gross."

She scrunches up her nose and takes another drink. "So?"

"Right. Yeah, you want me to tell you what's wrong."

She nods and bites into another cookie, the crumbs falling into her long wavy, mermaid-like hair. She brushes them off and stares at me, still chewing.

"Tom and I are breaking up."

"Mm-hmm." She splits another cookie and scrapes her teeth over the center. "But, like, for real this time?" She squinches her face, pursing her lips.

"Yes. For real this time. I *actually* told him. It's over."

She puts her half-eaten cookie down and wipes her hands together to dust off the crumbs. "Jeez."

"Yeah." I nod, eyebrows up. "Jeez."

"I know we've talked about it before, but what made you actually do it?"

"I had a panic attack."

"Seriously?"

"Seriously."

"You seem pretty chill considering the circumstances, though. Weird."

"Doctor Peterson gave me Xanax."

"Is that even legal?"

"I went for a doctor's appointment! It was totally legit."

"Should you be drinking?"

"I'm not driving or operating heavy machinery. Besides, I took them hours ago." I shrug.

"Be careful with those, dude. I've heard they're, like, super addictive."

"I know, but these are, like, the lowest dose. It's no big deal. I'm not gonna take them every day or anything."

She cocks her head, lifts a brow, and looks at me sideways. "OK." She stuffs the rest of the cookie in her mouth and opens the plastic bag of take-out she brought. I plate the Thai food, and we eat standing in the kitchen.

"Anyway, I'm moving back in with my mom."

"Does Joy know?"

"Yes, she knows. *She* asked me."

"Good luck with that. Once you move back, it's hard to get out."

"My mom isn't like your mom."

"You're right. She's worse." She refills the glasses. "Kiss your adulting days goodbye."

"Ugh." I set my fork down.

"So, when is your lease up?"

"I'm going to terminate early. I already bought boxes today."

She looks around the living area.

"They're in the bedroom."

"Were you seriously not going to tell me?"

I pinch my lips together, then take a long sip, finishing my glass. Sam downs her wine and divides the rest of the bottle between our two glasses. I grab the glasses and take them to the living room so we can sit.

"All right. Since you are now single and ready to mingle . . ." She digs her iPhone out of her small leather-tasseled purse. I'm sure it's thrifted. I could never pull something like that off. "Let me show you this dating app."

She giggles, swiping at her phone. "This, my friend, is Bumble. This is how everyone is dating now!" She plops down on the couch beside me.

I curl my upper lip in disgust before taking another long sip.

"Stop! Try not to be so judgy. I see the look you're giving me. I know that it's too early for you to date. . . . But I also know that you are way out of practice, so I just want to introduce you to it."

"It's way, *waaay* too early. I'm not even thinking about dating, let alone downloading an app for it."

"Shh! Let me just show you. Look with your eyes, not with your hands." She holds up her phone to demonstrate the app. "Never mind. Give me your phone."

"My phone? This is stupid."

"No, it's not. This is where you meet people. What, do you think you're just going to walk into a bar and meet the man of your dreams? No. Trust me. Just give me your phone."

"Fine." I hand her my iPhone and she beams. I immediately reach to take it back.

"No way."

She holds my phone over her head. The three inches she's got on me give her a longer wingspan. When I finally stop reaching, she laughs and types my pass code into the phone, and a few clicks later Bumble is downloaded. She begins a barrage of mind-numbing questions.

"Your dream dinner guest is?"

"Ryan Gosling. Wait, no, Chris Hemsworth."

"What three things make a relationship great?"

"Skip this one."

"Come on, Ruthie."

"If I knew, we wouldn't be here."

"Try."

I groan. "Um, empathy. A shared sense of humor . . . and kismet." I take another swig and remember the bottle of wine I bought earlier.

She raises a brow. "OK." She takes a drink. "Well, what about two truths and a lie?"

"I'm five-five. I speak fluent Spanish. And I love sports."

"You hate sports."

"Yeah. That's the lie. Duh. But they don't know that, and now they'll think I'm cool."

We both burst out laughing. When she finishes, she smiles and tilts her head as if to say, *You're welcome.* Then gives the app a test swipe. Still holding my phone, she prompts me to look at the first "contestant."

"Sa-man-tha," I say, emphasizing each syllable. "Give me the phone."

"No way. Not until you give it a fair shot. No one says you have to date these guys. I'm not even saying you have to talk to any of them. I just want you to give it a good look so that when you are ready . . ." She takes a sip of her wine, then moves her eyebrows up and down in a flirty little wiggle.

"Ugh, fine." I down the last of my wine and lean closer to her. "No. No. Nope. Uh-uh. *Nooo!* Sam, are you serious?"

"*Waaait!* You have to be patient. They can't all be winners. It takes time. We're *just looking.* Shh."

She continues to swipe left on countless men. Some with confusing group photos where you must click the profile to find out which friend is the profile owner only to discover it's the least attractive one. Men with their shirts off and abs flexed, men leaning against fancy sports cars, out-doorsy men, men holding pets, and strangely, lots of men holding fish.

"OK. Now, what about this one?" Sam holds up the phone and waves it around. The image of a man standing on a sailboat with bright eyes and strawberry-blond hair lights up the screen. "I know this guy is your type. What do you think?" she asks as she scrolls through his profile photos.

I feel my face burn.

"Ooh, you like him!" she says. "I'm going to swipe right."

"Nooo, you can't. Sam! You said we were just looking."

"We *were* just looking. . . . But now . . . I am just swiping." She slides the screen to the right. "Oops!" she says, giggling.

"Sam, I am going to murder you!" I laugh, although I feel I could just as easily cry. I snatch the phone out of her hand and close the app.

"I'm just trying to help."

"I know. I'm just not ready. Not even to 'just look.' I love you for trying . . . and for making me laugh . . . and for the little bit of eye candy, though."

"You're welcome. Well, I think my work here is done." She smiles, exposing too many teeth, and wipes her hands together.

I walk her to the door, and she hugs me too tightly before leaving. I lock the door, then uncork the bottle of wine from Rite Aid.

* * *

I wake to a throbbing headache. I open one eye and immediately regret it. Sunlight spills in through the blinds I forgot to shut last night. My stomach churns and I clutch my belly. *I think I'm going to be sick.* I rip off the covers and dart to the bathroom. I wretch into the bowl. Heaving and flushing. Gritty black cookie bits stain the sides of the toilet. Just looking at it makes me feel sick again. My nose stings with vomit. After a final flush, I sit on the floor and rest my head against the wall.

"Tom?" I shout.

Silence.

Suddenly the memories rush in. *We broke up.* The rooms spins. *I need to lie down.* I curl up on the bathroom floor and shut my eyes. *Just go back to sleep.*

Did I make a mistake? What if I don't meet anyone else? What am I even looking for? The thought of Sam swiping left so many times yanks me upright. I blink open my swollen lids, then dig my nails into my scalp, tugging at the roots of my hair. I let out a strained scream, then sob. *What is wrong with me?* I feel used up and dirty. Dehydrated and disgusted at myself for trying to sleep on the bathroom floor.

I drag myself up and stumble back to the bed. I pull the covers over my face. *I'm too old to start over.* I swipe at his side of the bed, then roll over onto his pillow. It's lumpy. I press my face into it and inhale deeply. It smells of his sweat and American Crew Hair Thickening Shampoo. I pull it out from under my head and clutch it to my chest. I feel like I'm in the movie *Groundhog Day*. But I'm the only person doing the same crap. At least this time there's no pizza box in the bed, though.

The kitchen sink is filled with sticky, brown-stained dishes, rice firmly glued on like a preschool macaroni art project. I don't bother to rinse them off and stick everything as is into the dishwasher and run it half-empty. I throw the empty Oreo bag and wine bottles into the garbage can along with the Thai takeout trash. I eat saltine crackers over the sink with a bottle of flat seltzer to calm my roiling stomach. It's two in the afternoon. I check my phone. The only new message is from Sam from last night, letting me know she got home safe. *I need to pack.*

I throw away everything in the fridge. Old plastic bags of cheese, ranch dressing, expired ketchup, a jar of pimento-stuffed olives—all tossed into a new white trash bag. Then I move to the freezer. Frozen-together Eggo waffles, freezer bags of probably long-expired chicken and ground beef, sticky sealed pints of Ben & Jerry's. The pantry comes next.

I fill another bag. Then drag the full bags of wasted food down the hall to the shoot.

When the pounding of my head becomes unbearable, I pop two Excedrin like Tic Tacs and swallow them with a sip of tap water. Once my brain stops throbbing, I wrap all the glassware in paper and place it into the first box labeled "kitchen." The dishwasher beeps just as the first cabinet is emptied. Steam smacks me across the face as I open the door. I roll out the bottom rack and notice Tom's 2010 Lakers championship pint glass. I pick it up and dry it thoroughly. Then throw it in the trash.

4

BUT, I'M A GROWN-UP!

've had the key to Mom's condo since she bought it years ago, using it when a piece of my mail was redirected from our old address or when I knew she'd be home soon. I open the door, balancing a box on my knee, and walk through the living area back to the guest bedroom. I set the box on the floor and flip on the light. It smells of dust and sea-breeze-scented air freshener. The room has been stripped bare. Picture frames, knickknacks, and beige bedding all removed to make room for my stuff.

"Mom?" Renée's voice echoes through the living room as she walks in after me.

"She's not here. She had to work today!" I shout back just as Renée steps into the room. "Sorry, I didn't realize you were right behind me."

"Do you need help unpacking? I thought Mom was going to be here to help you." She sets a box down.

"No, it's fine. I got it. Thank you, guys, for helping move everything over here."

"Of course."

"What are you going to do with all the furniture you left behind?" Joe asks as he sets the leather chair from my old living room next to the bed. He wipes the sweat from his brow with the crook of his elbow.

"Sell it, I guess." I shrug.

"All of it?" Renée's eyes widen.

"I don't know what else to do. Tom didn't want any of it, and I don't want to pay for storage."

"Is he going to help you at all?"

"Nope. He says it's not his problem."

"Wow," Renée says before exchanging side-eye glances with Joe.

"When is *he* moving out?" Joe asks.

"He pretty much already has. He took his clothes and his Xbox Monday while I was at work."

Renée wrinkles her nose. "So, on top of blaming you for everything, he's leaving you the mess?"

I frown and stare down at the boxes.

"Don't worry about it, Sister. Joe and I will help you with anything you need."

I nod at the boxes, my eyes beginning to burn.

"Do you need a minute?" she asks.

I pinch my lips together.

Renée looks at Joe and tilts her head, motioning to the door.

"Right." Joe follows Renée out.

I slump onto the mattress and rub my eyes with dusty fists. I finally stop crying when I hear the thud of heavy footsteps and murmuring in the entryway. I dry my cheeks with the backs of my hands and wipe my hands on my leggings. Then straighten my ponytail and hurry past Renée and Joe down the stairs to grab another box. I pick up a box labeled "Closet" from the back seat of Joe's truck and find my purse spilled open on the floor mat. Two lipsticks and the orange vial have rolled out. I toss the lipsticks back into the bag and read the bottle label: "Take as needed." I shake out one pill and swallow it dry before stuffing the vial back in my purse and carrying the box upstairs.

When Joe sets down the last box, he pulls his shirt over his face to wipe off the sweat, exposing his hairy belly button.

"Put your shirt down," Renée says. "Ruthie doesn't want to see your dad bod."

"Be nice!" I shove Renée's shoulder.

"I am nice." She pats her husband's belly.

"Thanks, babe." Joe rolls his eyes.

"So, what do you think?" Renée asks as she plops onto the mattress and pats the space beside her.

I plunk down and roll my shoulders forward. "It's weird. . . . But I don't know. I guess it's all right."

"It'll feel more like home once you unpack and make the bed." She leans back on her elbows and firmly pushes the pillow top as if she were in a mattress store taking a "test drive" on the merchandise. "Sure you don't need help unpacking?"

Joe's posture sags slightly.

"I'm sure," I answer.

"OK. Promise to call me if you need *an-nee-thing*." Renée hugs me goodbye, raising her brows as she peers into my eyes.

I break her gaze to nod at the floor.

"I would hug you, but I'm a little sweaty." Joe tugs the hem of his shirt to air it out, then offers his palm to slap, then fist-bumps me.

I walk them out, shut the door, and lean against it. Standing in the doorway, I take a long look at Mom's beautifully appointed home. She bought the condo after our house was sold in the divorce. New home, new her.

The condo exterior is nice but vanilla, part of a homogenous community of palm-tree-studded beige buildings. She gutted the interior, rebuilding and renovating from the studs out. Her second-story unit has high-vaulted ceilings and a living area that opens up to a large sun-drenched balcony. Natural light pours in, illuminating the pale blue walls adorned with framed images of Parisian scenes. A marble mantel, imported from Italy, sits over a fireplace that faces plush ivory leather sofas. And hanging above the large black dining table, an oversize Gothic smoke-colored chandelier sparkles. After her having lived inland for years, Mom's new place in Newport Beach, walking distance from Balboa Island, is her dream home.

It's nicer than my apartment and more expensive than I could possibly hope to afford. I feel ungrateful for hating it here. *I want to go home.* I trudge to the guest bedroom and throw myself facedown on the bed. When the mattress under my face grows too damp to tolerate, I get up to grab a tissue. Sniffling, I rip the tape off of the three "Closet" boxes and dig through clothes and accessories until finally I find it, buried between two blankets.

Teddy Bear, my dingy mustard-colored stuffed cat, was jammed inside a closet drawer when I found him while packing. I clutch him tightly to my chest and deeply inhale his musty aroma. I check his appendages for damage from the move. His legs are a little wobbly but no more than when I first packed him away. I tuck him under my left arm, then begin to unpack the box he came out of.

When I finish with the three boxes I ripped open, I pull the tape off a "Dresser" box. I pull a stack of semifolded pajamas from it, and a small glossy photo falls out. It's Tom's torn-off half of a four-frame photo-booth strip. I'd thrown away my half years ago after a fight. *How long has this been in here?* I shake my head. *Don't think about it.* I throw it into an empty box and finish filling the dresser. I pull the tape off another carton and throw the sticky wad into the box I've been tossing all the trash in. I'm sifting through the new carton when a sigh escapes my throat as my eyes begin to water. I stop sifting to look back through the trash box full of wadded tape and plastic bags until I find the torn photo strip. Both frames on the strip are nearly identical images of our faces pressed together in a drunk, open-mouthed, passionate kiss.

I set the photo down, then throw Teddy Bear at the bed. *What am I doing?* My chest tightens, and my breathing accelerates as I dig through my purse. I swallow a second Xanax dry and sit on the floor beside the bed, waiting for the room to stop spinning. When the tightness wanes, I take a deep breath. Then throw the photo back into the trash box and drag all the empty boxes outside to the dumpster.

I shower then get dressed in the closet. I try not to look in the mirror. The bathroom is split, with the toilet and shower separate from the dual sink vanity. The closet faces the vanity mirror. To avoid myself I'd have to close the door, but it feels silly since I'm alone.

The pretty blue sweater I thought would look cheerful hangs on me like a hospital gown. Both my sweater and my jeans fit looser than I remember. I apply mascara and blush, then stare back at the unfamiliar reflection in the mirror. *You're sad, not sick. Get it together.* I rustle through tubes and cosmetic cases for bronzer, then dust the brown powder feverishly all over my face. A loud thud of the door in the entryway startles me, shaking the bronzer out of my hand. The small round container crashes onto the tile below, sending tan-colored powder chunks everywhere. Mercifully, the bronzer stains only the tile, narrowly missing the white carpet of the adjoining bedroom.

"Hi, kiddo, I'm home. There's a package for you here. I just brought it in," Mom calls from the kitchen.

"OK! I'll be right there," I shout back as I drop to my hands and knees to clean up the dusty brown mess.

"Ooh, it's from Pottery Barn! What'd you order?" she continues, her voice growing louder as she approaches my open bedroom door. "Are you OK?" Mom drops her purse and bends over to grab my shoulders.

"I'm fine," I huff, pushing my hair back with the crook of my elbow. "I can't say the same for my bronzer, though." I shake my head, crouched over, wiping the floor with a russet-stained towel.

"Do you need help?"

"I'm OK, Mom. See? All cleaned up." I get up and point to the still lightly dusted, mostly clean floor.

"OK." She inhales a long breath and presses her lips together, glaring at the now off-white tile.

"Let's go open my package." I press my lips into a thin smile and lead the way out to the kitchen. "Where do you keep the scissors?" I ask as I open and shut drawers.

She opens a drawer by the sink and hands them to me. I cut open the box and pull out a pale blue ruched duvet and white cotton sheets. I run my fingers over the new soft fabric and smile.

"Do you want help making your bed?" Mom asks.

"No, thanks. I got it. Besides, I want to wash them first." I take the bedding to the laundry closet.

"Are you hungry?" Mom calls from the kitchen. "I was thinking of making some pasta."

"I'm not hungry!" I shout back.

"What'd you have for lunch?" she asks, walking into the hall beside me.

My jaw clenches and my lips pull back, exposing both rows of teeth.

"You need to eat." She narrows her eyes.

She crosses her arms, and my shoulders inch up as I expect her to say, *Or you're grounded.* She picks up her purse from the counter and heads to her room to change. She returns to the kitchen dressed in jeans to make dinner. I sit at the counter watching as she dices onion and tomato while linguini boils. When she starts cutting chicken, I get up.

"Do you need help?" I ask.

"Sure. You can open a bottle of wine."

"Which one?" I ask, eyeing the full rack on the counter.

"Let's drink a *good* one." She points to the cabinet in the living room with her knife.

"No. I don't wanna drink your good stuff. We're not celebrating anything."

"Yes, I am. My daughter moved in today."

"I feel like you should save the good stuff for when I move out."

"Don't worry. I'll open a good bottle then too."

I grab a bottle of Chianti and open it with her fancy one-touch electric opener. The aroma of sautéed onions permeates the living room and my stomach growls. I pour the wine and take a seat beside the end of the table.

"Thank you, Lord, for this food we're about to eat and for bringing my baby back home to live with me. Amen."

"Amen." I tilt my head to the side, pursing my lips. "Mom, you're killing me."

"What?" She grins, stifling a laugh.

I shake my head, then focus on twirling linguini around my fork. "Thank you for making dinner."

"My pleasure. It's nice having someone to cook for."

"It's nice having someone make *me* dinner for a change." I take a bite.

The scrape of forks twisting against spoons and the slosh of noodles become the only sounds.

Finally, I take a sip of wine and say, "It's weird, you know, living together again. It's weird because I'm a grown-up now."

"What? You? Impossible. No one told me. If you're a grown-up, I must be old, and I'm definitely not old." She puts her fork down.

"Mom, I'm serious. I mean, I'm not exactly excited about the circumstances, but I'm glad I'm here with you. And for the record, I am a grown-up. I've got a few grays to prove it."

"All right, that may be so. You might be a grown-up to everyone else, but you'll always be my baby. I remember when you were born. You were so beautiful I couldn't believe you were mine."

"No. Mom, no. No 'when you were born' stories." I laugh. "We need some ground rules if we are going to live together."

"I'm glad you mentioned it. I wanted to bring it up but thought I would wait until you were settled in. But since *you* brought it up, what were you thinking? To be clear, this is *my* house you're living in." She smiles and crosses her arms.

"Whoa, whoa, whoa. I was totally kidding. I was gonna say no baby stories and maybe take it as far as to ask that you please not humiliate me. I didn't think we were going to have this kind of discussion. You can't give me rules. I'm an adult now!"

"You may be an adult, but you're living with me, and I'm still your mom, roomies or not."

"Seriously?"

She nods. "I won't be so cliché as to number the rules for you, but to put it simply, you need to be tidy, courteous, and respectful. Don't leave messes around the house. I am not your maid."

"OK." I take a long sip of wine.

"I expect you to be home at a decent hour because you're a lady."

"Mm-hmm," I answer with the glass still pressed to my lips.

"Don't bring over boys that you don't want me to interrogate. Oh, and obviously no slumber parties. I don't want any of your girlfriends crashing my couch, and I certainly don't want any boys staying over." She twirls the linguini around her fork and takes a bite, completely nonchalant, as if we were discussing nail polish colors.

I toss back the rest of my wine in a single gulp. "Fair enough. I pride myself on being very tidy. No overnight guests—easy. I don't plan on dating while I'm living here so that's a nonissue." I pour myself a second glass. "But as an aforementioned adult, I think I should be able to come and go as I please without having to worry about checking in with my *mommy*." I point my glass at her, then take a long sip.

She mirrors me, taking a long drink of her wine. Then she takes another deliberate bite and chews slowly.

"Well?" I raise my eyebrows.

"I'm thinking." She shakes the table setting her glass down. "We can revisit that issue in the future if it becomes a problem. I do worry about you, Ruthie, but I am going to respect you as an adult."

"Thank you." I tilt my head back and look up.

When we finish eating, I help clean up. She washes. I dry, learning where everything is kept as I put the dishes away. A chime sounds just as I hang the dish towel.

"Mom, your phone went off."

"It's not mine. My phone's on silent. Are you sure it isn't yours?"

"My phone doesn't make that sound." I shrug.

She picks my phone up off the table. "It's yours."

"What is it?"

I spray disinfectant across the counter. The smell of lemony chemicals makes me grimace.

"It says, 'It's a match!' "

"What?" I drop my paper towel. "Let me see that."

My heart races, outpacing my sprint to the table. She hands me my phone and crosses her arms. A smile spreads across her face as she cocks a brow. I punch in my pass code and the phone vibrates. Still locked. I retype my pass code and fail again, then finally press my shaking thumb to the Home button. I have twenty-four hours to respond to Ryan from Newport Beach.

"What is it?"

"It's nothing."

Mom tilts her head, staring at me. "I thought you didn't plan on dating."

"I didn't. I don't." *Oh my God, she thinks I'm a slut.* "It was Sam. She downloaded a dating app to my phone. She liked some guy for me. I told her not to, but you know Sam. It doesn't matter. I'm going to delete the app anyway." Stomach acid rises in my throat, and my mouth begins to salivate.

"Are you OK?"

I shake my head and clutch my hand to my mouth. My stomach lurches and I run to the bathroom, making it only to the sink. Chianti-colored noodles spew out, staining the white basin. *Xanax and wine do not mix.* I wipe the sweat from my brow, then run the tap.

"Hey, are you all right?"

I put my hand up to stop her from coming closer. "I need a minute."

She retreats to the living room. I rinse out the sink, then splash my face with cool water and dry myself with a hand towel. Staining it brown with the bronzer I caked on earlier. My face is even paler now, after I've been sick. I finger-comb my hair and lean into the mirror. It's no use. My hair looks awful. I haven't washed it in close to a week. The roots are so greasy they look black compared to the rest of my dark brown hair. *No one else is going to want you.* I shake my head. Then smooth my sweater and exhale.

"Nice to meet you," I whisper to the reflection. I reach into my makeup bag and reapply blush, then lipstick. My belly flutters. "I'm sorry I'm so nervous. This is my first date in years."

I lower my gaze and look up through my lashes. My eyes are bloodshot and watery from the vomiting. I try to ignore it. Then toss my hair back and force a smile. Waxy pink stains are streaked across my teeth. I shake my head, wipe off the lipstick, and sag against the counter, my legs feeling weak.

"Ruthie?" Mom shouts from the living room.

"I'll be out in a minute, Mom. I'm changing into pajamas."

I change, then slump onto the sofa beside her and rest my head on her shoulder.

"Everything's gonna be all right." She pats my leg.

"Is it, though?"

"Yes." She wraps her arm around me. "And, no matter what you do, I support you. OK? I don't have to agree with you to support you."

"So, you think it's too early for me to date?"

"I'm not saying that."

I pull back from her and raise my brows.

"I just don't want you to get hurt while you're still healing. And if the thought of dating makes you sick, you're probably not as ready as you think."

"That's not why I puked." My voice is low and firm.

"So, my cooking is *that* bad?"

"No." I sigh. "Ugh. I just don't want to end up with framed pictures of my cats."

"What?"

"Nothing. Never mind."

I flip off the light switch. With my arms extended in front of me, I feel through the dark for the bed. My shin finds it before my hands. *Fuck.* I collapse onto the bed, curl my legs against my torso, and massage my shin. The stinging is a welcome distraction from the pounding inside my head. When the stinging finally stops, I lie flat on my back and stare up. It's darker than I remember it being here, and the silence is different. The change of contents has altered the resonance of the room.

I listen for something, anything, familiar from when I slept in this room last week, but it's all new. I take a few shallow breaths, listening to the sound of the air being drawn in and blown out. Then clutch Teddy Bear to my chest and shuffle from my back to my side. My heart aches. *I want to go home.* I tug the hem of the soft white flat sheet up to my eyes and wipe them dry. Then roll onto my back again and throw off the covers. My pajamas stick to my sweaty skin. I can't catch a deep enough breath as my breathing speeds up. I'm winded as though I've run up a flight of stairs. I force a yawn, trying to inhale deeply, then squeeze my eyes shut. *This is all my fault.*

5

LAST ONE IN HAS ROTTEN *EGGS*

oud, indistinct chatter coming from another room forces me awake. I rub my eyes and sit up. *I'm still here.* I pull back the mascara-stained sheets and check my shin. There's no bruise. I throw myself back against the bed and squeeze my eyes shut, then reopen them. Blinkingly look around the disarrayed room. A row of packed boxes line the wall along the floor. The channel changes on the TV in the living room and the volume increases till it's loud enough to wake a cadaver. *Seriously, Mom?* Rubbing my eyes, I feel the puffiness of the lids. Mascara smears across my knuckles in thick greasy streaks. I yawn and inhale deeply. A mild ache at the back of my head reminds me of the clamp I felt around my brain last night. I roll over to check the time on my phone, then remember I still have to respond to Ryan from Bumble. I stare at the screen as I calculate how many hours I have left. *Almost eleven.* I get out of bed, straighten my hair, and swing open the door.

"Do you have coffee?" I ask as I take a seat at the kitchen counter.

"Good morning. Yes. How'd you sleep?" Mom asks, smiling. Her eyebrows draw close together upon further inspection of my face. "Rough night, huh?"

"It was all right." I swipe under my eyes. *I should have checked the mirror.*

"Did you sleep at all?" She tilts her head.

I blink and look away to break her eye contact. "Honestly, I slept terrible, but it's fine. I didn't die. You know I'm a crier. It's no big deal. I survived my first night, and now this is my first day *really* living here." I shrug. "It actually feels pretty good. I think I'm even gonna go to church."

"Do you want to come to mass with me?" she asks, pressing the button to start the coffee maker.

I pinch my lips together and shake my head.

"You'd rather go all the way to San Juan Capistrano?" She leans against the counter.

"It's not that far." I pull at my ear, then press the earring back tighter.

"I don't know why you go to that Nondenominational church. There's no ritual, no saints, no *confession*." She shoots me a look, and I give her one back. "Well, without saints, who's going to pray for you?" she asks.

"I don't know, Mom. Do we really have to do this right now? I just woke up."

"OK." She nods gently. "Well, do you want to meet for lunch after?"

"I don't know. I'll call you after the service." I stand, backing toward the guest room. "I need to start getting ready."

"What about your coffee?"

I stop, let out a long, low sigh, and step toward the kitchen.

"Do you want breakfast?" she asks as she pours coffee then hands me the mug.

I shake the creamer, then pour into my mug. "No, I'm fine. I'll grab something before I leave."

"Are you sure? I can—"

"Mom, I'm fine," I interrupt. Then slam the creamer down on the counter.

She blinks slowly and goes completely still.

"Sorry. I didn't mean to snap." My shoulders slump. "You're right. I didn't get enough sleep. Honestly, I'm OK. I promise I can take care of myself."

She nods and sips her coffee.

I put the creamer back in the fridge, force a tight-lipped smile, and plod back to the guest room.

I arrive late, walking in as everyone is standing and shaking one another's hands. I scan the room, but with everyone out of their seat, it's impossible to tell if there are any available chairs. It looks like a hotel conference room, but instead of suit-wearing executives, the room is filled with pastel-wearing moms, polo-clad dads, and young couples. The stained-glass windows and pulpit remind me this is church. *I belong here.* As people begin to sit down, the seats fill. I look left and right counting the number of people still standing versus the number of chairs, then look back toward the door. An usher notices me. He holds up his pointer finger and mouths, "One?" I grit my teeth in a half smile, nod, and put up my pointer. He leads me to a single empty seat in the front row between two families.

"Is this the only one?"

He smiles and clasps his hands. "It's a full house."

"Thank you."

I grimace and nod hello to the smiling families on either side of me. Then draw my arms up against my chest and look ahead. Sitting cross-legged, I shift in my chair, then uncross my legs. I focus my eyes on the pastor, trying to steady my breathing. Forcing a yawn to catch my breath. Then rub my sweaty palms against the legs of my white jeans. The wet marks are obvious on my thighs. *Why did I wear white pants?* I look back up at the pastor, then look away when I think he's caught me. My face burns, flushing bright red. I sit up straight and stare into my Bible, swallowing the lump in my throat. *Just keep reading.* I read along as he speaks, keeping my eyes down turned.

I brought Tom to church once. We arrived early, but he led me to a row in the back anyway. He held my hand, pulling me down to sit while everyone else stood to sing. I was so happy he came, I pretended not to notice him using his phone as I read along with the congregation. In the weeks after, I fantasized about walking down the aisle of the church, him waiting at the end of it. But he never came back to church with me.

"Wasn't that a great message?"

"Hmm?" My eyebrows squeeze together.

"Wasn't that a great message?" the woman beside me repeats as she stands and straightens her dress. The rest of her family is standing and waiting on her.

"Oh. Yeah, it was great." I offer a tight-lipped smile.

She smiles and nods, then follows her adult children up the aisle. The room buzzes with a hundred voices, people excusing themselves and greeting one another. I shake my head and take a deep breath. *What was the message about?* I wait until the family on the other side of me reaches the aisle to finally stand. Then eventually pace out of the building behind an elderly couple. The wife waves me ahead as her husband ambles on, leaning into his cane, but I shake my head and smile.

My stomach growls as I reach my car. The heat emanating off the leather seats burns through my pants and against my back. I start the engine and turn the AC on full blast, then grab my phone from inside my purse. A new message from Mom.

"Will you be home soon?"

I turn off the engine and throw the phone back in my purse. I walk back toward the church and take a seat on a bench outside. Sunlight streaks through the leaves of the willow tree the bench is under. It's warm for autumn, but that doesn't stop people from wearing sweaters with their sandals. The bench faces a busy street, and I watch families and tourists wander by. A group of tween-age girls wearing too-short shorts and crop tops grabs my attention. *It's warm but not hot enough for a crop top.* I adjust the collar of my long-sleeved blouse and sit up straight.

"Ew, you like Jordan." The tallest of the tweens hurls the accusation at the flushed girl beside her. The three other girls laugh along with the first as they walk past.

I wrinkle my nose. *Ew, I like Ryan.* I shift against the stiff wooden bench, then pull out my phone and press my thumb over the icon for the Bumble app. All the icons on the screen start dancing. I watch the x shake, then press it. If I delete the app, I will lose all the data. *Cancel or delete?* I stare at the prompt, then let out the breath I've been holding. *Cancel.* I blacken the screen and set it facedown on the bench. The phone chimes.

New message from Mom: "Do you want to meet your sister and I for lunch?"

I reply, "Yes." I sag against the bench, then toss the phone into my bag and head back to my car.

Once I merge onto the freeway, I stay in the right lane. Cars pass and merge ahead, but I keep at a steady sixty-five. *Is he funny? Is he smart? What does he do for work? Should I send him a message? What would I even say?* I don't know how to date anymore. *He's going to think I'm an idiot.* Red lights flash and I slam on my brakes. The driver behind me throws both hands up, shakes his head, then gives me the finger. *Sorry.* Once he passes, I call Sam.

"Sam!" I shout into the Bluetooth microphone. "I matched with Ryan."

"Who's Ryan?"

"That guy, you know. The one you swiped, from Bumble."

"Ohhh, yeah. Nice. So, that's why you're calling me? You want to thank me for being such an awesome friend, right?"

"Yeah, yeah, sure. Look, I'm serious. What should I do? Should I respond? Do you think it's too soon?"

My words rush out, sounding like a disclaimer at the end of a prescription drug commercial, only louder and more forceful. *Side effects include shortness of breath, palpitations, nausea, dizziness, headaches, and vomiting.*

"Oh yeah, you should definitely wait until tomorrow. You don't want to look desperate." Her voice is firm.

"I only have like eight hours left."

"He swiped you yesterday, and you didn't tell me?"

I drum my thumbs against the steering wheel and bite my lip.

"I see how it is."

"C'mon, Sam," I whine.

"Wait until the last hour," she replies flatly.

"What?"

"Wait until the last hour," she repeats. "This guy took a week to swipe on you. So, either he is playing games, or he was seeing someone else and just got back to swiping. Either way it's kind of shady."

"Seriously?"

"Yeah. Welcome to the world of app dating. It's no big deal. You're not gonna marry this guy. He's just a rebound."

"And you don't think it's too soon for me to date?"

"Probably not."

"But what if I end up liking him?"

"You haven't even talked to him yet."

I arrive at Renée's just after 1:00 p.m. Renée and Joe, college sweethearts, met while studying engineering together. Like *real* grown-ups, they own a home and have two kids. I park on the street in front of their house, set my phone to silent, and get out of the car.

I knock twice before opening the door. Shrill cries immediately grate on my ears. Jacob has taken Rebecca's toy, and she's shrieking, strapped to her bouncer, trying to regain possession of what looks like a tattered stuffed rat.

"Jacob, give your sister back her rat. Come on, dude." I shut the door behind me.

"It's not a rat. It's an elephant. We need to wash it. That's why I took it from her." He pinches the matted fabric of the tail, holding the toy out in front of him. "It smells weird. I was going to give her this bear instead."

Jacob hands her the bear and gets up to give me a hug. Rebecca's red, teary eyes squint with a smile as she grips the bear with both chubby little arms.

"Oh, my goodness, you are getting so tall," I say. "Jeez Louise. You must have grown a foot since the last time I saw you."

"Yeah, I grow pretty fast." Jacob puts his hands on his hips and nods.

"Oh yeah?" I laugh, raising an eyebrow. "All right. Where's your mom? Is Grandma Joy here?" I ask and bend over to kiss Rebecca, who is now fully gnawing on the bear's ear. *That explains the weird smell.*

"They're upstairs in the loft, talking about boring stuff."

"Thank you, Jakey."

"I'm too old for you to call me Jakey! I'm six now. It's just *Jacob*, OK, Aunt Ruthie?"

"OK, if you say so," I singsong as I walk up the stairs.

How did my baby nephew grow up so fast? Jacob is short for his age and lean, with brilliant green eyes, a mischievous smile (missing three teeth), and a brown mop of hair that is rarely combed. While Jacob takes after my sister, Rebecca is the spitting image of Joe with dark hair and huge brown eyes. Both kids are so beautiful it makes my heart ache. As the older sister, I grew up assuming I would be first to get married and have children. But here I am, moved back in with Mom, having receded to the starting line.

Upstairs, Mom and Renée sit in a pair of dark brown leather sofas across from each other. Their half-empty wineglasses shake with their laughter. Renée, nearly doubled over, struggles to keep the glass from spilling. When she sees me, Mom taps Renée's knee and stands.

"So glad you could finally join us." Mom points to her watch. "Your sister needs to eat. I am *not* that funny." She chuckles as she hugs me. "Too much wine," she whispers, then points toward Renée with her eyes.

"Hiii!" Renée gets up and kisses my cheek, standing on her tiptoes. "Are those new shoes, or am I getting shorter?" she quips, tucking her shoulder-length brown hair behind her ear.

"They're old. I found them when I was unpacking." I take a seat beside her on the smaller sofa. "You can borrow them if you want."

"Can I borrow that shirt too?" my sister asks.

Mom lifts a brow and glares at Renée. Renée pinches her lips into a thin line, then pulls them back into a toothy smile.

"We were just talking about you," Mom says, eyebrow still raised.

Renée nods.

"OK?" I clench my jaw.

Mom clears her throat. "Renée was telling me about one of the engineers she used to go to school with."

"And?" I shake my head slightly. "What's that got to do with me?"

"Mom thinks you should meet him," Renée says.

"For what?" I ask.

Renée looks away and drinks the last of her wine.

My eyes widen as my mouth slackens. "Wait. Didn't you just finish telling me yesterday that it's too early for me to start dating?" I ask Mom.

"I never said that," Mom says.

Renée interjects, "No one says you have to go on a date tomorrow or anything. We were just *talking*."

"About *me*," I say.

"We're just worried about you. You've never been single for long, and we thought this time we might help—"

I cut Renée off. "I don't need either of your help." I narrow my eyes. "Thank you both for your interest." I pinch my lips shut as my cheeks flush. "What's for lunch?"

Renée scans my face. "Not so fast. What's that face you're making? What are you not telling us?"

I cross my arms and shrink back into the sofa. "Nothing. What are you talking about?" I bite the inside of my cheek.

"It's that guy from the match thing, right?" Renée leans toward me.

Pressed against the sofa, I have nowhere to retreat. My chin draws into my neck.

"Ha. . . . Yeah! It is. Look at your face." She squeals and slaps the sofa leather between us.

"Renée, that's enough," Mom admonishes.

Renée grits her teeth. "Tell us. Are you on Tinder? Did you talk to him? What did he say?"

"No, I'm not on Tinder. No, I didn't talk to him," I say. "He hasn't said anything. It doesn't work like that."

"Well, how does it work?" Mom asks and takes a sip of wine.

"I don't know. I'm still figuring it out." I shrug, then bite my lip. "Can we talk about something else?"

"No! Let's talk about *this.*" Renée slaps the sofa again.

"I know what she needs to talk. I'm going to get her a glass of wine." Mom gets up and walks downstairs.

Once her footsteps are inaudible, Renée leans toward me again. "Quick, tell me everything before she gets back." Hands clasped together, she bounces in her seat.

"Do you wanna know? Do you really want to know?" I whisper and lean toward her.

"Yes. Tell me, what does he look like? What's his name? Do you have a picture?"

I sit back and stroke my chin as if I had a beard, pretending to be deep in thought.

"Just tell me!" Renée shoves my shoulder.

Mom returns with a heavily poured glass and the rest of the bottle of rosé. "What did I miss?"

"Ruu-thieee was just about to tell me all about the guy from Tinder before you rudely interrupted." Renée giggles.

"It's not Tinder." I slap her thigh. Then take the glass from Mom.

"Ruthie, don't hit your sister." Mom pours wine into her and Renée's empty glasses.

"Yeah, don't hit your sister," Joe repeats, and laughs, imitating Mom, as he walks in from the bedroom.

"Hey, Bro-in-Law. How are you?" I ask and jump to my feet to hug him.

"I'm good. I just came in to say hello." He pulls back and walks toward the stairway. "I'll let you ladies get back to it. If you need me, I'll be downstairs with the kids watching the game."

"You don't want to join us?" I ask, hoping he'll redirect the conversation.

"Nope," he replies as he descends.

When he reaches the landing, he looks up at me, makes a fart sound with his mouth, chuckles, and runs down the rest of the stairs. *Aah, the brother I never wanted.* When I turn back around, both Renée and Mom are staring at me as if to say, *Shut up and tell us already.*

"So, what kind of food did you order? Is it coming soon?" I ask, grimacing.

"I ordered Mediterranean food. It'll be here in twenty minutes," Mom answers.

"What's his name? What does he look like?" Renée demands.

"All right, I'll tell you. If you will stop squawking, I will show you his Bumble profile. But that's it. After I show you, you both have to drop it. No more questions. No more probing. You cease the interrogation. Deal?"

"Deal," they concede.

"OK. His name is Ryan, and he lives in Newport. That's all I know. Now, I'm going to show you his photos. Don't touch anything. Actually, don't even touch the phone. I'll hold it for you both to look at." I sit back down beside Renée.

"Ooh, he's cute. Is that *his* boat in the picture? Is he rich?" Renée asks.

I blush. "I don't know. I don't even know his last name. He is cute, huh?" I bite my lip to keep from smiling.

"Like Aunt Hellen always says, 'One nail drives out another,' if you know what I mean." Renée wiggles her eyebrows.

"Renée!" Mom scolds.

"What? It's not my expression." She tilts her head and smirks before taking a long sip of wine. "Besides, she's not getting any younger."

Mom gives Renée a tight-eyed look.

Renée's chin dips to her chest as her posture slumps. "I'm sorry. I didn't mean it like that."

I clear my throat and cough. "It's OK. I know."

Mom leans over and pats my arm. "What your sister means is that we support you if you're ready to move on. We know this is hard for you. And we understand if you want to start dating."

"It's not even that I *want* to start dating." I shake my head. "Renée's right. I'm not getting any younger. I don't know what I'm doing anymore. I feel like I'm running out of time."

"But you're still young," Mom says in a way that sounds as if she's questioning her own words.

"I'm not, though. If I don't marry Tom, then I *have* to meet someone new. And not just anyone, someone that I *do* want to marry. How long will *that* take? A year? Five years? Never?" I throw my hands up, then cross my arms. "What if I get too old to have kids? What if my window closes? What then?" My voice catches as a searing tear rolls down my cheek.

"Food's here!" Jacob interrupts, shouting breathlessly as he runs up the stairs into the loft.

"Tell Dad we'll be right down," Renée tells Jacob.

Jacob turns around and runs back down, arms flailing behind him. I sit up straight and wipe my face. I swallow hard to clear my throat again.

Mom and Renée look at me blinkingly, both leaning in toward me as though visiting me in the hospital.

"It's fine." I drink half my wine in a single swallow. "I'm being silly. Everything's fine. Let's go eat lunch before it gets cold."

They both open their mouths as if to speak, but I ignore them and stand. Then jog down the stairs without looking back.

"Wait for me, Jakey."

OUT WITH
THE OLD . . .

With less than two hours left to respond, I sit cross-legged atop my bed and tap to open Instagram on my phone. I click the magnifying glass, then type "Ryan" into the search box. Beneath the couple of Ryans I already follow is a list of unknown Ryans. I scroll through dozens of strangers' photos searching for his strawberry-blond hair and bright blue eyes. When I reach the bottom of the list, I close Instagram, open Facebook, and repeat. *If only I knew his last name.* I close the app and throw my phone at the bed. Then lie back and stare at the ceiling.

I have fifty-four minutes left. I bite the inside of my cheek. *What will I even say?* I grab my phone, then drum my nails against the black screen. As I open the Bumble app, my stomach flutters. I close my eyes and take a deep breath. *It's just a message. He might not even respond.* I exhale slowly through my mouth, then type into the message box.

"Hi, Ryan, how's it going?"

I stare at the screen and reread the message I just sent. *Stupid.* My mouth goes dry, and I get up to grab a drink from the kitchen. *"How's it going?"* I grab a water bottle and slam the fridge door shut. Back in my room I slump against the headboard and take a sip. I pick up my phone as I drink. When the screen illuminates his response, I grip the bottle too hard and spill water on my chin and down my shirt. *Crap.* I mop at it with my palm, then use the hem of my shirt to dry my face as I open the app.

"Good. How's your Sunday night?" his message reads.

My eyes widen at the yellow bubble on my screen. I lick my lip, then bite down, keeping my teeth clenched against my lip as I type. "Really good." *Now what?* I tap at the screen with my thumbnail, willing the right words to flow out.

"Are you new to Bumble?" he asks.

He knows. I bite the cuticle of my thumb, then finally type, "Yes," and send a teeth-baring emoji.

"Welcome," he replies. "Before you get too comfortable, would you allow me to take you on your first Bumble date?"

I smile at the screen, tightly gripping the phone in my sweat-dampened hand. I tuck my hair behind my ear and look around the room. *Should I ask Sam?* I bite at my nail, chipping the pink polish, then reply, "Yes."

"Great. Send me your number, and I'll text you later this week to coordinate."

I message him my phone number with a smiling, blushing emoji. Then clutch my phone to my chest and let out a squeal as I throw myself back against the bed, kicking my legs through the air.

When my legs grow tired, I roll onto my stomach and message Sam: "The eagle has landed." I watch the screen, waiting for her ellipsis to pop up. When the screen goes black, I swipe over to my email to finally check for bites on the Craigslist ads I put up last week. Of the twelve emails I've received, only three warrant a response. Tina is interested in my bedroom furniture, Robert in the sofa and coffee table, and Edwin in the sofa, coffee table, and dining set. I reply to all three, hoping I can sell everything tomorrow evening, then close my email.

* * *

The next day at my office I open my inbox to find confirmations from Robert and Edwin. I send Tina a follow-up email, but when I don't hear back from her by the end of the day, I consider it a lost cause. I leave work thirty minutes early and take my old route *home*.

The drive seems longer than I remember. Without the radio on, all I hear is the sound of my uneven breathing and the occasional tick of my turn signal. As I turn down the street to my apartment complex, my breathing grows increasingly shallow, and my chest becomes tight. My fingers grip the steering wheel tighter as I begin to lose feeling in my hands and feet. *Just stop and park now.* I park in a guest spot in front of my building and kill the engine.

Tears sting my eyes and roll down my flushed face. I'm sweating. My blouse sticks to the skin under my arms and beneath my bra. I gasp for air. It feels like I'm drowning. I press the button to restart the engine, and the dash lights up with dozens of buttons. Arrows pointing up, arrows pointing down, Dashboard Vent, Play, Max AC, Forward, Stop. I smack all the buttons for the air-conditioning until finally the air punches through the vents and blows into my face. *I need my pills.* My shaking hands scour through my overfilled work bag.

I hear the pills rattling inside the vial as my hand violently thrashes through my purse. I twist off the cap, work three pills out with my finger, and put them into my dampened palm. *Three is too many. You don't know these people.* I pinch two pills from my palm and swallow them with a mouthful of cold coffee from my morning thermos. Then scrape the remaining pill from my palm back into the vial and twist the cap shut. The white powder inside will dry it off.

I wipe the black smudges under my eyes and dry the sweat from my forehead with a Starbucks napkin from my glove box. After I finger-comb my hair and reapply lipstick, I turn off the engine and force myself out of the car. Inside the elevator I rub my arms, wrinkling my blouse. I left my jacket in the back seat.

I pace down the hallway to our apartment. The space in front of the door where the welcome mat used to be is a shade lighter than the rest of the carpet. I take a deep breath, turn the key, and push the door open. It's dark and lonely and sad inside. Musty. It smells like sweat and cardboard. I flip the light on in the kitchen and set my purse down. The collar of my blouse clings damp around my neck. I roll up my sleeves and slide open the glass door to the balcony. The setting sun hangs low and red in the orange-hued sky. Leaning against the doorway, I squint at the sunset.

Inside my purse my phone chimes. New message from Edwin: "I'll be there in fifteen minutes." I check for unread messages and emails. Nothing. No missed phone calls. *It's probably best if Robert flakes since Edwin is on his way.* I throw my phone back inside my purse and sag against the counter. I hope Edwin will buy what's left. *Wait.* I stand up straight as my eyes blink rapidly. *What if he's a pervert or a serial killer posing as a secondhand furniture shopper?*

I grab my phone and message Renée. "If anything happens to me, it was Edwin from Craigslist."

I open all the drawers and cabinets in the kitchen searching for a knife, or scissors, or anything that resembles a shiv. *Empty.* I check all the drawers and cabinets in the bathroom and closet. Everything is empty. My phone chimes.

"What are you talking about? Where are you? Is everything ok?!" a text from Renée reads.

"Everything is fine. I'm selling my furniture to some guy off craigslist. I'm at my apartment. If I don't call you in twenty minutes, call me." I hit Send. "Then call the police," I add.

I jump and drop my phone when I hear a knock at the door. I tuck my hair behind my ear and take a deep breath before shouting, "I'm coming!"

Just ten more minutes for the Xanax to kick in. I adjust my collar and smooth my blouse before opening the door.

"Hi, I'm Edwin. Are you Ruthie?"

He extends his right hand with a broad smile. His big white teeth shine against his smooth cinnamon skin. I draw my hand up slowly before placing it in his. His giant hand feels as though it might swallow mine whole. He shakes it like a vending machine that owes him a soda, and I wobble from the impact. *He's probably not a serial killer.* Once I steady myself, I smooth out my blouse again.

"Yes, I'm Ruthie. Nice to meet you. Please, have a look. I'm selling everything that's left in here."

Edwin strides into the living area and stops between the dining table and sofa. I watch as his brow furrows while he examines the dining chairs. His huge athletic figure looks out of place in my little apartment. When he sits on the sofa, it reminds me of Goldilocks. *"This sofa's too small."* His lips purse when he lifts the coffee table. I imagine he's trying to determine from the weight whether it's solid wood or not. *"This table's too light."*

"I'll give you a hundred and twenty dollars for the dining set and a hundred and thirty for the coffee table and sofa," he finally offers.

"Sounds good." I cross my arms and clear my throat.

"Cool." He peels the bills from a thin folded wad of cash in a money clip and hands them to me before stuffing the clip back in his gym-shorts pocket. "I'm going to get my brother from downstairs, and we'll start moving this stuff out."

As I shut the door behind him, my phone starts ringing.

"Are you dead?" Renée asks.

"No, I'm not dead. How would I answer the phone?"

"Is he going to buy all your stuff?"

"Just the living room and dining stuff."

"What about your bedroom furniture?"

"He didn't offer me anything for it."

"Did he look at it?"

"No."

"Did you ask him about it?"

"No."

"Well, ask him! You don't want to go back, do you?"

"No." I sigh. "I gotta let you go. He'll be back any minute."

I hang up just as there's a knock at the front door. Edwin and his bigger younger brother have returned. They squat to pick up the sofa and carry it out without so much as a grunt. Then come back to pick up all the dining chairs. One in each hand, they march down the hall. The dining table is next, then lastly they return for the coffee table. Edwin pushes forward as his brother walks backward, angling the table to get it through the narrow doorway.

"Wait. Edwin!" I say.

"Yeah?" He grunts. "Is something wrong?" His eyebrows squeeze together.

"No, nothing is wrong. Um, do you have any more room left in your truck?" I bite my lip.

"I don't know. Maybe. Why?" His head flinches back slightly as he shoves the back end of the table through the door.

"Well, if you have room for it, I would literally give you the remaining furniture for free if you can just take it. Can you take it today? . . . I, um . . . have to get rid of it."

"Is something wrong with it?" Edwin raises his brows, then sets the coffee table down in the hallway, sweat beading on his forehead. Edwin's brother puts his sneaker on the coffee table and leans into his knee. I purse my lips and scowl at his foot. In response, he wipes his brow with the back of his hand and glares back at me.

"No, nothing is wrong with it. It's just . . . I don't want it anymore, I can't take it with me, and the lease is up. You would be doing me a huge favor if you took it with you."

"I mean, yeah. Sure. If you're sure you don't mind me just taking it. We just bought a house, and we could use it."

"Awesome!" I clasp my hands.

"Cool. We're going to take this table down and move stuff around in the truck. We'll come back up for the rest."

"Great!"

Edwin nods to his brother, and together they lift the coffee table and pace down the hallway. I shut the door after them, then run in place in the entryway to suppress the squeal I feel rising in my throat. My heart drums inside my chest. *I'm never coming back!* I've just grabbed my phone to message Renée the good news when there's a knock at the door. Still smiling, I swing open the door to find Tom. My heart sinks as my smile melts into a frown.

"What are you doing here?"

"I came to drop off my keys with the leasing office, and I saw our furniture being loaded into a truck. Do you know those guys?" He wrinkles his brow and runs a jerky hand through his hair.

"They bought the furniture." I cross my arms.

"You sold our furniture?"

"It was *my* furniture, and I didn't want to pay for storage." I turn around and walk into the living room.

He follows me in and asks, "Well, what are you going to do when we . . ." His voice trails off.

"When we what, Tom?" I focus my eyes on the setting sun outside the window, avoiding him.

His posture stiffens and his jaw clenches. "I know you're not ready to get married, but you can't be serious. I mean . . . you sold our furniture?" He throws his hands up, gesturing to the empty room.

"You didn't want it. Why should it be my responsibility to store it?" I face him.

"Because it's yours."

"Right. So, I sold it."

"But aren't we going to need it?"

"No." I shake my head. My eyes begin to water. "I don't think so."

His eyes narrow as he steps back. "You're going to change your mind, and when you do, I won't be waiting."

"I . . ." I exhale loudly. "I think you should go."

He lifts his chin, then turns around and walks out. The door shuts slowly, on its own, behind him. I lean into it and look through the peephole to watch his receding figure. A few seconds later, he's gone. I remain at the door staring at the gray carpet of the hallway long after his withdrawal. Then, with no furniture to slump into, I take a seat on the cold granite counter. When there's finally a knock at the door I don't bother to get up.

"Come in. It's open," I shout.

Edwin and his brother bound in, grinning broadly until they spot me on the counter.

"Everything OK? Did you change your mind?" Edwin asks, his smile dissolving.

"Hmm?" I shake my head. "No. I'm sorry." I force a smile. "Yes, everything is OK. Please take the furniture. Don't mind me."

Edwin smiles, but the smile doesn't touch his eyes. He responds, "OK, we should be done in two trips."

I nod and he mirrors me before shooting his brother a look that sends him back to work. Once they tow the mattress and bed frame down the hall, the apartment is empty. I walk from the living room back to the bedroom looking at the rectangular shapes on the carpet where the furniture sat for years. Then sit on the floor in the space where our bed used to be. *Did I do the right thing?* I wipe my face dry, then rub my hands together, tracing the naked space on my ring finger. I shake my head, stand, and dust off my slacks. Then flip off the light and lock myself out.

* * *

By Friday I receive a check from the leasing office for the return of my deposit. A small sum compared to what I had to pay to break the lease. I stuff the check into my purse and head to work.

"Good morning." Tammy pokes her head in my doorway, smiling. She enters with a mug of coffee in each hand.

"Good morning, Tammy." I force a smile. "Is one of those for me?"

Her toothy smile compresses into a thin line. "What's wrong?"

"Nothing's wrong." I take a sip of coffee. "It's Friday. Woohoo." I twirl my finger in the air as I roll my eyes.

"Stop. Tell me what's wrong right now, or I'll change the password to the Wi-Fi."

"That screws *everyone* up." I set the mug down hard on my desk.

"I know. But I'll do it." She laughs, then takes a sip of her coffee.

I groan. "It's this guy . . ."

She coughs midsip. "Ahem. What guy? You didn't tell me you started dating."

"I haven't." I shake my head and simper before finally asking, "Have you heard of Bumble?"

"Giiirlll! You're asking *me*? I am the queen of dating apps. I have them all. Bumble, Tinder, Hinge, Coffee Meets Bagel. I have no shame about it." She claps. "Yes! Tell me." Tammy, divorced last year, has been avidly dating in an effort to make up for the time lost in her failed marriage.

"Well, I sent him a message on Sunday, and he was supposed to text me this week to plan a date this weekend. I haven't heard back from him yet." I press my cheek into my fist, leaning my elbow on the desk.

"Mm-hmmm." Tammy takes a long sip and looks away.

"Mm-hmmm what?" I draw my eyebrows together and slap the desk.

"That's not a good sign. He's probably flaking on you. Or *worse*. He's probably going to invite you over to his place last minute. He might be looking for something . . . *casual*."

"That's OK. I don't mind dating casually. I'm not ready to get into a super-serious relationship yet or anything."

"I mean *very casual*. Watch out. If he asks you out for drinks, it means he wants sex at the end of the night, and he'll never call you again."

"What? No, that's stupid. I thought you said people call it 'Netflix and chill' when they just want sex," I say, my voice strained.

"I'm just telling you how it is, girl. You were with Tom for a long time. Things have changed since you last dated." She gets up from her chair and begins backing toward the door. "I just don't want you to be disappointed. Hopefully this guy isn't a total loser and will ask you out for dinner, though."

"Yeah, hopefully." I slump against my chair.

"Lunch at one?"

"Sure." I shrug.

Tammy heads back to her office across the hall. *How much could things have possibly changed? Sure, it's been a few years. And OK, now there are phone apps for dating, but so what? Dating websites have been around for years. How much difference could the introduction of apps possibly make?* I stare at the list of unopened emails on my computer screen. Then open the top one and read the first sentences: "Why has my rate gone up?! I need to cancel my policy with you!!"

I press my hand to my forehead and close the email. I look through my open doorway. *The coast is clear.* I open a new browser window and type into Google "how dating apps have changed dating?" My eyes widen when the screen populates with dozens of links. "Tinder Leads to Hookup Culture Among Millennials." I bite at the cuticle of my thumb. "Tired of Swiping? So Are We." "Could Bumble Actually Be Hindering Your Love Life?" I use my pointer finger to pull back at the hangnail I bit on my thumb. Then click the Bumble article and read: "With the ability to swipe through hundreds of potential matches, it seems that everyone is out looking for the bigger, better ~~deal~~ date." *Ouch.* My thumb is bleeding. I apply pressure with a tissue. Then close the article and open another. "Dating apps are leading to an alarming increase in STIs, especially in dense urban areas." I click the red x of the browser window and feel the color drain from my face.

I swallow hard and roll away from my desk. I stand, smooth out my dress, let out a long exhale, and sit back down. I ignore the hardening in my stomach and reopen my email. Then finally respond, "The rates can fluctuate with changing market conditions. It would be my pleasure to call you and answer any questions you might have."

I force myself to type responses between sips of the overly sweet coffee Tammy brought me. Between the whoosh of a sent email and the ding of a new one, my phone chimes. It's a new message from a number I don't recognize. I bite my lip and stare at the gray iMessage bubble. "Lunch at Luna tomorrow?"

"Ready?" Tammy knocks on the doorframe.

I lift my head up. "What time is it?"

"Lunchtime." She smiles and snaps her fingers. "It's one. Are you coming or not?"

I set my phone facedown on the desk. My cheeks burn. "I have to deposit a check." My voice cracks.

"He texted you, didn't he?" She raises her eyebrows and leans against the doorframe as she glances down at my phone.

"Yeah," I smile back shyly.

"So, did he invite you out for dinner?"

"Lunch."

"Good." She nods. "Well, come out for lunch. We can go to the bank after."

I nod and stand. "Can I have one more minute?" I purse my lips.

"One minute." She eyes me, then turns and walks out, her hair bouncing behind her.

I set my computer to sleep mode, grab my purse, and pick up my phone. My hands quiver as I type, "What time do you want to meet?" and hit Send.

7.

HONEYMOON PHASE

ripping over a hanger, I nearly fall out of the closet. I pick the hanger up and throw it at the colorful pile of clothing atop my bed. A slippery satin dress slides off onto the floor from the impact. *Definitely can't wear that.* I grab my phone and look at the time. I have less than an hour. I throw my head back and groan at the ceiling. Then, standing in my underwear, I dig through the mountain of clothes, sifting through blouses, dresses, and skirts. *No. No. No.* I grab a blue dress from the heap and hold it in front of the mirror again. It's still a no. I shake my head at the reflection and finally shrink into a seated position on the floor. Lowering my chin to my chest, I stare down at my hands. *Why didn't I buy something to wear?*

I look back up at the pale face in the mirror and bite down on my bottom lip. *Screw it.* I spring to my feet, pull on my bathrobe, and run down

79

the hall. The damp towel wrapped around my hair, bouncing with each step, falls off when I reach Mom's open bedroom door.

"Mom!"

"Yes, *dear*," Mom answers, seated on the sofa beside her bed. She scrolls on her iPad without looking up.

I throw myself, arms outstretched, facedown on her bed. "I've given up." My voice comes out muffled.

"Don't be such a drama queen." She looks up. "Don't you need to be ready soon?" Her brows lift when she sees my bathrobe and hair-towel ensemble.

"Yes," I moan as I roll over, lifting my head to meet her gaze. "But I have nothing to wear."

She sets her iPad down. "And you're sure you want to go?"

"Yeah. Why?"

"I was thinking about what you said at your sister's house." She pauses, searching my face. "You're sure you don't want to get back with Tom?"

I let out an exasperated sigh.

"OK. All right. Forget I asked." Mom gets up from the sofa and walks into her closet. The sound of hangers scraping and fabric swishing makes me sit up.

"What, Mom?" I ask when I hear her talking quietly. "I can't hear you!" I shout.

"I'm talking to myself. Give me a minute," she calls back.

I lie back on her bed and frown. Moments tick by and finally I clear my throat.

"Hold your horses." She flips off the closet light and steps out with a fistful of hangers.

I scrunch up my nose at a moss-green dress she holds up.

"No?"

"No." I shake my head.

"Well, what about this?" She holds up a pale pink blouse. "You could wear this with those white pants you wore last weekend." She adjusts it on the hanger, and the price tag falls out of the sleeve. "This would be perfect for your date."

"But it's brand new. I can't take your new shirt. You haven't even worn it yet. What else do you have that I could borrow?" I reach for the remaining hangers in her hand.

"I was going to return it. That's why I didn't pull the tag off." She pulls her hand away, then holds the hanger with the pink blouse up to my chin. "The color doesn't work for my complexion." She smiles and tilts her head. "But it's perfect for you. Take it." She forces the hanger into my hand.

"I feel bad taking your new blouse." I pout. "But I do love it." My lips draw into a sideways smile.

"Good, that makes me happy. Now go try it on to make sure it fits. You're running out of time, and you still need to dry your hair." She smiles again and shoos me out with a backward wave of her hand.

"Thank you, Mom."

Back in my room, I finish getting ready and tug on the new blouse over my white pants. I smile at the mirror and rip off the price tag. Then lean against the counter, double-check my teeth in the mirror, and exhale deeply. *Am I sure I want to do this?* I take another deep breath and furrow my brow. I need more deodorant. I smear on a second coat and spray on perfume. Coughing, I flap away the flowery mist. Then take one last look in the mirror and grab my purse.

"Bye, Mom!" I call out from the entryway.

"Wait! I want to see you before you go," Mom shouts back from her bedroom. The sound of her hurried footsteps grows louder as she approaches. "You look so pretty!"

"Aw, Mom." I look down as my cheeks flush and my lips stretch into a smile. "You're killing me. I gotta go." I reach for the door.

"What time is it?" She checks her watch. "You can't leave yet. You'll be on time. This isn't a business meeting, Ruthie. It's good to keep him waiting."

"There's too many rules for dating," I whine. "Besides, I like being on time."

"Listen to your mother. I know a thing or two."

She raises her eyebrows and gives me her most *motherly* look. Then puts a hand on each of my shoulders and redirects me to the living room. I slouch into one of the sofas and watch the clock above the television. Tick. Tick. Tick. I shuffle in my seat, picking at the cuticle on my thumb that was finally starting to heal. A dark red beady scab beside my shiny pink nail polish.

"Stop picking at your nails, Ruthie. You're going to ruin your manicure before your date." Mom crosses her arms.

"Ugh. I know. You're right."

I toss my head back and sag against the sofa, staring at the vaulted ceiling for what feels like eternity. When I look back at the clock, only a minute has gone by. I groan and let my arms fall to my sides, my hands slapping against the sofa cushion.

"Don't take your frustration out on my sofa." Mom chuckles.

"Sorry, Mom." I shift in my seat, then stand. "I need to pee."

When I return from the bathroom, Mom finally nods my dismissal.

Luna is a pretentious Mexican restaurant on the marina. It's the sort of place sugar daddies go to pick up impressionable Instagram-model types. On Taco Tuesday it's packed full of girls with wavy blond hair extensions and twice-divorced, silver-haired men with black American Express cards. But this Saturday afternoon the valet lot is relatively empty. A couple Mercedes and BMWs are parked beside the building, but there are no Rolls-Royces or Lamborghinis today. The attendant is leaning over the podium texting as I pull up. He looks at my four-year-old entry-model Lexus, then looks back down at his phone while I needlessly reapply lipstick and fuss with my hair. As I flip up the visor, I jump in my seat when the attendant finally opens my car door.

I exhale loudly. "You scared me." I close my eyes and clutch my lipstick to my chest.

"Your keys, miss?" Boredom oozes through his voice.

"Right. Sorry." I nod, dig through my purse, and hand him the key.

He hands me the ticket, and I hobble up the cobblestone driveway into the restaurant. The huge oak hostess podium is deserted. I look around for help, then look beyond the lanterns of the foyer, at the dining room. Beside the window, in a plush leather booth, I see his profile. I recognize him, elbows on the table, scrolling through his phone, from his Bumble photos. It's Ryan. I freeze and my stomach flutters. *Relax. Act casual.* I take a deep breath and dry my palms on my pants. Then pace toward his table.

"Hi, I'm Ruthie." I force a smile and offer my right hand.

"I'm Ryan."

His bright blue eyes light up as he flashes a wide toothpaste-ad-perfect smile. He sets his iPhone down and stands. He's taller than I expected. I step back with my hand still outstretched. Rather than shake my hand, he loops his arm around my back and hugs me. Pulling me in close enough to smell his sandalwood cologne. When he pulls away, he motions to the bench across from him.

"I'm pleased to meet you," I squeak out. *Sit down. Stop being weird. This is not a job interview.*

"Yeah. It's nice to meet you too. Would you like to sit?"

He takes a seat and motions again. I sit down, then scoot to the center of the booth. I take the napkin off the table, open it, then place it in my lap. Then realizing that his napkin is still on the table, I awkwardly refold my napkin and return it to its original spot.

"Everything OK? You seem a little nervous?"

I tuck my hair behind my ear and bite my lip. "I'm sorry."

"There's no need to be sorry. How about we get you a drink? This place has great margaritas. Have you been here before?"

"Twice."

"Just twice?" He shakes his head. "You haven't had their jalapeño pineapple margarita then."

"You're right. I haven't." I smile.

"Let's see if we can change that." He raises his hand, and a server approaches our table. He orders two margaritas and octopus ceviche. "You're much prettier than your photos, you know."

"Um . . . thank you." I blush.

"I mean it. That's one thing about meeting people through Bumble or Tinder—you never know what to expect."

"I can see how that would be frustrating." I bite the inside of my cheek. Then blurt out, "Have you met a lot of people on Bumble or, um, Tinder?"

"This isn't my first time, if that's what you're asking." He smiles warmly. "Anyway, tell me about you. You're trying Bumble for the first time. What made you download it?"

"I didn't." I let out a nervous laugh. "My friend downloaded it on my phone and started aggressively swiping despite my protests."

"The lady doth protest too much." He shakes his head. "Now, did you swipe right, or should I thank your friend?"

A tan hand places an icy green drink in front of me. I immediately grab the glass and take a long sip. My lips pinch the straw. I nod at the server as he walks away.

As I set my glass down, Ryan asks again, "So, who swiped?"

I smile, take another long drink, and set the glass down hard on the table. "It was Sam. It's all her fault. And if this date goes south, I'll be sure to give her an earful."

"And, if it goes well?" He crosses his arms and leans back in his seat.

"And, if it goes well, I'll thank her for you." I smile again, looking down at my glass.

"Great, I appreciate it. Now, I gotta know how someone as beautiful as you is still single."

"You're just lucky, I guess." I pick up my glass and notice it's half-empty. Then set it back down. "What about you?"

He runs his fingers through his perfectly coifed strawberry-blond hair and looks out the window to his right. "I don't know. I guess I just haven't found *her* yet," he says, more to himself than to me. Somehow, he sounds rehearsed.

I bite the inside of my cheek and feel a newly tender swollen spot. "So, are you looking for something? I mean, do you, like, ever see yourself wanting to get married someday. Like in the future. Obviously not like right away or anything." The words run together in a hurried string of sputtered syllables. *We would make beautiful babies.*

He laughs uncomfortably and looks down at his margarita. He takes a drink, then answers, "Yeah. I guess so." Then takes another drink.

"Cool." I look down at the table.

I tug my napkin from the table and replace it in my lap. I fold it longways before unfolding and refolding it widthwise. I tuck my hair behind my ear, then untuck it and finger-comb the crown. The inside of my cheek aches.

"So," he says too loudly as he straightens his posture, "how hungry are you?"

I open my mouth, but he interjects, "I'm starving. Do you like seafood?"

I nod. "Yeah, I like seafood."

"Great, do you feel like having some tacos too?" he asks, now staring at the menu as though studying for a test.

"Um, sure. I'm not super hungry, though."

The server sets down a plate. Red onion, tomato, and avocado mixed with purply bits of octopus are arranged in a glass bowl surrounded by chips. *It looks good. How bad could octopus be?*

"Are you ready to order?" the server asks.

I shake my head.

"Yeah. We're gonna start with an order of the pork belly tacos. Then we'll have the seared steak tostada. I also want to try the chipotle chicken enchiladas." Ryan looks up from the menu. "What was the special again?"

"A blackened Chilean sea bass served with cilantro lime rice and black beans."

"Let's finish with that." He hands his menu back. "And we'll have another round."

My mouth slackens, but I hand back the menu, and the server leaves. Ryan puts his hands together, fingers interlocked, and rests his elbows on the table.

"Do you enjoy sailing?" he asks and finishes the last of his margarita.

"I've never been." I shrug.

"You've never been? You live in Newport Beach, and you've never been sailing?" His eyebrows shoot up. Then a smile creeps across his face. "You have to. You would love it. There's nothing like it. I'll take you. What are you doing tomorrow?"

"Tomorrow?" I bite my cheek. The stinging makes my eyes widen. "I think I'm free. I have church in the morning, but I don't have anything planned after."

"Perfect. I'll take you tomorrow."

The server returns with the margaritas and the tacos. He sets the glasses down and scoots the ceviche over on the table to make room for the new dish. When the server leaves, Ryan grabs my plate and puts a taco on it, then serves himself.

"Don't worry. I washed my hands before I sat down." He waves both hands at me and smiles as though surrendering.

"I trust you."

He starts eating while I rotate my plate with the taco on it. I take a long drink of water, then pick a chip off the ceviche plate. I break the chip in half and take a small bite.

"Is something wrong?" he asks.

"No. Everything is great. It's just . . ." I bite my lip. "I have a nervous stomach. I haven't been on a date in a really long time." I eat the other half of the chip. "And if I'm being honest, I don't really know what I'm doing."

He shakes his head and starts laughing. "That's cute."

I scrunch up my nose.

"You're doing great. You look beautiful, and I'm having fun with you."

"I'm having fun too."

"So, tell me about yourself." He takes a bite of his taco.

I press my lips together then take another drink, staring down at the table.

"Do you want me to tell you about myself first?"

I nod. "Yes. Desperately." I laugh. "I don't think these margaritas are working."

"Be careful. They sneak up on you." He takes a drink and clears his throat. "What is there to know about me? Well, I'm an only child. I studied law at Pepperdine. I enjoy traveling. I like Mexican food. And I enjoy long walks on the beach."

I slap his hand and laugh. He grabs my hand and holds it.

"What do you want to know?" he asks.

"Hmm. Well, what do you do for work?"

"I'm an office manager at my dad's firm." He leans in and whispers, "I haven't taken the bar."

"Neither have I," I whisper back. "And I also like long walks on the beach." I laugh again. "See we have so much in common." I hiccup. *The margaritas are sneaking up on me.*

More food is brought to the table. There's enough to feed four people. I tell him where I went to school and what I do for work as I scoot rice and cilantro around my plate. He listens as he eats helping after helping of the spicy, colorful food. *Where does he put it?*

As he lifts a taco to his mouth, I watch his bicep move through the snug sleeve of his pale blue Henley. When he finishes eating, he throws his napkin on his plate and waves his hand for the server. A busboy hurries to our table to clear the dishes. When asked if we want a box, Ryan shakes his head dismissively.

"Unless you want it." He lifts his brows. "You didn't eat very much. Do you want something else? Do you want dessert?"

"No. Thank you."

Ryan nods to the busboy, and he takes everything away.

"So, I've already asked you out tomorrow. . . . And you've already agreed. But for the sake of your friend, I'm curious to know how you think this date went?"

I feel heat prickle my cheeks as I blush and smile at the table. I look down at my empty margarita glass. "I . . . I would say it went well."

"Shall we then?" he asks as he gets up from his seat.

As I get up and collect my handbag, I watch him open the bill holder and put two crisp hundred-dollar bills in it. *When did he get the check?* He returns his wallet to the back pocket of his perfectly snug jeans and offers me his hand. I take it, letting him lead, walking closely behind him as he navigates us through the now-crowded restaurant. My heart races in my chest. The heat of his hand shoots an electric current up the length of my arm and through the rest of my body.

Outside, the brightness of the day forces me to squint as we walk to the umbrella of the valet stand. The lot is now full of cars. A couple of Maseratis are new to the assortment. Ryan asks for my ticket, and I hand it to him. He gives it to the valet attendant with a folded twenty-dollar bill.

"Oh wait. No. I got it." I reach in my purse for my wallet.

Ryan shakes his head at me, then nods to the valet, who takes off running behind the restaurant with my key. Ryan shields his eyes with his hand and looks around, then grabs me by the waist and pulls me against him.

"Now you owe me." He smiles mischievously as he peers into my eyes.

"I . . ."

He leans down and softly presses his lips to mine. My knees buckle and he pulls me tighter against him. My heart thuds inside my chest, but all I can hear is the sound of my blood pounding in my ears. I feel feverish. Until he pulls away and I'm left nearly shivering. Squinting at the sun's reflection in my windshield as the valet drives up.

I get in my car and slam the door before the attendant can shut it. I tug on the seat belt, and it locks in place. I force a smile and wave at Ryan, who's watching me as he waits for his car. I tug again and buckle the seat belt. Then shift into drive as a shiny black Mercedes pulls up behind me. As I exit the parking lot, I suppress the squeal in my throat, waiting until the first traffic signal turns red. Once stopped, I look side to side and check my rearview mirror. Then finally let out a scream as I slap the steering wheel. My face stretches into a smile so wide my cheeks sting.

8

A DAY AT THE BEACH

I squeeze my eyes shut, resting my chin against my hands. Fingers tightly interlocked, they throb from the pressure between the knuckles. Tears run down my face, pooling under my jaw. They eventually drip softly onto the backs of my bare wrists and forearms, cold, wet splotches on my goose-bumped skin. I exhale loudly, drowning out the mic-amplified voice outside my head. *God, if you hear me, please help me. I don't want to be alone. Please give me a sign. What am I supposed to do?* The weight of a warm hand on my shoulder stiffens my posture. I wipe my face and open my eyes. The woman to my left is facing ahead with her eyes closed, her right hand resting on my shoulder as her lips move slightly.

My shoulders drop as I draw my chin to my chest and close my eyes. My heart heavy, I swallow hard, choking back the sob caught in my throat. My own voice is quieter inside my head with this stranger's hand on my shoulder. *I need a husband so I can have my own family. Please.* I pinch my lips together. *Dad, please pray for me. I need you.* I sniffle loudly, then open my eyes. Everyone's standing, looking forward with their heads bowed. The woman beside me included.

I stare down at her black orthopedic shoes. Then grab my purse and squeeze past her. *I'm sorry.* She doesn't flinch. I tread up the aisle past the ushers and push open the door. Then rush to the restroom and into the biggest stall and slam the door. Shakily forcing the latch shut. I lean against the wall, then double over. My lungs ache as I breathe too quickly. Inefficiently. Wheezing like a broken squeak toy. *Just breathe.* I press my lips together and force a deep breath through my nose, then exhale through my mouth. *Again.* I repeat until I can finally stand up straight. It smells like urine and commercial pink hand soap.

The restroom door opens. Sound spills in briefly, then is muffled again when the door shuts. A soft knock on my stall door makes me hold my breath. The black orthopedic shoes are visible beneath the door.

"Someone's in here," I blurt out.

"Sorry," she responds.

I listen as the adjoining stall door opens and shuts. *She just needed to pee. She didn't follow me. It's probably someone else with the same shoes.*

"I'm OK," I choke out.

"OK," the voice answers expectantly.

I look under the stall at the shoes pointing forward. I can't tell if she's sitting or standing in there. My shoulders sag. "Actually, I'm not." I pause. She doesn't say anything, and I continue. "Actually, I'm pretty shitty. Sorry for saying 'shitty.' " I sniffle. "I'm screwing up my life. And I don't know what's right anymore. I just don't want to end up alone."

The restroom door opens again. Worship music, chatter, and laughter fill the bathroom. My stall shakes with the slam of the third stall door.

"Sorry," I say hurriedly. Then unlatch my door and rush out.

I plod up the stairs. When I get to the landing, I reach into my purse for my keys when the door opens. I shuffle back a step.

"How'd you know I was here?"

"I could hear you stomping all the way up the stairs." Mom pulls the door open wide.

"Sorry." I frown and walk past her.

"Are you OK? Where've you been?"

"I'm fine. I went to church." I stop in the doorway of my room.

"Do you want to talk about it?" She steps toward me.

"Not really." I walk in and slouch onto the bed.

She comes in and sits beside me. "Come on. I'm your mom. You can talk to me."

I shrug. "I miss Dad." My face scrunches up as my eyes water.

"I know you do." She wraps her arm around me. "Sometimes I do too."

I pull back from her. My brows drawing together as my eyes narrow. I stand, then back toward the closet. "You *do not* miss Dad." I slam my purse down on the shelf. Then stand in the doorway with my arms crossed.

"What? You think because we divorced, I don't have *any* feelings about him?"

"You don't." I wave my hand and shake my head. "Let's not argue about it. I need to leave soon." I exhale loudly.

"Where are you going?"

"Out."

"Where?"

"Mom, I'm a thirty-three-year-old woman. I don't have to tell you where I'm going." My voice is firm.

She stands slowly. "OK. If you need me, I'll be in my room." She walks out.

"Mom, I'm sorry," I call out after her.

She stops in the hallway. "It's OK. It's OK. I don't take it personally. I know you've got a lot on your mind."

I pinch my lips together, then frown.

"I hope you have fun doing whatever you're doing today. I'm leaving for a conference tomorrow, so try not to be home too late. I'd like to spend time with you before I leave."

My shoulders slump, and I nod. "I'll be home for dinner."

Her smile doesn't reach her eyes, but she nods and walks to her room.

I stagger back into my room and shut the door. The faint sound of a chime inside my purse forces me to straighten up. *I don't have time to feel sorry for myself.* I swipe open the new message from Ryan. "Be there in 15."

I wad up a ball of toilet paper and wipe the smeared makeup under my eyes. Then reapply powder and blush before spraying on perfume. I stand back and look at my reflection in the mirror. *This outfit is for church.* I peel off my blouse and throw it in the laundry bin, then scrape the hangers across my closet. I back against the wall of the closet and stare at my clothes. *Not again.* My gaze darts around the small crammed space before landing on the last unpacked box on the floor beside my shoes. I drop to my knees and rummage through clothes as the phone chimes.

"I just parked. Which unit is yours?"

My heart races and my hands shake as I hurriedly type, "I'll be right down."

I pull a dry-cleaning bag out of the box and rip the plastic off a white blouse. I tug it on and change into a pair of shorts. Then grab my purse and a pair of sandals and run out of my room. I throw the sandals onto the floor and stuff my feet into them as I open the front door.

"Bye, Mom!"

I run down the stairs. When I reach the last step, I straighten my posture, run my fingers through my hair, then slow my pace to a saunter toward his car. When he sees me, he springs out of his car to open the passenger door. His shiny black Mercedes smells of artificial pine.

Once he shuts his door, my pulse speeds up. It feels like everything inside my skin is vibrating. As though I just dropped from the highest peak on a roller coaster, the force pulls the skin of my face back into a gummy smile. I look over to see him smiling back broadly. *Does he feel it too?* He starts the engine, and my heart stops for a moment before it resumes racing. He speeds through the green gates of the condo community, then turns down Pacific Coast Highway, southbound, heading away from the marinas.

"I've got good news and bad news. Which would you like first?" he asks, clearing his throat as he looks straight ahead.

"Umm. The bad news, I guess." I bite my lip.

"The bad news is that we can't sail today. The *Acquittal* wasn't seaworthy, and I didn't want to be late readying her."

"OK." I nod and force a smile.

"The good news is, I've got a chilled bottle of wine and packed a light lunch for us. There's a great spot I want to take you to."

He looks at me over the rim of his black Ray-Bans and winks before pushing them back up the bridge of his nose. I bite down hard on my lower lip but can't stop my cheek from pulling my mouth into a sideways grin. He presses a button on his dash, and the seat starts to warm up underneath me as he turns on the heater. I sit up straight, tug at my blouse, and open my mouth. Before I can protest, he lowers all the windows, then opens the sunroof. My hair dances wildly in the cool, salty wind. I wrangle my hair, pulling it to the side. I hold it in a messy ponytail, my elbow leaning out the window. I squint looking out at the cloudless sky. The sun, high and golden yellow, reflects off of the rolling waves of the Pacific.

"Do you want my sunglasses?" he asks, pulling them off.

"I'm OK." I squint back at him.

"Take them." He hands the sunglasses to me. "I don't need them."

He pulls into a large parking lot alongside PCH. I put the sunglasses on and look around at the mostly empty lot. *Where is everyone?*

"Those look great on you." He smiles, then lifts his chin and asks, "You ready?"

"As I'll ever be." I say shyly, then tug on the door handle.

"Wait for me." He smiles again and extends his arm, palm down, motioning for me to slow down. "I'll get it for you."

I take the sunglasses off and set them in his cupholder.

After he's shut my door, he pops the trunk. Inside is an overstuffed backpack, a beach blanket, and a small cooler. He asks if I wouldn't mind carrying the blanket, puts on the backpack, and picks up the cooler.

"What happened to the shades?" he asks.

I bite my lip, then answer, "I didn't want to lose them."

He shrugs. "It's a little bit of a walk. Let me know if you get tired and need me to carry the blanket." He smirks.

"I think I'll manage." I smirk back.

He takes my hand and leads me across the street to a sidewalk that lines a sandy hillside. When the pathway ends at the beach, we take off our sandals and continue barefoot. The warm, soft, grainy sand gives way to darker wet grit as we get closer to the water. When we reach the foot of a cliff, I turn around and he tugs on my hand as he stops.

"Where are you going?" I ask when he releases my hand, puts on his sandals, and steps on a rock.

"Up." He points at the cliff. "Come on, it's easy."

I squeeze my eyebrows together and put my hands on my hips.

"It's only like fifteen feet. You can do it. I'll help you."

He offers his hand and I take it. We walk up an uneven, rocky pathway, his arm steady as I hobble up the terrain slippery with sand. When

I reach the top, I exhale deeply. Then straighten my blouse and tug on my shorts.

"Where do you want to sit?" I walk along the narrow gravelly cliff top, looking for a place to set the blanket. I try to sweep a spot clean with my sandal.

"Oh. No, this isn't it." He chuckles, watching me. "We have to go down the other side."

"What?"

"Just wait and see," he says as he pulls my hand, drawing my body closer to his. He wraps his arm around my waist and looks down at me. Then brushes a stray lock of hair from my face and whispers, "It's worth it."

He gives me a chaste kiss on the cheek and pulls away. Then offers me his hand and leads me down the other side. When I reach the bottom, I stop looking at my feet and finally look up at a small stretch of sparkling beach. Blocked in on three sides by rocky cliffs, it's open only to the glistening water of the ocean. Small waves wash against the shore in misty blue-green swathes.

"So, what do you think? Was it worth it?" Ryan asks, smiling his Crest-white grin.

"It's beautiful." I shake my head and smile.

"I'm glad you like it." He squints at me and lifts his hand to shield his eyes. "You haven't even seen the best part."

He tugs my hand and guides me toward the underside of a cliff to a small wave-hewn cave. When he takes his backpack off, I finally set down the blanket. He opens the cooler and pulls out an iced, sweaty bottle of sauvignon blanc then a pair of plastic stemless wineglasses from the backpack.

"So, what else do you have in that bag?" I ask.

"What? This bag?" He lifts his brows. "Reach inside and have a look."

He holds the backpack open just wide enough for me to reach in. I stick my hand in, and he traps it between his own, holding the bag shut. I jerk my hand around, unable to pull away. He leans in and presses his lips against mine. I blink rapidly, then shut my eyes and melt into his kiss. My heart flips inside my chest as my entire body radiates heat. I lift my hand to his face, then realize he let it go. I pull my hand away. He sits up and peers down at me, his hooded blue eyes supplicating. *Should I reach back in?* I pinch my lips together. Then sit up straight.

"Come in the water with me," his voice commands, low and husky.

"I didn't bring a swimsuit," I whisper.

"Neither did I."

He begins to unbutton his shirt. I watch as he carefully undoes each button, inch by inch revealing his lean, muscular torso. He removes his shirt, stands, and offers me his hand.

My heart races. "I . . . I can't."

"Are you sure?" He bends down to kiss me softly.

I place my hand in his, and he pulls me up against him. He runs his hand down the nape of my neck, then his fingers through my hair. Once again he lowers his lips to mine. My breath catches in my throat. Every muscle in my body tightens as his hands move from my hair to lightly caressing the bare skin of my arms. When my arms stop tingling, I open my eyes to see him unbuttoning his shorts. He tugs them off. Then he's standing only in his boxer briefs. My jaw drops. *Get it together.* I close my mouth and blink hard.

"I really can't. I'm sorry." I frown.

"Come on, Ruthie." He leans in and gently holds my face in his hands.

I close my eyes and shake my head, then stare at the ground.

"All right, but you're missing out."

He moves toward the water and jumps into the shallow waves. I watch him splash playfully from a distance at the mouth of the cave, then slowly advance. Inching my way closer until I'm standing knee deep in the water trying to splash back at him as he squelches around in water up to his waist. The sun glistens off his skin and water-slick hair. *Just take off your clothes and get in already. You know you want to.*

"Come in. It feels great!" he says.

"I'm going to have some wine!" I shout back as I walk backward through the water.

Suddenly, I trip over a rock in the sand and fall bottom first into the shallow water beneath me. I slap the water and draw my head back to stare at the sky. I'm soaked from the waist down. The waves wash sand into my shorts.

"Are you all right?" Ryan shouts as he rushes toward me.

"I'm OK." I grit my teeth and look down. "Just a little wet." Sandy red-tinged water pools around my foot. "Shoot! I cut myself."

He pulls me up and cradles my waist. "Does it hurt?" His voice deepens as he raises his eyebrows.

"Not as much as my ego."

Once inside the shelter of the cave, he jumps into action. He pulls a towel from the backpack to dry my legs and sets a second down for me to sit on in my wet shorts. Then digs into one of the side pockets and produces a first aid kit. He cleans the cut on the bottom of my foot with an alcohol pad and places a large bandage over it. When he's done, he lifts my foot to his lips and gently kisses the arch.

"All better?" he asks mildly.

I nod.

"See? You should have just taken these off when I told you. You would have dry shorts right now." He grins and tugs on my belt loop.

He stands beside me and uses the damp towel he dried my legs with to wipe himself off. His short briefs cling to him in a way that sends a flush of color to my cheeks. I have to turn my head to avoid staring.

"It's OK. I'm not shy." He laughs, then wraps the towel around his waist to change out of his wet briefs back into shorts. He sits down beside me, still shirtless, and violently runs his fingers through his hair, shaking it dry, spraying droplets of salt water all over me.

"Now, about that wine you wanted." He grins as he grabs the wine bottle and finally pours us both a glass.

We sit in the shade of the cave drinking wine. After a while he reopens the cooler and pulls out a perfectly plastic-wrapped charcuterie board, a bag of red grapes, and pasta salad. Between bites we throw grapes at each other. He catches every grape in his mouth, while most of the grapes aimed at me roll down my blouse.

"Are you cold?" he asks before picking up his shirt and draping it over my shoulders.

"Thank you."

"It's my pleasure. I'd offer you my shorts, but then I wouldn't have anything to wear."

"Well now, we can't have that." I raise a brow.

"I wouldn't mind. Sure beats wearing wet clothes." He smirks, glancing at my damp shorts.

"I'm perfectly comfortable, thank you very much."

"Those goose bumps don't agree. I'd offer to take you home early but I'm selfish."

"I'm fine." I tuck my hair behind my ear and look down at the blanket. "I mean, I'm more than fine." I bite my lip. "I don't want to leave." My iPhone chimes. It's a new message from Mom. "Shoot, I've got to go!"

"Now?"

"Yeah, I promised my mom I would be home for dinner. She's leaving for business tomorrow and will probably be gone for a few days." I sigh. "I'm sorry."

"Don't be sorry. That's important. I get it."

He exhales loudly and sits up straight, brushing small flecks of sand off his arms. I tug his shirt off my shoulders and hand it back to him.

"What are you doing Tuesday?" he asks as he buttons his shirt from the bottom up.

"Tuesday? Uh, nothing. I don't think I have any plans."

"Great. Make plans with me. The Taco Tuesday at Mezcal's is incredible. I gotta take you. They have amazing margaritas and a killer taco menu. Say yes. Yes?"

"I don't usually go out during the workweek."

"We'll go out early. I'll have you home by nine thirty p.m., ten p.m. at the latest. You'll get plenty of beauty sleep. What do you say?" He lifts his brows and puckers his lips into a pout.

"OK, yes."

"Yeah?"

"Yeah, but I've gotta be home no later than ten p.m.!"

"Ten it is."

9.
NOCTURNAL PERMISSION

stare off into space, then set my mug down and look back at my computer screen. Row upon gray row of unread emails glare back at me. I roll the mouse wheel, scrolling to the bottom of the page, and open the oldest unread message. I apologize for my delayed response, roll my eyes, and repeat myself in even simpler language. *If I have to explain one more time, I'm writing it at a third-grade level.* I raise the mug to my lips for another sip of cooled coffee, then set it down again. It's empty. I roll away from the desk and slouch against my chair.

I look out through the open doorway, bite my lip, then pull my phone out from my purse. There's a twenty-three-minute-old "new message" from Ryan: "I can't wait to see you tonight."

A wide grin spreads across my face as I tap the screen to respond. "I," I begin before a knock on my open door stops my thumbs. I freeze, look up, then drop my hand to my lap.

"Hi, boss, come in," I choke out.

"Good morning, Ruthie." Martha looks down at me. "I see that you're busy. I don't want to interrupt you. Would you stop by my office after lunch?"

"Yeah." I clear my throat. "See you after lunch."

She purses her lips, then gives a tight-lipped smile and leaves. My stomach tightens. I throw my phone back into my purse, then stuff it inside a cabinet under my desk. Then slump over my keyboard and bite at the inside of my cheek.

My cheek grows sore clenched between my teeth as I type. I roll my tongue over the swollen patch to soothe it. My mouth has grown dry. I clutch my stomach when it gurgles and finally check the time. *Crap.* I open the desk cabinet, push past my purse, and pull out my small lunch cooler. I poke at the leaves of my sad spinach salad, taking a few bites, until the growling in my belly ceases, then toss the container back into the cooler and tug on my cardigan. I clutch at the ends of the sleeves. Then stand and take a deep breath. I nod to myself. *Just go in there and see what she wants.*

"Hi, Martha, is now a good time?" I ask, my voice just louder than a whisper as my knuckles tap lightly on her doorframe.

She swivels around from her computer screen to face me and smiles broadly. "Now is a great time. Close the door and take a seat."

She clasps her hands atop her desk as I shut the door. I take a seat in front of her enormous solid-mahogany desk, balancing on the edge of the leather chair, pressing my lips together to keep from biting at my cheek.

"Ruthie, I called you in here because I think that you might be ready for a bigger challenge."

My eyebrows shoot up. *Really?* I scoot back against the chair and clear my throat. "I appreciate your feedback. What did you have in mind?"

"Well, I have an opportunity for you. I have a client that needs insurance for his company of almost three hundred employees."

"Three hundred employees?" I sit up straight.

"Now, it's going to be a lot of work. Especially because it's your first time doing a commercial account this size. But if you close this deal, it'll be worth your while. What do you think?"

I close my mouth, realizing my jaw had fallen. Then shake my head. "When does their current policy expire? By when do I need to have the proposal ready?"

"Friday."

"Friday?" My mouth falls open again. *Close your mouth!* I press my lips into a thin line.

"It's up to you, Ruthie. I can give the prospect file to you, *or* I can give it to one of the guys that usually handle the big accounts. But I think you're ready to grow. The client has been really unhappy with their current provider. If we can just get in the ballpark on premium, you should be able to close it."

"OK." I nod, feeling my stomach flutter. "I'll take it."

"Great. Now go close this deal. If you need help, Geraldine can assist you." She slides an overstuffed file labeled "Widmer Consulting Group" across her desk to me. "I'll email you the rest."

I stand slowly and grab the file. "Thank you, Martha."

"Sure." She nods dismissively.

I pace back to my office cradling the file. *I can't believe she gave it to me.* I blink rapidly as I walk to my desk. *If I write this policy, it'll be a huge commission.* I sit down with a pad and pen, then open the yellowed manila folder. A wrinkled Post-it note stuck to an irrelevant tax invoice tops the stack of papers inside. I set it aside and leaf through old insurance forms and water-stained employee records. I look through every paper. My desk is covered in crinkled, dingy, unnecessary documents. I sag against my chair and stare at the ceiling.

I don't know if I can do this. I lean my elbow on my desk and rest my face on my fist. *If this ends up being a waste of time, I'll lose out on my usual commissions.* I shuffle all the documents together and stick them back in the folder. My email pings. *She said she'd email the rest.* I put my head down on my desk.

Just breathe. I can do this. I take a deep breath and reopen the folder. *Just take it one page at a time.* I search the aged documents for the most recent declarations page, pull it out, and shut the folder. I research until the office soundtrack of keyboard clicks and pages printing morphs into the bustle of rustling jackets and hurried "See you tomorrows." I'm staring at the numbers on my screen when the light goes out.

"Hey." I look up.

"Sorry. I didn't see you. I thought you forgot to turn it off." Tammy smiles, then flips my switch back on. "It's go time." She adjusts the purse on her shoulder.

"I'm gonna stay." I exhale loudly. "I still have a lot to do before I leave."

"What are you working on?" she asks, reaching for the open file. "Ooh, Widmer. That's a big one for you. No wonder you're still toiling." She chuckles and glances at her watch. "What time are you leaving?"

"Probably not for another couple hours. I want to finish reviewing everything and strategize before asking Geraldine for help tomorrow."

"Ugh, Geraldine." She points into her open mouth and pretends to gag. "Well, good luck, girl." She knocks twice on the wooden door and leaves.

After the last slam of the office door, only the faint sound of a vacuum cleaner running in the distance can be heard. I open my desk cabinet and reach into my purse. Then swipe open Ryan's message thread. "Sorry, I can't make it out tonight. I don't feel well," I type. Then backspace to delete it.

I stare blankly at the message screen in my hand. The blue line in the message box blinks impatiently. *Just tell him the truth.* I bite at my cheek. It stings and I stop. Then darken the screen and set the phone down. *Ugh. I am going to be an old maid forever.* I pick at my cuticle and stare at the phone, then grab it and call him. The phone rings four times before it begins to feel slippery in my hand. *Should I hang up? Do people call each other anymore? I should have asked Sam.*

"Hello?" Ryan answers, surprise in his voice.

Crap. I should've texted. "Hey," I respond. "How are you?"

"I'm good. What's going on?"

"I . . . I can't go out tonight. I'm so sorry to bail last minute, but my boss gave me an opportunity today that I just couldn't pass up, and I'm still here at my office."

"I can pick you up later"—he stifles a yawn—"if you need more time."

"No, I wish I could, but I can't. I need to stay focused tonight and be in early tomorrow. I'm sorry."

"That's all right. I'll see you later," he replies flatly.

"I'm free Friday," I blurt out.

"All right. Yeah. Maybe *Friday* then."

"OK!" My voice cracks. "Good night." The tone of finality when the phone beeps three times knocks the wind out of me.

I set the phone down on my desk and stare vacantly at my monitor as my heart shrinks in my chest. *It's fine. I'll see him Friday.* I tear a hangnail at my cuticle. *Or maybe not. He said, "Maybe* Friday." I blink at the screen. Then cover my face with both hands. I sigh heavily as my shoulders sink. My eyelids hot, I look back at the screen and open the latest email from Martha. It has nine attachments. I read the first sentence, then shake my head and try again. It might as well be written in Greek. I throw my head back and stare at the ceiling. *I am going to die a spinster.*

I flip on the light in the condo and let out a deep sigh. *Mom's gone.* I rub my arms over my cardigan, then turn up the thermostat. I shuffle to the living room and throw myself back on the long sofa, wrinkling my slacks. Then stare at the ceiling, ignoring the empty, gnawing feeling in my belly. *I could still call him.* I rest my hand on my chest. Close my eyes and take a deep breath. *No, it's too late. I'll look desperate.* I force myself to get up from the sofa, then change into pajamas.

The fridge is packed full. There are three types of bread, every variety of cheese ever made, a dozen cans of Perrier, another dozen Diet Cokes, leftover takeout, and a slew of condiments. I pull out a plastic container and smell-check the contents. I tilt my head and purse my lips, then stick it in the microwave. The rubber stopper makes a loud thump when I pull it out of a half-full bottle of merlot. I smile at the glug-glug-glug sound as I pour the wine. When the microwave beeps, I finally notice the cheesy, oily smell of the leftover casserole. Then burn my fingers when I pull the container out. I scoop the yellow and green oozy mass onto a paper plate.

I eat sitting cross-legged on the sofa, my glass, the remainder of the bottle, and a handful of old Easter chocolates I found set on the coffee table. I unwrap a fourth egg-shaped chocolate and toss the foil into the pile I've made as an episode of *Friends* ends. I click on the next season, skip down to "The One Where Joey Tells Rachel," and pour the last of the merlot. When Netflix asks me for a third time if I'm still watching, I finally wipe my eyes and check the time. Then drink a final sip and throw my plate away.

* * *

2:07 a.m.

What! What is that? A loud thud shakes me awake. I rub my eyes and sit up, looking around my dark bedroom. Everything looks in order. My heart skips when I hear it again. Then again. The persistent pounding is coming from outside. My eyes widen and my pupils dilate. *Oh my God. Someone is trying to break in.* My heart pounds inside my chest, my breath loud and raspy between the thuds. I freeze. I'm home alone. I clutch Teddy Bear against me and shakily pull open my nightstand drawer. *I have exactly zero weapons and even fewer self-defense skills.*

Trembling, I pick my phone up off the nightstand. *I need to call the police.* As soon as I unlock the screen, multiple alerts appear. Five missed calls, all from Ryan. The pounding continues. My mind races. I swipe away the alerts and press nine and one on the keypad when the phone vibrates in my hand. An incoming call from Ryan. I press the screen to dismiss it but accidentally answer. The pounding stops.

"Hello?" My voice shakes as I sit up.

"Ruthie!" Ryan shouts from outside, his voice echoing into the receiver.

"Is that you?" I swallow hard and hold my breath.

"Yeah. Let me in," he says, his voice too loud for any time of day in this neighborhood.

I shake my head and close my eyes. Then whisper into the phone, "Stop shouting. The neighbors will hear you."

"Please open the door," he slurs.

"Do you know what time it is? I have to work in the morning. What are you doing here?"

"Please just open the door."

I grunt into the phone and hang up. *Maybe if I ignore him, he'll leave.* I lie back down and squeeze my eyes shut. A loud thud forces them open, and I sit back up. The thudding grows faster, more insistent. I throw the covers back and stand. Then stuff Teddy Bear under the bed. I turn on the light and check the mirror. Then frown at the reflection, my skin pale and eyelashes drooping. I tie my hair in a knot and put my bathrobe on. I open the door to find him leaning against the wall, drunk and glistening with sweat. *Annoyingly, still sexy.*

"What are you doing here?" I ask.

"What are *you* doing here?" he echoes mockingly.

"I live here! Ugh, this is ridiculous. Here . . . just . . . come in." I open the door wide enough for him to enter. He leans in to kiss me, and I take a step back. "Why are you here?"

"I wanted to see you."

"How did you know which door was mine?" I ask.

"Lucky guess."

He leans forward again, this time landing a wet sloppy kiss on my mouth. He tastes of whiskey and cigarettes. I step back and push him away. He looks down at me in a stupor, then slowly tilts his head and runs his hand through his hair. His lips pull into a sideways smile. My breath catches in my throat. He rubs his knuckles against the stubble on his cheek. And my knees weaken. *I'm just tired. I'm not falling for it.* I bite my lip.

"It's two in the morning," I say. "Now is not really a good time for me."

"Come on, Ruthie. I tried to pick you up earlier, but you canceled."

I clear my throat. "Did you drive here?"

"Mezcal's isn't that far."

"You shouldn't be drinking and driving. You could get a DUI or worse. That was really stupid."

"I know. I'm sorry. I just really wanted to see you. I couldn't wait until Friday. I know it was dumb. I'm sorry."

He takes my hand and pulls me toward him. Putting his hand on the small of my back, he looks down into my eyes. My heart speeds up. I blink, my eyelids hot. I look away.

"It's OK," I say with a sigh. "I just really need to get to bed. I have to get up early tomorrow to work on my proposal."

"Can I sleep here?"

I cross my arms and frown.

"Just sleep. I promise. I'm tired and I don't think I can drive home from here without falling asleep at the wheel." He presses his hands together in a pleading gesture.

"Seriously?" I shake my head. "Can't you order a Lyft?"

"There's none around for at least forty minutes. It's after two in the morning."

"I know what time it is," I snap, then throw my hands up. "Fine. You can sleep here, but *just* sleep. OK? And you have to go when I get up."

"What time are you getting up?"

"Five thirty."

"Five thirty?" He lifts his brows.

"Are you in or out?" I cross my arms.

"In."

He grins and wraps his arms around me. I take a step back to release myself from his embrace. Then lock the door and walk back toward my bedroom. I yawn and rub at my tired eyelids, ignoring the fluttering in my heart. He shuffles behind me. When he reaches the foot of my bed, he takes off his jacket, then pulls his T-shirt over his head. I bite down hard on my lip, then flip the light switch as he tugs off his jeans. I take a deep breath, then retie my bathrobe before getting into bed.

"Do you always wear so many clothes to sleep?" he asks softly, lying beside me wearing only his briefs.

"I do when a stranger sleeps in my bed."

"Give me a break, Ruthie. I'm *not* a stranger."

"I met you Saturday!"

"That was *days* ago."

"Good night, Ryan." I roll away from him.

I squeeze my eyes shut and press my lips into a thin line. My heart pounds in my chest. I feel hot but tug the covers up to my chin. *When was the last time I had sex?* I think back, counting the weeks, then realize it's been close to six months. Tom and I stopped having sex long before we broke up. Ryan shifts on the bed beside me, and my eyes spring open. My face flushes, growing hot, and I adjust the collar of my bathrobe. My skin is burning up. As if he knows, he rolls over and presses his body against my back. He kisses the nape of my neck, tugging down on my bathrobe. I feel the hair rising on my arms and neck, tingling as my skin forms goose bumps.

"Stop." My voice trembles.

He trails kisses from my neck to the lobe of my ear. Then whispers, "Do you really want me to?"

I hold my breath, feeling light-headed, every cell in my body electrified by his touch. I feel like a hot red neon light buzzing bright in the darkness. I shake my head against my pillow, then turn over to face him.

The alarm's bleeping is loud, and aggressive, and persistent. I slap my phone off the nightstand, then realize the sound is coming from the alarm clock on my dresser. I drag myself out of bed and smack the Snooze button. I crawl back into bed and roll to the center. Then sit up straight. *Where's Ryan?* I pull back the covers. *Did he leave a note?* Nothing. Just Teddy Bear buried under the sheets. My cheeks burn up. I quickly tuck him behind my pillow and look around the room.

"Ryan?"

I get out of bed, adjust my bathrobe, and walk out to the living area. When I find the door unlocked, my heart sinks. I lock the door and sag against it. *He left.* The alarm beeps loudly from my bedroom, and I stomp back to turn it off. Then pick my phone up off the floor. No new messages. I slump onto the bed and wipe a lock of hair away from my face. *I need to get to work. There's no time to cry.*

I start to tug down my pajama shorts, then stop when I hear a knock at the door. I pull the shorts back on, tuck my hair behind my ear, and run to the entryway, slowing down when I reach the tile of the doorway to look through the peephole. *It's Ryan.* I wipe the sleep out of my eyes. Then force my grin into a straight line and open the door.

"Hi." I exhale. My lips pull back into the grin I tried to suppress. "Where'd you go?"

He clears his throat. "I ran out to grab coffee." He shrugs, empty handed. "I, uh, forgot my wallet."

He tilts his head, motioning inside, and I step aside to let him back in. He strides past me into my bedroom, and I follow, watching as he kneels beside the bed and reaches under.

"Where's your friend?" He lifts his brows and smirks, looking at the bed.

My eyes widen as I squirm, my right arm crossing my body to nervously rub the opposite elbow.

"Don't be shy." He smiles as he lifts his wallet. He stands and tucks it into the back pocket of his jeans. "It's cute. I found him on the floor beside your bed this morning, so I tucked him under the covers for you. What's his name?"

"Teddy Bear." I shrug.

"But it's a cat. Shouldn't it be named Teddy Cat? . . . Or better yet, Ryan Cat?" He grins sideways.

He then pats his thighs and backside, checking his pockets. Then pulls me by the hand toward him and wraps his arms around my waist. He leans down and kisses my forehead.

"I know you gotta be at your office early, so I'll go." He releases me.

"So, I'll see you Friday then?"

"Uh, yeah. Friday." He nods. He tugs my hand and leads me toward the door.

10

HELLO, IS IT ME YOU'RE LOOKING FOR?

The Widmer office is twelve minutes away according to Google Maps. I open my desk cabinet and pull out my purse. Then reach in and feel for the Xanax bottle. When my fingers wrap around it, I press my lips together. *I can do this. I don't need these.* I shake the vial and take a deep breath at the sound of the pills rattling. Then tuck the proposal folder into my purse.

I pull off of PCH into the parking lot of the enormous, black-mirrored tower building alongside the marina. Then drive around the entire lot before looping around to do it again. When I see the taillights of an Infiniti light up near the entrance of the building, I push up my turn signal and stop. Then drum my fingers against the steering wheel until it finally pulls out. The Infiniti turns toward me to exit, allowing a Porsche to pull into the emptied spot. I honk at the Porsche, my turn signal still blinking, but it doesn't move. Instead, the brake lights darken. I wait for a moment, watching the gray-haired man in a black polo sit in the driver's seat. Then flip off my turn signal.

I drive to the rear of the lot, then squeeze into a space only a Smart car could reasonably fit into. I flip down the visor and slide open the mirror. My eyelashes blink furiously as I smear on a thick layer of lipstick and plaster on a smile. "You can do this," I whisper to myself as I set my purse on the floor beside the cracked open door of my car. Then narrowly manage to squeeze out. If I were at my former weight, just six pounds heavier, I'd be trapped in my parked car right now.

I stand at the tail of my car and tug at the hem of my dress. Then smack off the dust I got on my rear from scooting against my car. I shake my head at the backside of the Porsche driver as he walks toward the building. *What a dirtbag.* I pace toward the huge glass double doors of the entryway, wishing I were the sort of person who keyed cars.

As soon as the glass doors part, cold air spills out carrying the aroma of automatically pumped commercial air freshener. My heels clack against the black marble, inharmonious with the classical music playing in the background. I scan a brass-encased monitor and touch the screen to scroll to Widmer. Then press the button for the top floor when I enter the elevator. I stare at the buttons to avoid my flushed reflection in the brassy walls.

When the doors open, I lift my chin, square my shoulders, and force myself to stride out. I push open the heavy glass door of the company's suite. Behind the large stone reception desk, a matching stone wall with a metal logo reads "Widmer Consulting Group" in bold capital letters. There are glass doors on either side. One leads into a conference room and the other down a hallway.

"Good morning. I have an appointment with Paul Widmer at eleven thirty a.m." I clear my throat and look down at the tiny pixie-like receptionist.

She jumps in her seat. Then presses her lips into a thin smile and sets her iPhone down. She rolls her mouse erratically over a bright pink pad. "Ruth?" She looks up and squeezes her brows together. "Smart State Insurance?"

I nod.

"Please have a seat. Paul . . . erm . . . Mr. Widmer will be right with you." She motions to the black leather sofa in the reception area. "Can I get you something to drink? Coffee, water . . ."

I answer, "Water. Please."

She opens a small metallic door beside her desk, then hands me a water bottle. I walk back into the reception area, set my bag atop the sofa, and stand beside it.

Before the door opens, I see him, the gray-haired man wearing a black polo. My jaw clenches as he swings the glass door of the hallway open. My eyes tighten as my nails bite into my palms.

"You must be Ruthie." He smiles broadly, his teeth the size of Chiclets. I watch his eyes scan over my body before he reaches for my hand. He says, "Martha speaks very highly of you." He gives an overly firm handshake. My body tenses reflexively and my dress suddenly feels too snug. *I wish I'd worn pants.*

"She's very kind." I force a smile. "But I do hope to impress you with the proposal I've put together."

"Shall we then?"

He ushers me through the glass door of the conference room. It feels like a fishbowl. Around a large oak table, twelve leather executive chairs are neatly tucked in. *How many people have been fired in here?*

"You're kinda young to be an insurance agent, aren't you?" He rolls out the chair to the left of the head of the table and motions for me to sit.

I clear my throat and force a chuckle. Then sit. I feel his eyes on me as I pull my laptop out of my work tote and open it.

"Well, aren't you?" He crosses his arms.

"I'm older than I look. I've been writing insurance for years." I pull out the presentation folder and set it on the table in front of him.

"OK." He opens the cover and looks at the first page before looking up at me. "Are you married?"

I let out a strained laugh and shrug, hoping I misheard. He stares expectantly and I feel my heart begin to speed up. A slight tingling starts at the tips of my fingers. *I should have taken a Xanax. Even just one would have helped.*

"Pardon?" I finally manage.

"Are you married?" he repeats, his Chiclet teeth gleaming in the blue-tinged light shining from the ceiling. "I ask because it doesn't look like you've had kids yet."

My teeth grit as my body grows rigid.

"I mean, you just look so young, and kids would've aged you. I would know. I've got three boys. I look like I could be their grandpa."

I sit up straighter. "No. I'm not married. And I don't have kids."

"That's the secret of prolonged youth." He nods, then turns his eyes back to the folder.

I feel my nostrils flare as I exhale loudly. "Why don't you tell me why you're shopping for a new carrier when it looks like you've had the same policy for nine years."

He leans back against his chair. "I don't like my broker. He was a friend of my ex-wife's, and I don't want to do business with him anymore."

"I see." My forehead wrinkles. I straighten my face and press my lips into a smile before responding, "Well, I did identify some gaps in your coverage, and I'm confident that the proposal that I've put together will win your approval."

"He fucked my wife."

My eyes widen and I gasp before I can stop myself. I cough to try and mask my surprise. Unsure if I should pity him, I wonder if maybe he deserved it. He doesn't say anything. I feel like a taut guitar string ready to snap. Finally, I clear my throat.

"Yeah. She was probably too young for me." He chuckles, then looks at me, and my face grows hot. "Do you do home insurance?" he asks.

"Hmm?"

"I've got a beautiful house right on the water. I'd love to show you." He smiles wickedly. "For an insurance quote, I mean."

Is he serious right now? "Let's focus on this quote for now, and we can review your home policy at another time." I grimace. "If you'll look at page nineteen, there's a breakdown of the premium expense. He picks up the folder and eyes the page, his expression stern as he looks over the numbers. I fidget in my seat, fighting the urge to pick at my cuticles. When he finally sets the folder down, he gives me a squinty-eyed expression I'm sure is meant to intimidate me. It's working.

"Well, Ruth, I'm not going to lie to you. It is more than the offer of renewal I received from my broker."

"I understand." I press my lips together. *Look here, dirtbag. You're not going to take a week of work and my parking spot without giving me this deal.* My eyes narrow and I clear my throat again. "Mr. Widmer, our policy may be a little more than your current offer of renewal, but as we've discussed, there are gaps in your current coverage that my proposal corrects. And your broker *fucked* your wife. Aside from price, can you give me one good reason why you shouldn't switch?"

He shakes his head, then lets out a nervous-sounding laugh, his cheeks puffing out as he exhales. I swallow hard, then push the folder closer to him. He eyes it, then crosses his arms over his chest. I bite the inside of my cheek, then watch the way his brows furrow and straighten. His lips purse, then his forehead wrinkles. *Please don't tell Martha. Please don't tell*

Martha. I straighten my posture and place both hands on the table, as if to get up.

Finally, he slams his hand on the folder. "I'm going to give you my business."

"Really?" I ask, voice shaking.

"Really. What do you need me to sign?"

I wait until the elevator doors shut before letting out the squeal I've been holding in my chest. Then dance in place until the elevator dings open on the main floor. When I get to my car, I open the door wide, the spot next to mine now empty, then slam it shut and squeal again. I message Ryan, "I closed the deal. I can't wait to celebrate with you tonight!"

The TV is turned up loud inside the condo. Loud enough that when the travel host swirls the wine in his glass, I can hear the liquid swish on television. Mom, seated on one of the sofas, pauses the show when she sees me.

She sets down her wineglass. "How did it go?"

I drop my work bag on the floor with a thud and lift my hands. "You are looking at one very rich insurance agent!" I squeak out, smiling.

"Congratulations. I knew you could do it." She lifts her glass. "I just opened that bottle on the counter. Have a glass with me."

I pour myself a glass of the pinot noir and sit across from her on the love seat. "How was your conference?"

"Long." She takes a drink of her wine. "I don't want to bore you." She laughs. "I'm glad to be home. How was the rest of your week? All you talked about on the phone yesterday was this appointment."

I bite my lip and take a long drink of wine. "It was long. I don't want to bore you," I echo, then shake my head and laugh.

"What time is your date tonight?"

My brows lift. "I don't know. I haven't heard back from him yet." I spring to my feet and grab my work tote from the entryway. Then dig out my phone from the pocket. I have no new messages. My heart sinks. "Should I call him?"

"Give him a little more time." She smiles and nods. "Go and start getting ready for your date. I'm sure he'll message you soon."

I sing into my loofah, pretending it's a soapy microphone, while TLC's "No Scrubs" plays. Suddenly the song stops midchorus, and my phone chimes over the speaker. When the song resumes, I rinse off, grab my towel, and stumble out of the tub, dripping a trail from the shower to my nightstand. I smile at the screen. A new message from Ryan.

Damp, naked, and shivering, I open his text: "Sorry I can't make it out tonight. I have a headache." I darken the screen, then throw the phone at my bed. Slumping onto the mattress, I press my face into my hands. Then wrap the towel around me like a blanket. *Does he really have a headache? Does he still like me?* I frown and let out a sigh. I'm interrupted by the shrill ring of my phone. I sit up straight, grab the phone, and slide to answer without looking.

"Hey."

"Oh, hey, Sam." I sigh loudly. "I thought you were someone else."

"I'm gonna guess Ryan from your disappointment."

I groan into the receiver and flop over sideways on the bed.

"What happened?"

"He flaked."

"When? Just now?"

"Yeah, he just sent me a text saying he has a headache."

"Can't he take an aspirin and meet you later? You know, like a grown-up?"

"I don't know. I guess not."

"Well, screw him. Did you close that big deal you were working on?"

"Yeah." I muffle a sigh into my pillow.

"Get dressed. We're going out. Now that you're rich, you're buying me a drink."

"Come on, Sam. I can't go out. I'm over it."

"Don't be lame. I'll be there in thirty minutes whether you're ready or not."

I hang up and slide open the screen to message Ryan back: "Sorry you're not feeling well, let me know if you need anything." Then roll off the bed and drag myself to the closet. I shrug on a beige sweater and jeans, then slump back on the bed. Thirty-six minutes later there's a shave-and-a-haircut knock on my door. Sam's smile quickly melts into a frown once she's eyed me up and down.

"What are you wearing?" she asks, her eyebrows squished together.

"I don't know . . . clothes? I didn't know you were gonna be so dressed up." I shrug, looking at her tight black romper.

"Yeah, no. You need to start over. You can't wear that. We are going out out. Put a dress on." She shakes her head, then squeezes past me toward the closet.

"Do I have to?" I slump onto the bed and stare at the ceiling.

"Yes. I want to go to Luna."

"I went just last week."

"I know. But we're celebrating." She pops her head out of the closet to look at me. She lifts her brows and shakes her head again when she sees my scrunched-up whiney expression. "What? Do you want to celebrate at Taco Bell?" She steps out into the hallway and holds up a tiny formfitting black dress. "Here. Put this on."

"I love Taco Bell. Can't we just go get burritos?" I throw my back against the bed.

She grabs my hand and pulls me up to a seated position. Then puts the dress in my hand. "Go." She presses her lips into a line and points to the closet.

"Fine."

It's dark, and loud, and crowded. A sea of Botox, breast implants, Rolex watches, and Burberry dress shirts (probably picked out by Nordstrom salesgirls). The sound of Spanish music playing over the speakers drowned out by chatter and laughter. Sam grabs me by the wrist and drags me through the restaurant, pushing past wrinkle-free, martini-toting husband hunters. I mouth "Sorry" whenever I catch a glare. Then breathe a sigh of relief when Sam finally grabs a stool at a bar table. I wait until the bald man beside the second stool puts on his jacket and nods at me to take his seat.

"What are you gonna have?" Sam asks, looking down at the menu.

"I kinda want a burrito." I giggle.

"I meant to drink. I'm going to have a margarita."

"Oh. Well, yeah, me too. Last time Ryan ordered me a pineapple jalapeño one. It was really good. I'm gonna have the same thing."

Sam waves at a passing server. He stops and leans in to take her drink order. When he leaves, she reclines against her seat. "So, what's going on with this Ryan guy? You really haven't told me anything about him since your first date."

I bite down hard on my lower lip. "I don't know. I really like him." I shrug. "Do you think I should text him again to see how he's feeling?"

"No." She raises a brow and glares at me. "He's *not* your boyfriend. You can't trust these *app* guys. They come and go." She shakes her head dismissively.

I drop my chin and look down at the menu.

"You didn't sleep with him, did you?" She raises both eyebrows, blinking rapidly. Her posture stiffens.

I slump and press my lips together, my face hot.

She leans across the table and tugs at my hand. "Hey, it's OK." She smiles weakly, then squeezes my hand like I'm a six-year-old waiting at the doctor's office. "It's fine. If you like him that much, he must be a good guy. I'm sorry for jading you with my dating trauma." She laughs.

I bite at my lip again as my cheeks pull into a smile.

"Anyway, we are supposed to be celebrating." She bangs the table with her palm. "That's it. I'm ordering shots."

"Shots?" My face scrunches up.

She nods and smiles.

"Ugh. OK, but I have to pee. I'll be right back." I get up just as the server returns with two salt-rimmed green margaritas.

The line for the restroom wraps around the wall. I reach into my clutch and send Sam a text: "FYI there's a line for the bathroom."

The phone chimes in my hand. Sam says, "No sweat, I found a cute guy to keep your seat warm." I reply with the eye-rolling emoji and throw my phone back in my bag. The line moves and I shuffle forward. My bladder stings. *Don't think about it.* I press my knees together and look around at the crowd. Then suddenly I see *his* strawberry-blond hair by the hostess stand.

"Hey. Ryan. Hey!" I shout and wave.

He turns in my direction. His brows dart up when he sees me. He looks around, then walks toward me. "Hey, Ruthie. What are you doing here?"

I smile up at him. "Sam dragged me out to celebrate." I furrow my brow and frown. "What are you doing here? I thought you had a headache."

He runs his hand through his hair and sighs. "Yeah, I do. I just came to pick up some food to go. I live around the corner. I was actually just about to step outside to wait because it's so loud in here." He presses his hands over his ears.

"Do you want me to wait with you?"

"No, no, that's all right. Looks like you're next in line. I'll give you a call tomorrow. Have fun." He kisses my cheek and turns around.

"It's your turn," the girl behind me slurs and pushes me forward.

When I finish washing my hands, I shake them out at the sink, waiting for the two girls blocking the paper towel dispenser to move. Then look at the mirror and pretend not to notice them huddling. *Use a stall.* I roll my eyes. *Newport.* The taller girl passes a rolled twenty-dollar bill to her friend once she's cleared the first line. She steps toward the mirror, rubs her nose furiously, then reapplies lipstick.

"Does Ryan have any more coke?" The second girl looks up and finger-teases her hair.

"Yeah, he's got another gram on the boat. He just texted me. He's outside waiting. Grab your bag. Let's go."

My heart sinks. *It can't be the same Ryan.* I bite the inside of my cheek and watch them in the mirror. Their heels clack loudly as they exit. I wipe my hands on the sides of my dress and follow them out, my heart pounding. The tall one pushes the entrance door open, and I hold my breath as I watch them leave. I stand beside the door and look out the bubble glass window as the girls step into the back seat of his black Mercedes. My hands shake as I push the door open in time to watch Ryan hand the valet cash.

My heart stops when he looks back at the restaurant. *Did he see me?* He lowers his head and steps into his car. My face flushes as tears sting my eyes. I reach into my clutch, my fingers searching for the vial. I bite the inside of my cheek. *I didn't bring my Xanax.*

I push through the crowd, squeezing past bare backs glistening with sweat and damp designer polos. Sam has leaned over the table, laughing at something my "seat warmer" said. I glare at him then pick up the two full shot glasses in front of Sam. I down one, cough, then grimace. It's tequila. I down the second.

Sam's mouth gapes open. "Are you OK?" she asks, eyes wide.

"I need to go home."

"OK." She nods.

When the Lyft stops in front of the condo, my head is swimming. Sam opens my car door and lifts me up by the arm. I step too hard getting out of the car and my heel breaks, causing my leg to buckle.

"Please don't come with me." I swallow hard. "I'll pay for your ride home. I just really need to be alone." I hiccup and feel the sour burning of stomach juices rising in my throat. I swallow it down.

"Are you sure?" Sam asks, head tilted.

I nod and push her back toward the idling Corolla. "I'll call you tomorrow."

She backs toward the Lyft, then gets in. She watches me from the window as the car U-turns and drives away. I step out of my shoes and walk barefoot across the parking lot, gravel digging into the soles of my feet. Then throw the shoes over the wall of the dumpster enclosure. They bang against the cement floor.

I trip on the final step up to the condo and scrape my knee. Inside, I throw myself onto the bed fully dressed. *I'm too old to be doing this crap.* I muffle a sob with my hands. Then stare up at the ceiling before forcing myself to get up.

I peel off the dress and shrug on an oversize T-shirt. It's Tom's. Then brush my teeth and wash my face. I open the medicine cabinet and grab moisturizer, then stare at my reflection when the cabinet door shuts. I pull the skin back on my forehead, then around my eyes. *When did I get all these wrinkles?* I lean into the counter, then rub at my smile lines with my fingers. My eyes water. *I can't compete with these Botox, boob-job, Pilates girls.*

I feel a tear rolling down my cheek before I see it in the mirror. *Pathetic.* I close my eyes and my whole body sags. *I don't want to do this anymore. I can't live like this.* I slump onto the floor, and my knee stings when it bends, stretching the torn skin. New tears wet my eyes. I straighten my legs out and press my back against the vanity.

Everything is uncomfortable. I'm suddenly aware of every inch of flesh, all of it oversensitized. My hair hot and sweaty against my nape. The T-shirt collar hanging against my neck. The sleeves tickle irritatingly at my arms. And the cold tile beneath my legs. It's not cold enough, though. I wish I could peel a layer of skin off. I'm sure I would feel cool then.

I sit until my ass falls asleep. Then stand up on wobbly legs. Reach back into the medicine cabinet and pull out the orange vial of Xanax. I open it and shake it into my hand. White powder swirls out along with the pills. There are only eight left. I stare at them. Then imagine tossing them all into my mouth and swallowing them. *It's probably not enough to kill me.*

I pinch the pills one by one and put them back into the vial. I don't want to be wasteful. The last pill I put in my mouth and swallow with a handful of tap water. Then I grab my phone.

"Hello?" his voice answers.

11

MISERY LOVES COMPANY

Tom's voice is raspy and strained. Like I've woken him up from a nightmare and he's still deciding whether this phone call is real. I tug at the hem of the T-shirt and let out a sigh as I crawl into bed. I listen to the sound of his ragged breath.

"I miss you." I pinch my lips together as a tear rolls down the side of my face and into my ear.

He sighs deeply. Then it's silent. I swallow hard and wipe at my wet face and ear. Then he finally responds, "I miss you too."

"I don't want to do this anymore." I squeeze Teddy Bear to my chest and roll to my side.

"Ruthie." He exhales loudly. "I really can't have this conversation with you right now. It's late and I'm tired."

"I'm sorry. I'm sorry about everything. You're right. I don't know what I'm doing. I'm sorry I called you." I sniffle into my pillow.

"It's OK, Ruthie. I'm just really tired. If you want to talk, you can call me tomorrow."

When the call ends, I roll onto my back and clutch the phone to my chest with Teddy Bear. The light of my lamp makes a halo on the ceiling. *Why am I like this?* I bite my lip, then stare at my phone. I open my messages, then text Ryan: "I thought you were different." Then set my phone to silent and put it facedown on the nightstand. I switch off the lamp.

* * *

The pounding in my head eventually forces me awake. I squint one eye open. It's morning. Gray light sneaks in through the slats of the shutters. I moan, then sit up and rub my eyes. When I look down at Tom's T-shirt, I toss my head back and let out a loud groan. Then peel it off and throw it at the floor before lying back down. I roll onto my stomach and bury my face in the pillow. *Crap.*

I turn over, sit up, and grab my phone off the nightstand. I hold my breath, then swipe open Ryan's response: "Sorry." I can feel the color drain from my face. I feel like a sagging old balloon with a needle pricked in me. Instead of a loud pop, the air comes out in a slow hiss. My eyes burn. With my thumb, I navigate to my recent calls. Outgoing call to Tom: three minutes. *I'm such an idiot.*

I drag myself out of bed, shrug on my bathrobe, and open the medicine cabinet. Eye the orange Xanax bottle before reaching for the Excedrin. I shake out two pills, then grab a water bottle from the kitchen. *I can't believe he faked a headache to hang out with those coke-snorting trash bags.* I swallow the pills and chug the water. Then slump on the edge of the bed. I shake my head, then grab my phone. New message from Sam.

"Are you alive?"

"Barely," I text back. Then grab Tom's T-shirt off the floor and toss it in the laundry bin.

"Well, glad you're not dead. I need my car back. If you pick me up, I'll buy your breakfast burrito."

"Fine, but I want Taco Bell. You owe it to me." I toss the phone into my purse.

I double-park in front of Sam's place. Then press the button to turn on my hazard lights and text Sam. The overcast sky is too bright for my aching, bloodshot eyes. I squint through the lenses of my sunglasses, then pull the bill of my cap down. My hair, a ratty tangle, strings down my back in a ponytail over my faded UC Irvine alumni tee. I look down at my sweatpants and frown. *I really should have put real pants on.* I'm light-headed, but the rest of my body feels heavy. I used to be able to pound shots all night, then wake up and shake it off with a Red Bull when I was young. But today even tugging the sweatpants on was work. I turn off the engine of my car, then stare up at Sam's apartment. The graying pink two-story building is sandwiched between vacation beach homes.

When the door of the metal gate clangs shut behind her, I sit up straight and unlock the doors. She slumps into the passenger seat. Her giant black round-rimmed sunglasses make her look like a fatigued fly. She tugs the seat belt over her black PINK sweatshirt, looks ahead, and nods. Her leggings, part of a matching ensemble, are hangover chic. I turn off the hazard lights, then make a U-turn back toward PCH.

"Where's Taco Bell from here?" I stop at the signal.

"You act like you've never been around Huntington." She squishes her eyebrows together and points left.

"Give me a break. I'm still learning where everything is in *Newport*."

"How long did you live in Costa Mesa?" Her voice is sarcastic. "It's literally the next city over." She laughs.

I shrug. "I guess I was living under a rock."

"A rock named Tom."

"I thought you liked Tom." I bite the inside of my cheek.

She raises a brow and purses her lips. "I tolerated Tom. But now that it's over . . ." She shakes her shoulders in a jig, then stops. "Ooh." She presses her hand to her lips. "I need to eat something before I dance like that." She smiles into her hand. Then points left at the light.

I turn into the parking lot. "Is it cool if we eat in the car? I don't want to be seen looking like this." I grimace at her. She nods and I pull into the drive-through. When I park, she hands me back my take-out bag and I tear the paper off my burrito. Then rip open a packet of hot sauce with my teeth, pour it on, and bite. I close my eyes and chew slowly.

"Get a room." Sam glares at me, then grins.

"Dude, I'm so hungry. I didn't eat anything last night, and this burrito is giving me life." I squeeze more hot sauce over the beans and cheese.

"So, are you going to tell me about last night?" She tilts her head and bites into her burrito.

I take another bite and lower my hand. Then look out the windshield at the painted white brick wall of the parking lot. I swallow hard. My mouth spicy, I lick my lips, then set my burrito atop the paper bag in my lap.

"I ran into Ryan." I press my lips together. "It's like you said—these app guys come and go." I sigh and look down at my lap.

Sam sets her food down, then looks at me.

"I sent him a text last night saying, 'I thought you were different,' and his response was 'Sorry.' That's it. Just 'Sorry.' " My eyes water and I throw the half burrito into the bag and crumple it.

"He's not the only guy, though. You can't let this one douche get to you."

I wipe away an escaped tear and sit up straight. "I know. I just really thought—" I swallow hard. "I just really wanted to believe I had a shot with him. I know it's stupid. I didn't even know him." I let my head fall against the headrest. "I just really wanted it to work this time." My ponytail itches against my neck.

She shifts in her seat, turning her body to face me. "Dude, you can't rush this stuff. That's how you got into trouble with Tom. After your third date, you told me you wanted to marry the guy, and look how that turned out."

I drop my chin, then narrow my eyes at her. "This is totally different."

"Why? Because it's a different guy?"

"Because I'm older now. I'm a different person. I've matured."

She crosses her arms. "It's the same. The only difference is that this guy didn't string you along for years. At least this loser had the courtesy of showing you who he really was early on. I've been your friend forever. I know you." She lowers her stare.

"But I do love Tom."

"I know you do." She shakes her head. "But you know he's the wrong fit. Do you remember when you used to drag me to look at wedding dresses and bridal expos?"

I press my lips together.

"You stopped wanting to go *after* Tom proposed." She purses her lips. "You didn't think that was weird?"

"I was busy with work."

"Too busy to plan the wedding you already planned out?"

I slump in my seat.

She sighs loudly. "I know you want to get married, with the house, and the kids, and the career." She tilts her head. "It's what we all want."

She throws her hands up. "But who do you know that has all that stuff right now?"

"Renée."

"OK. Well, your sister is a freak of nature. Aside from Renée, who else do you know that has it all figured out?"

I bite the inside of my cheek as my brow wrinkles. "Ashley."

"Selling diet tea on Facebook doesn't count as a career."

"Well, at least she's married and has kids." I shake my head. "Sam, aside from us, everyone we know is married. This is it. The music stopped. There is nowhere to sit. This game of musical chairs is over, and we are out."

Now Sam slumps in her seat.

I let out a noisy exhale. "And I called Tom last night."

She sits up, her posture rigid. "You didn't." She narrows her eyes at me.

"I did. He was sleeping, but he said I could call him today if I wanted to talk."

"Ruthie, you can't call him. You will regret it." She presses her lips into a thin line. "Sure, you can marry him and have kids. But you will have to cook, clean, and shop for him for the rest of his life all while working full-time."

"I like working."

"Did you like acting like his mother?"

"Wow. That was harsh." I narrow my eyes at her. She purses her lips and blinks slowly. Finally, I sag and let out a groan. "Fine. I won't call Tom." I throw my hands up. "I'll just be a spinster forever."

I turn off the TV, roll onto my side, and switch off the lamp. It's quiet. The only sounds are my breath and a cricket chirping somewhere outside. Mom wished me good night hours ago. I tug the covers up to my chin and close my eyes. *Just go to sleep.* I yawn. Then hear a vibration on my nightstand. I rub my eyes, then pick up the phone. An incoming call from Tom. An old photo of him smiling at the camera lights up my screen. I bite the inside of my cheek. It's raw and chafed from a day spent overthinking in bed, achy and nauseated, watching romantic comedies. I slide to answer.

"Hey . . . I'm sorry for calling you last night." My voice cracks.

"It's OK. I didn't hear from you today. I just wanted to make sure you were all right."

"I'm fine. I was just *really* busy."

"So, how have you been?" he asks, his voice low and soft.

"All right, I guess. You?"

"Same. Look, Ruthie . . . I didn't call to exchange small talk," he says with a sigh. "Can I see you?"

I sit up and switch the lamp on.

"Hello?"

"I'm still here," I whisper into the receiver, then clear my throat.

"I want to see you. Can I see you this week?"

I sigh loudly.

"It's not a marriage proposal. I'm just asking you to dinner."

"When?"

"Wednesday night. Massimo's at seven?"

"OK."

I hang up and lie back down. Then press my hands together and place them under my cheek on the pillow. I stare at the lamp. *I didn't call him. He called me.* I bite at my cheek and it stings. My eyes widen. *Sam is going to kill me.* I switch the light off and squeeze my eyes shut.

* * *

I can't count the number of times I've been to Massimo's. All we have to do is nod at our server, and they know what to do. Whenever they've hired someone new, all it's taken is two visits for them to memorize our order. The yellow stucco facade and black awnings used to make me smile after a long day at the office. A second home, only here, I didn't have to cook. It was one of the only restaurants Tom and I could agree on. When I asked him to try the new Indian restaurant that had opened by our apartment, he rolled his eyes. "Indian food is for Indian people. Nobody else wants to eat that stuff." I did.

I park behind the restaurant, then scan the lot for his Audi. I let out a deep sigh and turn off my car. It's 6:37 p.m. I had to leave early to avoid Mom. I tug the pink blouse she gave me straight, then check my reflection in the mirror of my car visor. It's 6:39 p.m. My eyebrows draw together. *I should take them now, so they have time to metabolize.* I reach into my purse and pull out the vial. Then take one and swallow it with water from a half-empty questionably old bottle. Watching cars drive in and out of the parking lot, I pretend to look at Instagram while I wait for his car.

At 6:54 p.m. his Audi drives into the lot. As I expected, he parks in the second row facing the restaurant. I shrink in my seat, and he walks out of view. I rifle through my handbag and grab the vial again. *I need another one.* I swallow the second pill dry.

There's a glare in the glass of the door. I squint, but all I see is my own reflection. I pull open the door. A family sits waiting on the bench near the host stand. A Rat Pack track plays in the background, part of a playlist that's on a continual loop. The smell of cheese and garlic hangs in the air. I purse my lips, clutch my bag against me, and walk up to the hostess.

"Hi, I'm meeting my—" I squish my eyebrows together, shake my head, and let out a strained chuckle. "Someone. I'm meeting someone here."

Her eyes move from mine to over my shoulder. I turn around. His hazel eyes bore into mine, and my heart sinks. He shuffles in place, then shoves his hands in his pockets and smiles awkwardly. I feel my lips pull back into a toothy grin, mirroring his. I lean forward and he pulls a hand from his pocket. When he leans in, I turn my face away. We both stumble for a moment, then embrace in a single-armed hug. My arm wraps farther than I remember. *He's lost weight.* I stand up straight and smooth my hand over my blouse.

"Tom, your table is ready," the hostess interrupts with a tight-lipped smile. Her long brown hair whips as she turns around.

He nods and we both follow her to the dining room to a low-lit small corner booth. My eyebrows shoot up, and I press my lips together when we reach the table. Before I can say anything, Tom sits. He motions at the seat across from him. I look at the hostess and pinch my lips into a smile, then sit down.

"Peter will be taking care of you tonight." She mimics my expression, drops the menus, and leaves.

I smooth my hands over the red-checked tablecloth and exhale. His skin looks dry and tired, like mine. *He's been drinking and he hasn't been sleeping.* He sets his elbows wide apart on the table with his fingers interlocked. His green button-up shirt is new. It's the kind of shirt I would pick out for him and that he would return.

"It's good to see you." He smiles shyly.

I look down at the table and nod.

"You don't have to say anything. I know you are going through a lot." He sighs. "What I'm trying to say is, I don't expect anything. I'm just glad you're here."

I look up. My eyebrows gather, and I squeeze my eyes shut when I see the pained expression on his face. He reaches across the table for my hand, and I pull it away. My fingers twist together in my lap. He gives a weak sideways smile, his eyes watery.

"I like your blouse."

"Thank you. My mom gave it to me," I respond, looking at the table, then open the menu. Peter brings a glass of pinot noir and a beer to the table, and Tom nods at him. "No. I don't want the piccata tonight." I shake my head at the server. "Could I have another minute?"

Peter nods and walks away.

"I thought you loved the piccata here," Tom says.

"I changed my mind." I pick at my thumb cuticle in my lap.

"Don't pick at your nails." He lifts his eyebrow and glares at me.

"Don't tell me what to do, Tom." I cross my arms. "Besides, it's none of your business."

His posture stiffens and his shoulders rise. He lets out an impatient snort, then shakes his head and laughs sarcastically.

"We don't have to do this. You asked me to meet you here," I say, my voice rising.

"Do you just say yes to everything I ask you?"

I grab my purse and scoot toward the edge of the seat.

He stretches his arm across the table palm down, fingers spread, as though trying to calm an anxious pet. "Please don't leave." He tugs at the collar of his shirt. "I didn't mean it."

I set my purse back down and frown at him.

"Look, I know you were unhappy, but I can change." He clears his throat. "I want to change. I don't want to lose you."

"You are who you are. We've had this conversation before, and nothing ever changes."

"I'll try harder. I'll do more of the things you want." His eyes are now feverish and overbright. "I'll help around the house more. I'll spend more time with your family." He runs a jerky hand through his hair. "I'll go to church with you. Whatever you want, I'll do it." His voice is choked.

My shoulders slump, and I shake my head. "I don't want to make you do anything anymore. I'm tired of trying to make you someone you're not." My words rushed, I draw in a breath and release it. "And I'm not myself when I'm with you."

"Tell me then, who are you?" A tear rolls down his cheek.

"I don't know anymore."

12

GRIEVED MINDS THINK ALIKE

park my car against the curb in front of Renée's. The two-story house is typical of an Irvine family neighborhood. It's an ivory stucco tract house with a Spanish tile roof. With a three-car garage for their two cars and storage for their bikes, Jacob's street-hockey gear, his old Power Wheels police car, and unused toys destined for donation. A basketball lies on the green grass of their freshly mowed lawn. I stare up at the brightly lit windows, then shut my eyes when my face reddens.

I swallow hard, then flip down my car visor and wipe the smudged makeup off my cheeks. *Should I call first?* I smear on a waxy white coat of lip balm, then open the car door. I knock three times, then step back and stare down at their monogrammed welcome mat. Joe opens the door.

"Renée, your sister's here!" Joe shouts, and steps back, opening the door wider. "Whoa, what happened to you?" His brows shoot up.

"I had dinner with Tom." I shrug and sigh, stepping into the entry-way. It smells like chicken and broccoli masked by citrus kitchen cleaner.

"Oh man." He shakes his head, then turns toward the stairs and shouts, "Get down here! Your sister needs you."

"I'm coming!" Renée shouts as she jogs down the stairs. "Sorry, I was helping Jake finish his bath." She leans in to kiss my cheek when she reaches the entryway.

"I'm sorry for not calling." I frown.

Her brows draw together. "You know you are always welcome here. Come in. Sit down." She sits in the living room and pats the cushion beside her on the sofa.

"Do you want anything to drink?" Joe asks, still standing in the entryway.

"I'm OK. Thank you," I answer.

"I'll bring you water anyway," Joe says before retreating to the kitchen.

"So, what happened?" Renée asks, her face full of motherly concern, as if she just found out I was being bullied at school.

"Nothing happened." I bite the inside of my cheek. "I had dinner with Tom, and everything is the same." My eyes water and I stare up at the ceiling. "I just couldn't go home. Mom thinks I'm at Bible study, and I don't want to explain myself to her." I let out a deep breath and my shoulders slump.

Joe sets down two glasses of water on the coffee table, careful not to make eye contact, and walks upstairs.

"Where are the kids?" I look around the quiet living room. The toys have been picked up and are neatly stacked in a wicker basket by the television.

"Well, Jacob's getting ready for bed, and Rebecca's down for the night." Renée sighs.

"Already?"

"It's almost nine." She shrugs. "It's late for us." Her lips curl into a half smile.

"You're right. I should get going." I take a long drink of water and set the glass down too hard on the table.

"No, it's fine. Rebecca sleeps through everything. That kid's a tank." She laughs. "Hey, you know what you need?"

"A brain transplant?" I answer dryly.

"I'm being serious. You *need* a girls' night." She claps.

"No. I really don't. I went out with Sam last Friday, and I'm still hungover." I laugh.

"But this'll be different." She puts her hands together and pleads. "Please. I need a girls' night. The baby has been sucking the life out of me, and I know Lauren needs a girls' night too. It'll be fun. The three of us haven't gone out together since before Rebecca was born."

"Great." I roll my eyes. "Yeah, it'll be super fun to party with my happily married sister and her recently engaged best friend. I won't feel like a total spinster loser at all." I scrunch up my face.

"Oh . . . I didn't tell you . . ." She pinches her lips together.

"What?"

"Lauren gave Andrew the ring back."

"What?" I furrow my brow. "You're lying." I shake my head.

She purses her lips and picks up her glass. "I'm serious." She takes a sip. "There must be something in the water." She forces a laugh and sets her glass down.

"Whoa, that's big news. They've been together a long time."

"Yeah, eight years." She nods, then shrugs. "Anyway, I think it'll be good for you guys to get together. I'll ask Joe to stay home with the kids this weekend. Is Friday or Saturday better for you?"

"Can it at least wait until next weekend? I don't think my liver can take a girls' night right now."

"Next weekend is Halloween," she says dismissively while looking down at her phone, her thumbs furiously typing. "So, this Friday or Saturday?"

"I don't care. Since you've already committed me, go ahead and ask Lauren which day is better for her."

"Saturday," Renée says without looking up from the phone.

"OK. Saturday. I'll just clear my agenda of sulking and sobbing and pencil you in for the evening," I reply sarcastically.

"It's going to be fun."

"Sure." I slump against the sofa.

She looks up from her phone and stares at me.

"What?"

"You never told me how you gave Tom the ring back." She narrows her eyes.

I shut my eyes and lean against a throw pillow. "I didn't." I pinch the bridge of my nose. When I open my eyes, Renée is still staring at me. I sit up. "He took it." I exhale loudly. "I left it in the box at home. And when I came home from work, it was gone. Along with all his other crap." I shake my head. "It's not a big deal." I shrug. "It was an ugly ring anyway."

"I thought you liked that ring." Renée squishes her brows together.

"Yeah? Me too. I also thought I wanted to marry Tom." I lift my brows. "Surprise." I press my lips together. "I don't." My eyes water. "I really don't know what I want or what I'm doing anymore."

"That's why it's good that you guys took a break. Maybe when you guys get back together—"

"What?" I interrupt. My jaw clenches, and I let out a noisy breath. "I'm *not* getting back together with Tom."

"Well, why did you meet with him then?" She frowns.

"Because he asked me to," I snap.

"OK." Renée takes a drink.

"I don't know why everyone keeps thinking I'm going to get back together with him. I'm not. I've wanted to break up with him for three years now."

She looks at me expectantly. When I don't say something immediately, she pats my knee as if to say, *You can tell me.*

"I didn't . . . because I thought I was too old to start over at thirty. Every year . . . every birthday, I would blow out my candles and wish for a different life. Maybe I am too old, but I don't care anymore. I have to try. I can't live with myself if I don't."

A single lamp lights the living room inside the condo. I turn the switch off, then look down the hallway to Mom's bedroom. Light spills out through the crack under her doorway. My bedroom is black. I flip on the light and smile at Teddy Bear atop my bed. Then shrug off my purse and sit slouching over on the bed. My breath catches in my throat when I hear a knock at the door. I press my hand against my forehead.

"Come in." I throw my head back and look at the ceiling.

Mom pushes the door open slowly, only to shoulder width. She stands in the hallway. "I know it's late. I just wanted to let you know that I'm leaving tomorrow morning for business."

"Again?" My brows draw together. I swallow the lump in my throat.

"Yes. This time it's for a business meeting. Anyway, please pray for me because I really need it to go well."

"Of course, I'll pray for you. I know it'll be great. Where are you off to?"

"I'm flying to Chicago. I won't be back until Monday."

I stand, push open the door, and throw my arms around her. "I'm really going to miss you."

"It's only a few days." She smiles and pats my back. "You won't even notice I'm gone."

* * *

I open the fridge and stare at the selection of bread and cheese. All the leftovers are gone, eaten in the first two days after Mom's departure. I pull open the freezer drawer, sigh at the frozen packs of meat, then shut it. I need to eat. I'm meeting Renée and Lauren at nine, and I can't drink on an empty stomach. *I don't need a repeat of last weekend.* I swipe open my phone and scroll through a list of restaurants, looking for something to order. Stopping when I see Little India Grill, I bite my lip and smile at the screen.

I'm in my bathrobe, tweezing my eyebrows, when the doorbell rings. I set down the tweezers and run toward the entryway. "I'm coming!" I shout, walking briskly through the living room. As soon as the door opens, the rich smell of cumin and turmeric escapes through the steam-sweaty plastic bag and tugs at my belly. "Thank you." I smile at the delivery driver and shut the door.

I finish eating and stick the Styrofoam box in the fridge for tomorrow. Then resume tweezing my brows. It's a quarter to eight. When I finish squirting setting spray over my makeup, I finally check my phone. I have thirty-two new messages in a group chat with Renée and Lauren. I roll my eyes as I scroll through the gray bubbles filled with exclamation points, dancing GIFs, and emojis. Then hold my breath and type, "What are you two wearing?"

"Black skinny jeans with strappy heals and a cute top," Renée types back almost instantly. Lauren sends a headless selfie of a black bell-sleeve tunic dress.

I throw my head back and groan at the ceiling, then look down at my phone and type, "Where are we meeting? Can I get away with wearing leggings?"

Both gray bubbles say, "No."

"Lauren got us a table near the bar at Gather," Renée writes.

"See you girls at nine!" Lauren replies with the dancing girl emoji.

I shrug on a black V-neck sweater over black jeans and order a Lyft. When the car stops in front of the valet stand of the wood planked restaurant, I frown. The warm yellow light from the illuminated metal "Gather" sign on the building shines down on bored millennials below it. A half dozen people looking down at their phones, a few vaping, and one smoking an actual cigarette.

"Could we drive around the block and come back?" I ask, brows scrunched together, as I lean over the back of the passenger seat. I look at the digital clock on the center console. It's 9:12 p.m.

"We're already here and I have another ride to pick up." The driver shakes his head and taps the screen of his mounted Android phone.

"OK." I nod and open the car door. The night air is cool, carrying the sweet scent of candy mixed with smoke as I walk up to the small host stand. The rail-thin hostess doesn't look old enough to work. She's wearing too much eye makeup and a choker as if to make herself look older. She points inside the restaurant toward the bar, then turns her eyes back to the seating chart on her tablet while the security guard checks my ID.

It's dim inside. Strung Edison bulbs illuminate the dark shiplap walls. It smells like alcohol and something greasy, like pork lardons. Another lit-up metal "Gather" sign hangs on the wall across from the bar. Under the *G* I see Lauren's blond highlights, her face turned toward Renée, who is looking down at her phone. I feel a vibration inside my purse, ignore it, and walk toward them.

"Finally!" Renée shouts and pushes a copper mug toward me.

"We were waiting for you." Lauren smiles brightly.

"*She* wouldn't let me drink until you got here." Renée lifts her brows and gives Lauren a sideways smirk.

"I hope I didn't keep you waiting too long." I pull out a wood and metal industrial-looking stool and sit down across from them.

"No—" Lauren starts to say.

"Yes," Renée says, cutting her off. She squinches her brows together and takes a long drink from her tumbler. "Mama needs a drink." She laughs. "If you had kids, you'd understand."

I pinch my lips together and take a drink, then grimace. *I hate ginger beer.* I take another long sip.

"Do you want me to get you something else?" Lauren asks, her brows raised, as if she's done something wrong. "I just got you the same thing I was drinking."

"No. It's great. Thank you, Lauren." I nod and smile. "So, how are you?"

Her face turns red as she curls her lips into a frowning expression I thought only Muppets were capable of. Her eyes water and she takes a drink. The copper mug eclipses most of her face.

"Never mind." I swallow hard. "Hey." I smile. "Why don't we do shots?"

"Yes. Definitely yes." Renée grins, exposing too many teeth.

"I don't know." Lauren shrugs and looks down at the table.

"Yes. She needs it." Renée widens her eyes at me and nudges Lauren's shoulder.

"What should I get?" I ask.

"What did we used to get back in the days?" Renée tilts her head.

"Fireball," Lauren says into her mug.

"Gross." I frown, remembering the hangovers. I shake my head, then clear my throat. "All right, three shots of Fireball coming right up." I down the rest of the Moscow Mule, gag slightly, then head for the bar.

I squeeze between two plaid flannel shirts. Black and red to my left has a full thick beard. Black and gray to my right, a five o'clock shadow. I read the chalkboard mounted above the rows of glass bottles. "Good Vibes Only." *OK.* I roll my eyes then wave my hand at the bartender. He holds up his pointer, and I shift my weight. When I order the shots, his waxy black mustache curls back with a mocking smile. *Good vibes only!* I grip the three small glasses using all my fingers, then pace back toward the table.

"Ta-da. Shots." I set the glasses down.

"You didn't see him at all, did you?" Renée asks with a sideways smile.

"See who?" I ask, feeling the hairs on the back of my neck stand up. "Is it Ryan?" My face flushes as I look toward the open door of the entrance.

"Who's Ryan?" Lauren lifts her brows.

"No, it's not Ryan," Renée answers, her voice stern in response to my nervous expression.

"You seriously didn't see that guy staring at you at the bar?" Lauren asks.

"What guy?" I ask, scrunching up my face.

"The cute one. Crap, he's looking over here. Don't be obvious," Renée says, looking down at the melted ice cube in her whiskey glass.

"Quick, pretend we're talking about flower arrangements," Lauren says.

"Why would we be talking about flower arrangements? No one's getting married." I shake my head.

"I don't know. I can't think of anything else." Lauren frowns.

"What's he doing now?" I mouth to Lauren, who has the best view of the bar.

"He's talking to his friend." Lauren bites her lip. "He keeps looking over here."

"What does he look like?" I ask.

Renée slaps my arm. "He's coming over here."

I stand up straight and tuck my hair behind my ear. *Don't be weird.* I squint at Renée and Lauren, my lips pressed in a hard line. "Let's take the shots."

"Now?" Lauren's voice rises to a screech.

"Now," I say, lowering my voice and nodding slowly.

I feel a tentative tap on my shoulder just as I finish swallowing, the cinnamon burning all the way down my throat and chest to my belly. My face scrunches as I stroke my neck, then force my grimace into a thin smile. I turn to face him. Then wave him back. I lower my head to cough into my elbow.

"Sorry." My eyes water as my lips curl into a weak smile.

"Are you OK?" he asks, his eyes wide.

"I'm great." I stand up straight. "We're celebrating, and we just took shots." I clear my throat.

Renée and Lauren lift their empty shot glasses, smiling half-heartedly.

"What's the occasion?" He smiles broadly.

"It's Ruthie's birthday," Lauren sputters.

"Her dirty thirty." Renée tosses her head back and laughs.

I shoot her a look that could melt the polar ice cap, but she just laughs harder.

"Can I buy you a birthday drink?" he asks.

I press my lips into a thin line, then finally nod.

He returns from the bar with two icy, wet copper mugs. Hands full, he tosses his head to shake his wavy brown hair away from his face. His warm brown eyes, framed by thin laugh lines, light up when I smile at him. I thank him for the Moscow Mule, suppressing a sulk with every sip. The bar grows louder as it becomes more crowded. He and I stand beside the table, shifting with the current of people squeezing past, while Renée and Lauren sit and drink, whispering into each other's ears.

My body feels fuzzy. It's warm in here. I bite my lip. *He's cute.* I step closer to him when a server shuffles behind me. "Sorry," I slur as I press against him. His eyes glossy, he leans in toward my ear.

Then Renée grabs my arm and shakes me. "We gotta go!"

My eyes widen. "Why? What happened?" I shake my head.

"Lauren is freaking out. and she wants to leave."

"What? Why? Isn't she having fun?" I argue, my brain a cloudy bowl of soup.

"No, she's not. She misses Andrew, and she's already tried to call him."

"I'm not ready to leave yet." I press my lips together and point to him with my eyes.

"It's late and the bar's going to close soon anyway. Come on, Ruthie. Let's go."

"I'll catch up with you guys. I can take a Lyft." I grit my teeth.

She lets out a loud exhale and shakes her head. I watch as they collect their handbags. The table is littered with empty glasses and mugs. Renée drinks the last of her whiskey, then slams her glass down and pushes past me. "I'll call you later." She glares at me as she grabs Lauren's hand and drags her toward the entrance.

I blink slowly, my eyes hot. I pull my head back to look up at him, then smile. My head feels heavy. *Kiss him.* I lick my lips. *Just kiss him.* I lean into him and press my lips hard against his. His mouth is cold from his drink. I close my eyes and feel my body sway in his arms.

I pull back and give a sideways smile. "Are you coming or going?"

"Coming or going where?" he asks, his face confused.

I point toward the entrance and take another sip of my drink.

"Coming?" He furrows his brow, then takes my hand and leads me to the entrance.

Outside the smell of candy vape and cigarette smoke has grown stronger. I clutch my mouth. He pulls the door open to the back seat of a stopped gray Prius. I sit down, then scoot over.

"Are you Chad?" the driver asks as he taps at a phone mounted on the windshield.

He ignores the driver and turns to me. "Where do you live?"

"On PCH. Mm, maybe three miles from here." I hiccup. "Are you Chad?" I giggle.

"Are you Chad?" the driver repeats, his voice brittle.

"No. I'm Matthew." He pulls a twenty-dollar bill from his jacket pocket and hands it to the driver. "The lady lives about three miles away on PCH. Think you can make it work?"

"Sure." The driver shrugs. "North or south when I get to PCH?"

"Whichever way left is," I respond.

"South." The driver nods, then taps the screen of his phone off.

13

TRICK OR TREAT?

The Prius stops outside the gate, and I push open my door. I stumble out as Matthew hands the driver another bill and steps out on the opposite side. I punch the security code into the metal box of the gate system. The speaker starts ringing. *Oops.* I press wildly at the keys until the ringing stops. Then try again. And push the handle when the gate lets out a loud buzzing tone. "Are you coming?" I hold open the door and gesture widely for him to come inside.

Matthew lifts his brows, then looks around. The taillights of the Prius are bright in the distance of the otherwise dark street. He shoves his hands in his pockets and paces toward me. He follows me up the sidewalk leading to the condo. When we reach the stairs, I look back at him and press my index finger to my lips and mouth "Shh" before grabbing on to the handrail and stomping up the steps. I'm dizzy. I lean against the wall of the entryway and dig through my purse.

"Hey, are you OK?" Matthew asks. I lean into him and press my lips hard against his. He pulls back and shakes his head. "Let's just get you inside." He reaches into my purse and pulls out the keys, then opens the door.

I left all the lights on. It's bright and smells like Indian food mixed with the flowery scent of my perfume. My stomach reels. *I need to lie down.* I stagger toward a sofa and slump against the cushions. In the kitchen Matthew opens and closes cabinets, the doors banging loudly, until he finally pulls out a glass. He fills it with water from the tap and brings it over. I sit up straight and take a sip. He sits down beside me.

I shake my head. "I'm sorry. I can't do this." I set the glass down.

"You should really drink the water."

"I will. What I mean is, I can't do sex."

"*Do* sex?" He lets out a chuckle.

"*Have* sex, I mean. I can't do it. I want to. I like you, but I just can't." I hiccup. Then put my hand over my mouth.

He lets out a loud sigh, then leans back against the sofa. He rubs his hand over his forehead and down his face, then drops it to his lap. He turns and smiles at me. "It's all right."

"Really?" I hiccup again.

"Yeah." He reclines against the sofa and closes his eyes. "Is it all right if I lie here for a minute?"

"Um . . . sure." I take another sip of water, then slump back against the sofa. My eyes shut.

＊　＊　＊

My face is hot. My cheek stinging. *Wake up. Wake up.* The sound of clapping at odds with the pain I feel in my face. I squish my eyebrows together, then force my eyelids apart into a squint. A blurry figure stands over me.

"Wake up. Ruthie, wake up."

"Stop," I slur, and swat the hand away from my face.

"Wake up!"

I scrunch up my face, then open my eyes, the lids like sandpaper over my dry pupils. I sit up straight on the sofa.

"What are you doing here?" I rub my eyes.

"I called you a hundred times. We couldn't get a hold of you! Why did you bring him here?" Renée shouts.

I look around. "Where is he? What did you say to him?"

"Nothing. He left when Lauren and I got here and woke him up. Ruth, you can't go home with random strangers. You're so lucky nothing happened to you."

"You're not my mom!"

"He could have raped you. Grow up."

"You're making a big deal out of nothing. Nothing happened."

"How do you not understand how dangerous that was? You have no idea what kind of person he is. He could be a rapist or a murderer."

"But he isn't." My voice is firm.

"How do you know he wasn't a thief?"

"Because he just wasn't. I got to know him. He's a nice guy."

"Oh, you *know* him. What's his name?" She crosses her arms.

"Chad." I rub my face. "No. It was Matthew."

"You brought home a total stranger whose name you don't even remember." Renée's face flushes red. "I didn't come here to argue with you." She sighs. "Lauren needs a place to crash for the night. She can't go home, or she'll call Andrew. I had to take her phone."

"Where is she?"

"In the bathroom. It's late and I can't take her home with me. I'm tired of babysitting." She hands me Lauren's phone. "Don't let her have it. I'll call you in the morning." She walks to the door.

I follow her to the entryway. "Please don't tell Mom about this."

"I won't." She exhales loudly. "Promise you'll be more careful."

I look down at the floor and nod. She gives me a tight hug, then leaves. I shut the door behind her and lock it. Inside my room, I tug off my sweater, then shrug on a T-shirt and sweatpants and pull out an extra set.

"Lauren, I've got pajamas for you," I call toward the bathroom and yawn as I get into bed. The bathroom door opens slowly and Lauren steps out. Her eyes are red and swollen. Her makeup smeared. She sniffles as she grabs the pajamas off the bed.

I sit up. "Are you OK?"

"No." She sighs and slumps onto the foot of the bed. "I miss Andrew. I know you won't let me call him tonight, but I'm going to call and apologize in the morning."

I wipe my hand over my face and sigh. "Trust me, you don't want to do that." I let out a low laugh, then shake my head. "I was *you* last weekend. I did the exact same thing. I went out, got drunk, felt lonely, and called my ex. The feeling will pass, and then you're going to regret it."

"No. I won't. You might be ready to start over, but I'm not. I can't be like you." She stands and pulls the sweatpants on under her dress, then looks down at me. "I'm going to marry Andrew." She grabs the T-shirt, walks into the bathroom, and shuts the door.

I let out a breath I didn't realize I was holding, then sag against the headboard. My eyes water and I switch off the lamp. Then roll onto my side with my back to the bathroom and choke down the lump in my throat. *I can do this. I won't marry Tom.* I squeeze my eyes shut.

⁕ ⁕ ⁕

I kneel on the floor in my closet and pull the lid off a plastic storage bin filled with costumes. I pull out a blue gingham dress and bonnet. Then the red bandana and striped stockings of a pirate getup. Underneath is the eye patch and vest of Tom's costume. *Tom always dressed up with me.* I stuff all the clothes into the bin, snap the lid shut, then sit on the floor. I drop my head into my hands, my cheeks smooshed between my palms. *Why did I agree to meet Matthew tonight? How could I forget it was Halloween?* I didn't even remember giving him my number when I received his text. I reach up to the shelf and pull down my phone to call Sam.

"I don't have anything to wear," I say, my voice whiney.

"Why is it so echoey? Are you in the bathroom?"

"No." I moan and stand. "The closet."

"Don't you have a ton of costumes, though?"

"I guess. . . . They just all feel incomplete without . . ." My voice trails off.

"Oh. Well, no sweat. I have just the thing for you." Her voice is loud and full of enthusiasm.

"Great," I answer dryly.

"See you in an hour."

I set down the curling iron when I hear Sam's knock. Her tight nurse uniform makes me question what's in the paper bag she brought. She sets her purse on my bed, then opens the bag and pulls out a pair of handcuffs. I cross my arms and roll my eyes when she hands me a gray romper and sheriff badge.

"Cute, right?" Sam smiles. "See, now *we* have coordinating costumes. You don't need no man." She laughs.

"How do these coordinate?"

"These are both careers of strong, independent women." She shrugs.

"Sure, these highly sexualized costumes don't objectify women at all." I smirk.

"Shut up and put it on. You were a naughty schoolgirl four years ago. Don't start this crap."

"I was in my twenties. Those were different times."

"You were twenty-nine. Give me a break. What, have you suddenly shriveled up into a prude?"

I roll my eyes again, then take the romper and cuffs into the closet. "If my mom didn't already think I'm a slut, she's definitely going to now." I step out into the hallway wearing the costume and a pair of knee-high black boots.

"She thought my nurse costume was cute." She crosses her arms. "You need to stop being so self-critical. You are not the old lady you think you are. No, we're not twenty-two anymore, but we're not grandmas either. I swear, you've aged more in the couple months since you left Tom than in the last five years. Put those handcuffs on your belt and let's go."

I link the cuffs on the plastic belt of the romper and tug the shorts down. *These are going to give me wedgies all night.* I follow Sam out through the living area and let out a deep breath once I lock the door. *Mom didn't see me.*

I haven't been down to the bar scene on the peninsula in years. Not since before I met Tom. Every Friday and Saturday night is the same here: Sloppy and stumbling twenty-somethings waiting in line to get into small, sweaty, standing-room-only bars. Leaving one bar and jaywalking across the street to get to an equally humid bar. The same people every weekend. At the end of the night, the parking lots reek of vomit and sometimes urine. Girls puke on the sides of buildings; their best friends hold their hair back. Holiday weekends bring even bigger crowds. Before the popularity of ride-sharing, we'd chew minty gum and risk DUIs. The names of the bars have changed, but it's otherwise the same.

Gary's pub, a redbrick sports bar at the top of the peninsula, usually draws a slightly less sloppy crowd. But it's Halloween, the sour smell of vomit already on the breeze mingled with the ever-present evening aroma of flavored vape. The Lyft stops in the street to let us out.

We run across the pavement in heels, beating a group of girls dressed as slutty Power Rangers to the bouncer. As soon as we walk in, I feel sweat begin to bead on my forehead. *Somebody needs more deodorant.* I scrunch up my nose. Sam tugs my arm, weaving between damp polyester costumes to a table near a makeshift DJ stand. The giant speakers blaring EDM make my ears ring. I stand at the table and smile awkwardly as Sam hugs a half dozen people I don't know.

"What do you want to drink?" Sam shouts over the music and pulls out a barstool from under the table.

"I don't care. What are you having?" I shout back.

She shrugs, points for me to sit on the stool, and muscles her way to the bar. I smile and nod at her friends, then wipe a stray hair away from my face. My curls are falling flat in the humidity. I keep my feet tucked under the table to keep them from getting knocked around by passersby.

Sam sets two blue drinks down on the table. Then smiles, lifts her brows, and points to the left with her eyes. "It's Niko," she mouths, her face flushed. A tall brontosaurus looms beside her. *I don't care how cute he is. It must smell so bad inside that costume.* I force a smile and wave.

"He bought us drinks!" Sam shouts, and grins.

"Thank you." I nod at him and lift my glass. Then lean into Sam's ear. "What is this?"

"It's an Adios!" she yells into my ear.

"Gross."

"Don't be rude. I like him. Just drink it." She picks up her glass and drinks.

I watch her nose scrunch up as her lips pucker around the straw and cover my mouth to suppress a laugh. He leans into her ear and says something that makes her nod and smile, then he walks away.

"What time are you meeting with Matthew?" she asks.

I take a drink, cough, then answer, "I don't know. Why?"

"Niko broke up with his girlfriend."

I shake my head and shrug.

"I think he likes me." She takes a long sip of her drink. I squish my eyebrows together. "You know I've liked him for a long time. This is my chance." Her lips pull back in an apologetic smile.

"We just got here. When are you leaving?" I crunch hard on an ice cube.

"Not *right* away. Can't you text Matthew and just ask where he's at?"

"I don't really want to. I don't want to look desperate. We haven't even gone on a date yet." I take a long drink and crunch down on another ice cube. "I was actually planning on flaking so I could stay with you." I tilt my chin down and look her in the eyes.

"Don't look at me like that." She turns away. "Fine. I'll stay. But you're buying the next round."

I smile, then stand. "Easy."

After I get the drinks. I hold the two glasses in front of me, then lift them over my head when I squeeze between people, holding my clutch under my armpit. I set the glasses down at the table, then look around. Everyone but Sam and Niko is exactly where they were when I left. I tap the shoulder of a cowboy I saw her hug when we sat down. "Have you seen Sam?" I shout. He shakes his head. I wave at the girl across from me and ask her if she's seen Sam.

"She went out to the patio. Sam'll be right back!" she shouts, her face paint melted and indecipherable. I nod and smile. Then press my lips to the straw of my vodka soda. The bass thumps so hard my whole body feels like it's vibrating.

I shake the melted ice around my glass, then eye the drink I bought for Sam. I pick it up and take a sip, then check my phone. Red and green lights reflect off the screen. No new messages. I take another sip, then lift the glass over my head and push my way through the crowd. The floor is sticky beneath my boots. Outside, the smoky breeze feels good against my flushed face. I tug at the hem of the shorts, then squint and search. *I'm going to kill her for this romper wedgie.*

I fan a vanilla-scented vape cloud away from my face, then see the yellow felt spines of Niko's costume. As I near him, he stands up straight with his back to me. He's wearing Sam's red cross headband backward. I sidestep and hide behind what I think is a gorilla and peer over his hairy shoulder. And see Sam's smiling face looking up at Niko.

She's so happy. I pinch my lips together and turn around. Then push to get back inside. I look around the room. Rotating LED lights shine off the sweat-glistening, smiling faces. I frown, then suck down the rest of the vodka soda in my glass. I squeeze my way up to the bar. My hair lies limp and stringy against my shoulders. Everything is sweating. I stuff a bar napkin down the front of the romper, then use another to wipe my forehead. When I catch my reflection in the mirror of the bar, my nose wrinkles and my lip curls. *I look like crap.* I order another drink.

I toss my head back and stare up at the lights shining down red, green, blue, and purple. My hair sticks to my forehead and against the back of my neck. I close my eyes and shake my body in time with the throbbing beat. One hand swaying in the air, the other clutching my drink against my chest. I open my eyes. *That vest looks familiar.* I down the last of my drink and set my glass down on a table littered with trash and glasses.

"Excuse me!" I shout and pull at the shoulder of the guy's striped shirt. The stranger turns around and recoils from my touch. *Wrong pirate.* "Sorry. I thought you were someone else," I slur. Then shake my head. *I need to go home.* I thumb open my phone and stare at the Lyft app, then look down at the text icon. I bite my lip, then press down on the text bubble.

"Cn u come get me?" I watch the screen, then smile when the ellipsis appears.

"Where are you?"

"Gary's."

"Give me thirty minutes."

I see him before he sees me. Even from far away I can see that he looks tired, his pale face a stark contrast to his black T-shirt. I watch him as he searches the bar. When his eyes land on mine, he gives a weak smile. *Tom.* I smile back and push my way toward him. "Are you ready to go? I'm parked illegally," he says, his dark-rimmed eyes full of concern.

I look over his shoulder in the direction of the patio, then pinch my lips together and nod. He takes my hand and pulls me through the sweaty mass outside. The streetlights are bright. He tugs me toward his car, the hazard lights flashing. *Don't puke.*

When he gets in, he leans over me and lowers my seat. I stare out the open moonroof as he buckles my seat belt, then starts the engine. It's cold, but I say nothing. The fresh air keeps the acid in my belly from rising to my throat. I close my eyes, forcing them open only to check the street signs when the car stops. *He's driving me home.*

He presses the code into the security gate and drives in. He parks, then helps me out of the car and up the stairs. I flip off the lamp Mom left on in the living room and lead him back to my room. Then flop onto the bed, my feet dangling off the side. Tom stands in the doorway and scans the room, his eyes land on the chair I brought from our apartment. His lip curls.

"So, this is *your* room now, huh?" he says.

I sit up, leaning on my elbows. "It's temporary." I shake my head. "Will you please come in and shut the door?"

He takes a slow step inside, then shuts the door behind him softly. "Look, I don't know if I should stay."

"Why?" I ask.

"I don't know if I can be *here*." He looks around. "In *this* room with you. It doesn't feel right."

I lay my head back down on the bed and look at the ceiling. "It's just a room, Tom. It's where I have to live right now." I put my hand over my eyes as the room begins to spin.

"Do you want to get into bed?" he asks.

I nod with my hand still over my face. He unzips and tugs off my boots, then pulls back the covers on the bed. I don't move.

"Do you need help"—he swallows hard—"getting undressed?"

"Yes." My voice is whiney.

He unbuckles the plastic belt and sets the handcuffs on the night-stand. Then unzips the romper and pulls out the damp, wrinkled napkin I stuffed down my cleavage earlier. He lets out a low laugh. "Are you saving this for something?" He holds the napkin up.

I feel my face flush, then sit up. "No." I snatch it from his hand, wad it up, and throw it at the floor. "It was hot in there." I shrug off the romper, step out of it, and leave it on the floor before crawling under the covers. *I wish I wore a matching bra and underwear.* I pull the duvet up to my chin.

His face flushes. He rubs the back of his neck and stares down at me. Then clears his throat and asks, "Should I go?"

I press my lips together, then shake my head. He flips off the light.

14.

SLUMBER PARTY

My hand fumbles over the nightstand searching for the water bottle I know isn't there. *When will I ever learn?* My mouth dry, I roll from my side onto my back. My brain throbs behind my eyes. I haven't experienced this many consecutive weekend hangovers since I was in college. When I hear the toilet flush, I sit up straight. My heart sinks. *What have I done?* I look around for confirmation of what I fear to be true. Short auburn hairs are scattered on the pillow beside mine. I bite the inside of my cheek and look down at the floor. Teddy Bear lies facedown atop a messy pile of *his* clothes and the gray romper. *Oh God.* When the bathroom door opens, I pull the duvet up over my bare chest. Tom steps out into the bathroom vanity area in his underwear to wash his hands.

"Good morning," he says softly. Then closes his mouth, sucks air in through his nose, and hocks phlegm into my sink. The sound of his wet spit against the porcelain makes me scrunch up my nose and shake my head. *Disgusting.*

"Sorry." He cups his hand under the spout to rinse the sink. "I think all the smoke outside the bar last night aggravated my allergies." He turns off the water, then walks toward my bed. He pulls back the covers and sits down beside me.

"I think you should go," I choke out.

"It's early. I'm sure your mom's not even up yet," he says.

He reclines against the headboard and scrolls on his phone. I press my lips together and stare at him. My posture stiffens. Finally, he looks up at me, lifts his brows, and frowns.

"Tom, I want you to leave." My heart races.

He sits up straight, pulling on the covers, and I put my arm down to keep the sheet from exposing my nakedness. "You're not serious," he says, his eyes cold.

I bite the inside of my cheek, then nod slowly. He pulls off the covers and stands, his pale chest and gut spattered with auburn hairs and freckles. He rubs at the back of his neck before throwing both hands up. "I don't know what you want from me," he says. "I'm trying to be patient, but my patience is wearing thin. I want to make this work. I love you. Tell me what to do here."

"That's just it. I don't want to make it work. Last night was wrong. *This* is wrong." I cross my arms, my chest tightening as my belly churns.

"I don't understand how everything could be all right for the last six years, and then suddenly you wake up one day and it's not. Now everything is wrong."

"It's always been wrong. You've been patient for a couple months. I was patient for years. You knew I wanted to get married, and you dangled it like a carrot over my head. Keeping me waiting. Keeping me working for it. I thought maybe if I cooked enough, or cleaned enough, or did enough, it would make you want to marry me." I clench my fists and my muscles tighten. I gasp for a breath.

"I *do* want to marry you."

"But I don't want to marry *you* anymore. When you proposed, I began to realize that I was working too hard for too little in return. I know *now* that I did more than enough. Yes, I love you. Yes, I still miss you. But, it's over, Tom." My words shoot out like water from a hose with a thumb pressed over the spout. My breath is shallow and ragged.

"I told you at dinner that I can change. You have to give me another chance."

"No, Tom. No." I put my hands over my ears and squeeze my eyes shut. *I can't do this anymore.* The duvet slides down to my waist. Tears burn my face when I realize I'm exposed. *I need my pills!* I pull back the covers and get out of bed.

"Where are you going?"

"I need my pills," I say, my naked body now trembling as I stagger toward the closet.

"What pills? Are you taking drugs now?"

I shut the door and stand against it. Tears pool under my chin. I gasp for air, but it doesn't feel like enough. My face hot, the rest of my skin is covered in goose bumps. *Just get the pills.* The tingling starts in the tips of my fingers as I search for my clutch. *Don't scream. Don't scream.* I swallow hard. He knocks on the door.

"Leave!" The shrill scream rises from my chest and scratches the inside of my throat as it escapes. "Get out," I say, sobbing.

"I'm not leaving." His voice is firm behind the door. "I have what you want."

I hear him violently shake the pill bottle. "Nooo!" I scream. Adrenaline rushes through me. The tingling in my fingers spreads into my hands and arms, then from my feet up to my thighs. I crumple to the ground against the door, clutching my knees to my chest, my whole body shaking as I struggle to breathe. The closet spins. When the handle turns, I hold my breath and squeeze my eyes shut. The pressure from the door being forced open pushes hard against my back.

"Please don't!" I cry out between sobs. I press both palms against the carpet and use all my strength to push myself against the door, but I can't keep it shut. He forces it open, and I let out another scream. I'm hoarse, the muscles in my throat strained and sore. My naked body shivers cold, soaked in sweat as I look up to see his fingers wrapped around the door.

"Get out of my house!" Mom screams, her voice distant outside my head.

"But, Joy—" His fingers retract, and the door slams shut behind my back.

"Get out or I'll call the police" are the last words I hear before everything outside goes silent. The noise inside my head is like the test sound of the Emergency Broadcast System. I press my fists against my ears. Everything is black. My heart pounds in my chest as I spin down, down, down.

I suck in a breath and finally feel my lungs fill. It's like I've been plucked out of a pool after spending too much time facedown in the water. I hug my knees against my chest, then wipe the damp, stringy hair away from my face. The tears are still running, but I can feel my fingers and toes. *How much time has gone by?*

I force my eyes open. Four empty purses lie in a heap on the floor, along with a few stray tubes of lip balm and a torn-open tampon. I take a deep breath, then stand and shrug on my bathrobe. Then stack the purses back on the shelf. I brace myself, then open the closet door.

I exhale deeply. He's gone. The gray sheriff romper is still on the floor with Teddy Bear, but Tom's clothes are gone. On the bathroom vanity counter, my clutch hangs open. My cell phone, lipstick, and wadded up bar napkins are in the sink. *Where's my Xanax?* I dig around the clutch. Only the keys rattle inside.

My bed is disheveled. The sheets and duvet hang down to the carpet. I lift the covers and search the bed. *Nothing.* I drop to my knees and lift the bed skirt, but only a box of old photos greets me. *Where are my pills?*

"Mom?" I yell out, my voice shaky, as I stand, then collapse onto the bed. Doubled over, my shoulders bowing over my chest. I rub my hands over my face.

"Are you OK?" Mom pushes my bedroom door open, her face ashen.

I nod, then cry. Forming a sentence requires energy I don't have.

"He's gone now. It's OK. I'm here." Mom wraps her arm around me.

I wipe my cheeks and under my runny nose but it's no use. More tears and snot come. I cry until I'm depleted. My cracked, dry lips sting, a reminder of my desperate state of dehydration.

Finally, I whisper, "He took my pills."

"No, he didn't. I have them." Her voice is soft. She pulls them out of her pocket and hands them to me. "Running low already, huh?" Her brow is wrinkled. Her face has more lines and seems more aged than I remember.

I shrug. "I *need* them."

She nods. "Do you want to talk about why Tom was here?"

I toss my head back and close my eyes. "He picked me up last night."

"I thought you went out with Sam."

"I did." I sigh loudly. "I did go out with Sam."

"What happened?"

"She ran into this guy that she's had a crush on forever. And—I don't know—she just looked so happy." I shake my head. "I was happy for her. But I was jealous because I felt so lonely. I don't remember the last time I was *that* happy. You know, as happy as *she* looked. . . . And so, I called Tom."

Mom nods again.

"I know it was stupid. I'm sorry for bringing him here. I'm sorry about what happened."

"It's OK. I'm just glad you're all right. I didn't know what to think when I heard you scream. I didn't know if someone broke in or what. I gotta tell you I was a little relieved when I saw Tom's skinny body." She laughs. "I knew I could take him."

I suppress a smile.

"I don't know what you ever really saw in that guy."

"He was all right once."

"Well, I hope you said everything you needed to because I don't think he'll be back anytime soon. I told him if he ever set foot in this house again, I'd slap a restraining order on him."

"Mom!"

"Well? What would you do if you found a grown man in his underwear trying to force his way into your daughter's closet?"

I roll over and pull the covers over my head ignoring the sound of my phone's vibrations echoing in the sink. My entire body aches. It feels like I've run a marathon but with nothing to show for it. I squeeze my eyes shut and pray for sleep.

Did Tom tell his parents where he was going when he left so late last night? Did they care? Did they know he was coming to rescue *his drunk and sloppy ex-fiancée? What do George and Marcy think of me now?* I imagine George telling Tom to forget about me. He'd clap him on the back and say something like *It's all right. You'll do better next time.*

Marcy seemed to like me. She bought me scarves and socks every Christmas. She invited me into her kitchen to learn how to make Tom's favorite peach pie. The recipe never did stick. I tried to bake it a couple of times back home in our apartment. Something always went wrong. Once I burned the crust and left the filling undercooked. Another time it was so salty it was inedible. I'm still not sure how that happened.

I can't blame Tom for being the way he is. Tom was their miracle baby. Marcy had been declared medically barren. She waited on him hand and foot. His father painted his room with every change of Tom's whim. They went to every soccer practice, Little League game, and school concert. Tom was the first kid in his neighborhood to get a Nintendo. For George and Marcy, Tom was truly special, and they spoiled him for it.

What will Tom tell them when he gets home? I sit up straight. *They must hate me.* I rub my eyes and pull back the covers. *Don't think about it.* I grab my phone out of the sink and swipe it open. I have four missed calls from Sam and thirteen new messages. Eleven of the messages are from Sam, some from last night and the rest from this morning. All of them asking where I am and telling me to please call her. The other two new messages are from Matthew. Both are from last night, asking if I still want to meet up. I leave the clutch and its contents on the bathroom counter and slump on the bed to call Sam.

"What the hell?" she answers.

"I know. I'm sorry."

"I've been so worried about you. I asked everyone where you went, but nobody saw you leave. I was scared something happened to you. I didn't know what to do. You can't scare me like that."

"I know. I know. I'm really sorry. I'm OK. I got home all right."

"When did you leave?"

"Sometime around midnight."

"Why didn't you tell me you were leaving?"

"I—" I let out a noisy breath. "I didn't want you to see who I was leaving with."

"How ugly could Matthew be?" Her voice is sarcastic.

I lie back and look up, biting at the inside of my cheek.

"Ruth?"

"Tom picked me up," I say. Then press the phone hard against my ear, turning up the volume. The only sound is her slow, measured breath. I sit back up. The inside of my cheek feels raw.

"I can't talk to you right now."

"I'm sorry. I swear I broke it off this time."

"I can't keep watching you make the same mistakes. It's exhausting. I know you're going through a tough time, but you seem to like making it harder. I want to be a good friend, but . . ."

"I said I was sorry." My eyes sting with new tears.

"Last night I left Niko and went home in a panic worrying that you might be locked out of my apartment. I stayed up waiting for you while you were at home with Tom. You don't think about anybody but yourself."

"That's not true."

"Since you first broke up with Tom, yes, it *is*. You've been completely self-absorbed. I miss my *friend*."

"I'm here."

"OK, what's new with *me*?"

I press my lips together.

"You don't know, because you don't listen. What about your mom? How did her trip to Chicago go?"

I don't know. My breath comes out in short bursts as tears run down my face.

"I'm your friend, and I love you, but I can't keep watching you 'break up' with Tom and pop Xanax. I'll talk to you later."

The phone beeps three times in my ear before I can argue. I look down at the dark screen. *Should I call her back?* I set the phone down. *She's right.* My phone vibrates and I pick it back up. Incoming call from Rite Aid.

My prescription is ready. I let the call go to voice mail, then tug on a pair of leggings and an oversize sweatshirt. I grab the clutch and its contents from the vanity counter and shove everything into another larger purse. Then swallow a Xanax with a handful of tap water.

It was tough getting Dr. Peterson to refill my prescription this time. He asked me to come back to his office for a follow-up appointment and a potential referral to a therapist. But I assured him I was fine. I was confident I wouldn't need them much longer. Now I'm not so sure.

I wrestle the keys out of the clutch inside my purse and open my bedroom door. Walking briskly through the living room toward the entryway. I get as far as the dining table before Mom stops me.

"Where are you off to?" Her voice comes from the kitchen.

"An errand."

"I thought you weren't feeling well," she says.

"I'm not." I walk to the entryway and reach for the door.

"OK." She steps out of the kitchen to meet me in the entryway. "I hope you feel better. Call me if you need anything." She smiles weakly, drying a decanter with the dish towel I brought back for her from the Paris Las Vegas years ago. She stuffs the Eiffel Tower into the neck of the bottle. *I can't believe she still has that thing.*

My hand drops to my side. "Mom?"

"Yeah?"

"How did your meeting in Chicago go?"

She sets down the decanter. "It went well. Remember I told you that I wouldn't have to fly back for a while? Which is great because it's starting to freeze out there." She grins.

I frown and shake my head. "No, I don't remember."

"Well, that's OK. You've had a lot on your mind." She offers a tight-lipped smile.

"No, Mom, it's not OK. I've been a really crappy person lately. I'm a crappy friend, a crappy sister, and a really crappy daughter."

"No, you're not."

"Yes, I am! I'm selfish and thoughtless. I've already broken two of the three rules you gave me to live here. The only reason I haven't broken the third is because I happen to *be* a tidy person. Which may be my only redeeming quality these days. Let's face it. I suck."

"You do not suck. And I hate it when you use that word, by the way. This is an adjustment period. Think of this version of you as being 'Transitional Ruthie.' " She gestures with both hands.

"Well, 'Transitional Ruthie' sucks. I don't want to be crappy anymore."

"So, don't. Decide right now that you're going to do better, and you will. I don't see any reason why you can't."

"I did end it with Tom." I shrug. "Like, *really* end it."

"See? Step one: complete. What's your step two?"

My shoulders slump. I shuffle to the counter and pull out a barstool. "Don't refill my prescription." I sit down and hunch over.

She smiles warmly and nods. "And step three?"

"Suck less?" I squish my brows together.

She lifts her brows and gives me a look that says, *You can do better than that.*

I draw in a deep breath. "I need to stop thinking about myself so much and start being more present with the people I love."

She gives me a smile that says, *Atta girl.*

15.

IF I COULD TURN BACK TIME

It's been a whole week since I last spoke with Sam. As part of plan "Suck Less," I've tried calling her three times, but she won't take my calls. I've sent her a few messages and a couple (what I thought were super funny) memes. And . . . nothing. The radio silence has grown deafening. I want to tell her I have a date tonight and to ask her for advice. But mostly I just want to ask how she's been.

I twist the wand around the tube of mascara. Then brush the goopy bristles against my lashes until they stand straight and black. *Call her.* I look down at my phone on the counter. The black screen reflects my frown. I stuff the wand back into the tube. *I need to get dressed.*

I tug on a sweater and grab a scarf. I'm late but I spray on perfume and switch out purses anyway. Shuffling my wallet, keys, and lipsticks one by one from my work purse to a brown leather one that matches my boots. I grab my phone off the counter, bite the inside of my cheek, then leave.

I was surprised when Matthew asked me out again after Halloween. *Maybe he mistook my lack of response for playing hard to get.* He messaged me Tuesday and invited me out for a drink. He told me to pick the place. I picked Gather.

By the time I pull up to the valet stand, I'm seventeen minutes late. I hand the attendant my key. Then wave my hand in front of my face as I walk up to the restaurant. The smell of weed permeates the smoky vape haze. Inside it still smells of lardons and alcohol. The same buffalo-plaid-and-beanie-wearing patrons huddled around the bar and rustic wood tables.

It's darker than I remember. I can't decide if it seems more romantic or gloomy in this lighting. Somewhere between the mood lighting of a fancy Newport Beach steak house and a musty Santa Ana bikini dive bar. "Gooey" plays in the background, the words barely audible over the sound of loud conversation.

I walk through the bar half expecting to find Lauren and Renée. The table where we sat is now occupied by seven girls celebrating, gold metallic balloons in the shape of the numbers two and five bunched between bouquets of pink and gold latex. They snap photos for Instagram and Snapchat. They're careful to hold the balloons down beneath the illuminated Gather sign.

When a stool frees up at the bar, I set my purse down. I stand behind it and scan the bar before reaching into my bag. A new message from Matthew reads, "I see you." I smile at the screen, then toss my phone back into my purse. *Where is he?* It's crowded. Every table is seated. Tight groups of people crouch over their drinks murmuring in one another's ears.

I squint, looking around the restaurant, until finally I see a hand waving. He scoots to the end of the bench at a low wooden picnic-style table and stands. I grab my purse, tuck my hair behind my ear, and walk toward him. As he leans in to kiss me, I turn my face and kiss his cheek. He lets out a noisy exhale and an uncomfortable laugh. Then sits on the bench and scoots down to offer me the end seat.

"Do you know these people?" I ask, looking around at the table full of strangers.

"No, it's a communal table. I didn't make a reservation, and this was the best they could do." His brows draw together in a contrite expression.

I nod and try to ignore the people seated around us.

"That's for you." He points to the copper mug set at my place setting.

I bite down on my lip, then say, "Thank you, but, I don't like Moscow Mules." I grimace, my lips pulling down to expose my lower teeth.

"You don't?" His face scrunches up.

"No. I don't. I only drank them last time to be polite. First to Lauren and then to you. I'm sorry."

"That's all right. I'll drink it. When the server comes back, you can order whatever you want," he says. "So, how was your Halloween?"

"It was awful." My posture sags. "I'm sorry for flaking on you." His eyes, the color of toffee, melt me. He lifts his brows as if to say, *Go on.* My face grows hot. I shake my head and say, "I got into a fight with my best friend. . . . She's mad at me for leaving her at the bar."

"That doesn't seem like enough of a reason for her to still be upset."

I shrug. "Well, I also scolded her for sleeping with her ex."

"Is he a bad guy?"

"Not exactly."

"So, what's the big deal?"

"She shouldn't have done it. It was really stupid of her. She should have ended it sooner and moved on." My eyes water, and I pick up the copper mug and take a sip.

He puts his hand on my shoulder. "I think you're being a little hard on your friend."

"You don't understand. She keeps making the same mistakes. It's like she enjoys the suffering." I take another long sip. "She's actually really smart. That's why it doesn't make sense that she would have spent so much time in a dead-end relationship." I let out a sigh, then pinch my lips together.

"It sounds like you really care about your friend. Why don't you just call her?"

"I've tried."

"Try again."

"When? Now?" I squish my brows together.

He nods, then takes a drink of the honey-colored liquid in his glass. The single ice ball, cracked and melting, swirls clear liquid into the whiskey. I reach into my purse and pull out my phone. Then turn up the volume and strain to hear with my ear against the receiver, listening to it ring and ring before it finally goes to voice mail. I throw the phone back in my purse, then swallow down the last of my drink.

"Wow. You're really upset." He sets down his glass. "Do you want another drink?"

I shake my head and look down at the table. "Are you hungry?" he asks. I shake my head again. "How about some fries?" he says. I smile weakly.

He waves and catches the attention of a passing server. When he asks about ordering fries, the server frowns and tells him the kitchen is closed for the night. Matthew turns to look at me, his face apologetic. "Do you want anything else then?" he says. I sulk, and he asks for the check.

"There's a great little burger place by my house," he says. "Why don't we pick up some fries, and I'll open a bottle of wine?"

"Hmm." I bite the inside of my cheek. The raw flesh stings, and I make a face.

"Come on."

Outside, he pulls out his phone. "Lyft'll be here in seven minutes," he says. The streetlights shine down on the parking lot. It's cold. I breathe in and blow out through my mouth. The vapor hangs in the air in a white puff before dispersing. I pull the scarf out of my purse and wrap it around my neck.

"I can drive," I say finally, rubbing my hands over my shoulders. "I only had one drink. I can drive." I walk toward the valet stand.

He follows me, scrunches up his brows, then asks, "You drove?"

I shrug. "I didn't want to drink too much. It's my way of holding myself accountable." I hand the valet my ticket, and he sprints toward the lot behind the building.

The thick greasy smell of french fries fills my car. Matthew points left and right, wagging fries in his hand between bites, until we turn down a quiet residential street. A neighborhood of modest two-story family homes with manicured lawns and painted shutters. I slow down when I see a kid-shaped yellow sign that says, "Drive Like Your Kids Live Here." A single basketball hoop punctuates the street.

The majority of the homes have a weathered look. The homes of older parents where childhood bedrooms have been converted into offices or home gyms. The kind with dusty treadmills and spiderwebby Bowflex machines. He points to a house with a blue porch swing, and I park along the sidewalk.

"Are your parents home?" I ask and bite into a fry.

"They don't live here."

"Is this *your* house?"

"My dad owns it, but we live in it. My brother and roommate aren't home." He opens the passenger door and grabs the paper bag of fries. I open my door, step out, and follow him up the driveway.

"Here. Take off your shoes," he says as he shuts the door behind me. I tug off my boots and set them beside the rack full of men's shoes and sandals. It smells like sweaty socks and the faint odor of pets masked by air freshener. A grandfather clock ticks loudly in the foyer. He flips on a light and walks toward the kitchen. I linger walking through the foyer and stare at the great room filled with outdated furniture. A pair of large floral-print sofas and glossy pine tables reek of the late eighties.

I wander into the kitchen as he pulls out a Brita pitcher from the fridge. He pours water into two mismatched glasses before reaching for a bottle of wine. The brown bag of french fries looks sad and oily atop his kitchen island, but I reach in and grab one anyway. He drinks his full glass of water in a single drink. Then pops the cork on the wine bottle and pours into his emptied water glass and then into a crystal goblet. It's the kind of goblet that his parents would have registered for at Sears.

He takes a long sip of wine, then sets his glass down and pulls off his green sweater. The hem of his crisp white T-shirt lifts up just enough to expose a sliver of toned midsection. I look away and take a long drink of wine. He drapes the sweater over a stool and shakes out his hair.

"I should probably go." I set down my glass.

"You just got here."

"I know, but it's getting late." I reach into the paper bag for one last fry. A loud snort makes me jump, and I drop the fry back into the bag. "What was that?"

Matthew grins and leans against the counter. "Relax. It's just my dog," he says. "Come here, girl!"

A small tired-looking pug hobbles into the kitchen. Her paws slip on the smooth tile floor. Her weak legs seem barely able to withstand the weight of her sagging little body. She bumps into Matthew's leg, then collapses onto the floor beside him and yawns.

"What's her name?" I squat down to pet her. Her fawn-colored fur feels silky under my fingers.

"This blind old girl is Emmy."

"How old is she?" I pet her head softly.

"She's sixteen and on her last legs."

He picks her up gingerly and nuzzles her side. I take another sip of wine. *I wonder if he's good with kids too.* I swallow hard, then say, "I never asked. How old are you?"

"Thirty-four," he says. "How old are *you*?"

"That's a rude question to ask a lady." I cross my arms.

"You asked how old I am and how old Emmy is. I think it's fair to ask."

I bite my lip. "Twenty-nine."

He smirks. "Didn't you just celebrate your dirty thirty?"

Crap! I feel my face flush. Then groan. "I'm thirty-three."

"Are you sure this time?"

"Yes. Do you want to see my ID?"

"No, I trust you." He takes a sip. "Why lie and say twenty-nine, though?"

I slump in my stool, slouching over the island counter. "Because guys in their thirties don't want thirty-year-olds. They want twenty-some-things." I take a drink. "My dating pool has shrunk to kiddie size, and it's mainly forty-year-olds looking for second wives." I shake my head.

"That can't be true."

"It is. Think about it. How many thirty-plus girls have you dated?"

He takes a long drink, then shakes his head and refills his glass. "I don't know." He takes another sip, his expression pensive. "I guess I haven't met too many single girls over thirty."

"That's because they're all married. Or engaged. Or dating forty-year-olds already." I smile weakly and take another sip of wine. "I really should get going." I set down my glass and drape my scarf around my neck.

"Is it because I'm too young for you?" he says. "Now who's the ageist?"

"You're not too young for me. I think I'm just too old for you." I shake my head again. "I think you're sweet. but I'm tired of 'dating' already. I don't want to meet up for drinks and casual sex. I'm terrified of dick pics. And if you text, 'You up?' I won't be. I'll be asleep, cuddling my teddy, probably slathered in night wrinkle cream and spots of zit medication. I *like* you. And I don't want to pretend that I don't so you'll keep hanging out with me. If I die a spinster, so be it."

"I didn't invite you over here for sex." He smiles awkwardly.

I lift a brow and tilt my head. *Really, dude?*

"I mean, I'm a guy, so of course I wouldn't mind it, but that's not why I invited you. I like you too. I just wanted to cheer you up with wine and fries since you were so bummed about your friend."

I blush and bite my lip to suppress a smile. He puts his hands on my waist and peers down at me. Then says, "And I promise to never send you a dick pic." He puts his right hand over his heart and lifts his left hand.

I can't help but laugh. Then I say, "Thank you."

He stands on the sidewalk with Emmy swaddled under his arm as I start my car. He waves a final time as I drive away. In my rearview mirror, I watch him wait for me to reach the stop sign before he finally walks up his driveway and back inside. I turn left, then stop in front of the house with the yellow kid sign. *Where am I?* I open Google Maps and tap "Home" on the menu. I follow the prompts on the screen until I reach PCH and realize I'm in Huntington.

My left-turn signal ticks as I wait at the intersection for the green light. The fog is dense, reflecting back the light of my headlamps. The left arrow lights up, but I ignore it, then flip my turn signal right. When the traffic light turns green, I cut across the vacant right lanes and make an illegal right turn.

I hear the siren before I see the red and blue lights in my rearview mirror. My heart races inside my chest as I press the Hazard button and pull over to the shoulder. My body cold, I feel sweat form along my hairline. *I only had one drink at the bar and a half glass of wine at Matthew's.* I bite at the swollen spot inside my cheek and shift into park. *But over how much time?* I look at the digital clock on my center console. It's 11:36 p.m. *Just over three hours.* I hold my breath as the officer steps out of his car and walks up to my passenger window. I press to roll it down, and the officer shines a flashlight inside my car.

"License, registration, and proof of insurance," he says flatly.

I pinch my lips together and nod. Then peel my fingers from the steering wheel and open the glove box. A mess of Starbucks napkins spills out. Tears prick my eyes as I stuff them back in and reach for my documents. I sniffle but can't keep the tears from rolling down my face.

"Do you know why I pulled you over?" the officer asks, his face devoid of expression. I wipe my face and nod slowly. "Is there a reason you made that illegal turn?" he asks.

I nod again, take a deep breath, and say, "It's not going to sound like a very good reason to you." He looks at me as if to say, *Try me.* I blurt out, "When I stopped at the light, I just felt lonely. I was supposed to turn left to go home, but I decided to turn right because my friend lives this way. I know it's late. I wasn't even going to try to see her. I just wanted to drive past her apartment and pretend everything was OK." I wipe the tears from my face.

He exhales deeply. Then holds out his hand for my documents. I hand him the registration and insurance. Then look at him and say, "My license is in my purse." He nods and I dig for my wallet, then hand him my license. He flashes his light over it.

"Is this Costa Mesa address correct?"

"No." I shake my head. "I live in Newport with my mom now." I let out a noisy breath. "I'm going through some *personal* stuff."

He taps his left hand on the window frame, then walks back to his car. I let out a sigh. *It's just a ticket, not a DUI.* I cross my arms over my chest and rub my shoulders. My heart slows. Time ticks by and I bite at my thumb to keep from chewing on my swollen cheek. An eternity later the officer reappears in my passenger window.

"I'm going to let you go with a warning," he says.

"Really?" My stomach leaps.

"Going through a divorce is not a reason to break the law, no matter how upsetting. But I'm going to let it go this time. Go home. And drive safely." He hands me back my documents. This time when he taps the frame, I notice the thin band of pale skin on his ring finger. I look down and nod.

At the next traffic signal, I finally make a U-turn and drive toward home. *I'll try again tomorrow.*

16

SHE LOVES ME NOT, SHE LOVES ME

I parallel park across the street from her apartment building. My car wedged between a Jetta and a pickup truck. The salty air is cool despite the sun's cloudless presence. I pull the tag of my zipper and zip my jacket up to my neck. Then pace up to the pink building and tug the ratty twine loop of the gate latch. The metal gate creaks open to a cement courtyard and kidney-shaped pool of teal water.

A cat-shaped welcome mat lies beneath the screen door of Sam's apartment. I open the screen and knock on the gray door behind it, then step back and let the screen swing shut. A neighbor steps out of his apartment in sweats toting a black trash bag. I smile awkwardly at him. Then open the screen, knock again, and shout, "Sam?"

My shoulders slump. I step off the cat mat, and the screen door slaps shut. My chin lowers to my chest as I walk back to my car staring down at the pavement ahead. Inside my car it's warm and I tug the zipper of my jacket down and take a deep breath. *Come on, Sam. What do you want from me?* I drop my forehead to the steering wheel. My eyes widen as I gasp, then sit up straight and open the glove box.

I pull out a napkin and pen. Then write across the thin brown paper, "I meant it when I broke up with Tom this time. I'm never going back. I need you, friend." Then open my purse and pull out the orange prescription bottle. I wrap the napkin around the vial. Then march back up to Sam's door and place it under the mat. I smile at the lump under the cat's nose, then leave.

* * *

I tapped my phone screen all day Sunday checking for new messages or missed calls. But only the time and date against my floral wallpaper lit up the screen. No new alerts. Today has been the same. Between emails I've been sneaking peeks at my phone. I look at the blank screen, frown, and stuff the phone back into my purse. Then shove it into the cabinet under my desk.

At home I step out of my pumps. Toss my purse onto the bed and slump into my reading chair. Then throw my head back and stare at the ceiling. The tag of my blouse itched against my neck all day. I couldn't wait to get home and peel it off. Now that I'm here, I ignore it. A vibration buzzes inside my purse. *It's probably Renée.* I let out a yawn and close my eyes.

The phone buzzes again, and I force my eyes open. Then stagger to my feet and dig through my work bag. I have two new messages from Sam. My thumb races to punch my pass code into the phone. The first bubble simply reads, "Hey." The second, "I got your note." With my shoulders hunched over the phone, I smile at the screen. Then hold my breath when an ellipsis appears. "Do you want to come over?"

"YES!" I type back. Then throw my phone into my purse. I pull my blouse over my head and unbutton my slacks as I hurry to the closet. I take off my pants, then wad up my clothes and toss them into the dry-cleaning bin before tugging on jeans and a hoodie. Tripping over my flip-flops as I rush back to the bed, I grab my purse and spring out the door.

Soft yellow light glows from the windows of Sam's apartment. I look down at the flattened cat mat, then pull open the screen door and knock. This time I hold the screen door open as I wait. "Coming." Sam's voice sounds musical behind the door. The knob turns and I smile. When she opens the door and smiles back at me, tears wet my eyes and I laugh. She lifts her arms and we hug. It feels like opening a Hallmark card with a thoughtful message and personal note from someone you love.

"I'm sorry." I sniffle.

"I'm sorry too."

Inside, it's warm and smells like pumpkin spice candles, sweet and a little smoky. She shuts the door behind me, and I stand in her entryway. The two-bedroom apartment is snug. Sam and her mom have long outgrown the space. Books, DVDs, and boxes of puzzles and games spill out of a bookshelf. Cat toys are scattered across the floor, though I've only ever seen Alfred in photos. "He's a scaredy-cat," Sam had said with a shrug. She sits down on the big beige couch and tugs a knitted blanket over her lap. Then points at the second blanket, draped over the arm of the couch. I sit down beside her and tug the blanket over myself.

"Where's your mom?" I ask.

"She's on a date." She rolls her eyes.

"What happened to the last guy? Mike or whatever."

"Who knows?" She stands and heads to the kitchen. On the wall behind the table, her mom has hung a sign that says, "It's always wine o'clock." Sam opens a cabinet and pulls out a bottle of red and two stemless glasses. She pours, then corks the bottle and leans over her oven. The buttons beep loudly as she sets the temperature. She brings the two glasses to the living room and hands me one before sinking back into the couch. "I'm going to make a pizza," she says, and smiles. "Oh, before I forget." She leans over the coffee table and pulls my vial of Xanax out of her purse. "You left these here." She hands me the vial, and I set it down.

"I—"

"You don't need to say anything," she cuts me off. "I appreciate what you were trying to do. I was worried about you. But you should have them when you need them."

I tuck my hair behind my ear and nod slowly. "Thank you, Sam."

She takes a sip of wine and peers at me over the rim of the glass, her eyes smiling. Then she sets the glass down on the coffee table and her face changes. Her eyebrows pull together forming a deep crease between them. She bites her lower lip, then finally says, "I have to tell you something."

"OK." I sit up straight. My pulse quickens at the sight of her expression.

"You might want to take one of those pills." She nods, eyeing the bottle I set on the coffee table.

I grab the vial and stuff it in my purse. "Just tell me."

"I saw Tom holding hands with some girl on Saturday. I didn't get a good look at her. It happened so fast. They walked past my store. And I know he saw me. It was so weird," she blurts out and visibly stops breathing. Sam's been the general manager at Jim's Surf for years. She's had a few brushes with fame. Celebrities shopping last minute there for swimwear and hats, but somehow a Tom sighting seems strange.

"Is that it?" I raise my brows. Sam lets out a noisy breath and nods. I feel my shoulders drop. Then I shake my head slowly. Sam's lips curl into a nervous smile.

"So, you're not mad?" she asks.

I shake my head again and smile. "No. I'm not mad. I'm relieved that's what you *had* to tell me."

The oven beeps loudly, and Sam jumps in her seat. She gets up and heads for the kitchen. Then cuts the plastic wrapper off a frozen pizza and puts it in the oven before pressing more buttons for the timer. She flops back onto the sofa and sags against the cushions. She says, "I thought you were going to be so upset. I worried about telling you. It's part of the reason I didn't call you back sooner." She waves her hand around as if to erase an imaginary blackboard, then leans forward and grabs her wineglass off the coffee table.

I take a sip of wine. "I mean . . . it's a little sad. But it's fine. I'm fine." I pat her knee. "Anyway, enough about me. Tell me about you and Niko."

Her face flushes and she pinches her lips together. Even without the participation of her mouth, I can see the grin in her eyes. "I really like him," she says.

"I know. You've liked him for a long time."

"Yeah. But I, like, really, *really* like him."

"That's great." I nod slowly and take a long drink of wine.

"I thought you'd be happier for me."

"I am."

"You're gonna meet someone too."

"Yeah. Hopefully."

"What's going on with Matthew? Have you heard from him?" She finally takes a sip of wine.

"I was out with him on Saturday when I called you."

"You called me from your date?" Her eyes widen.

I shrug. "He told me to."

"Did you tell him we were fighting?"

My face scrunches up into an uncomfortable smile.

"Did you tell him *why*?"

I grit my teeth. And she looks down and presses her hand to her forehead, then says, "Never mind. Don't tell me."

I let my head fall back against the cushion. "Anyway. I'm super happy for you. I hope it works out with Niko."

"Me too." She slumps against the cushion and turns to look at me. "I hate how much I like him. I've never felt like this before. So . . . vulnerable."

I turn my head and look her in the eyes. "I think it's only when we feel our most vulnerable that we can feel the deepest sentiments of hope and love. Most people go through life on autopilot, never experiencing the deep lows or immense highs that life has to offer." I sit back up. "I lived like that." We sit in silence for what feels like a long while.

Finally, Sam looks up at the ceiling, then closes her eyes and says, "Maybe you're right."

"I know I'm right. I'm older than you. It's called life experience, baby." I let out a laugh and drink the last of my wine.

"Ooh." She wiggles her fingers in the air like a magician. "A whole three years." She sits up straight. "Do you want *my* advice now?"

"Probably not."

"Too bad. I'm giving it." She finishes the last of her wine, then stands and looks down at me. "Stop putting so much pressure on yourself. When it's the right time, the right guy will come along. Have fun with Matthew. You're probably not going to marry him and that's OK."

"But—"

"No buts. Freeze your eggs if you have to. But stop trying to make a square peg fit in a round hole." The oven timer beeps loudly from the kitchen. "Time's up."

* * *

I park along the sidewalk and look out at the blue porch swing beside his door. It's lit up by a single lantern mounted on the wall. *Did his parents sit in front of this house watching them play on the lawn?* It's easier to picture Matthew's little brother as a child since I've never actually met him. Neither he nor their roommate ever seems to be home. Granted, I've only been over a handful of times over the last few weeks. Sam was right. I *am* having fun.

I walk up to his door and knock. A soft bark sounds in the distance, then grows closer until I hear barking behind the door accompanied by Matthew's low voice. The door opens and he steps back and smiles. "Sorry it took me a minute. Emmy's been a little jumpy lately."

"That's OK." I kneel down and pet her before stepping out of my sandals and setting them beside the shoe rack.

"Just let yourself in next time. You don't have to knock."

I stand up straight. The look on my face must be one of shock or discomfort because he immediately says, "Or not. I just thought it might be easier."

I tuck my hair behind my ear and nod. "Yeah, maybe next time." I kiss him chastely on the lips.

"Do you want a glass of wine?" he asks and turns toward the kitchen. I follow him. "I bought that red blend you like."

"That sound's great. I had the longest day at the office, and I could use a drink." I sit down at the island counter.

"Oh yeah? What happened?" he asks as he uncorks the bottle.

"I'm just really busy. On top of my usual workload, my boss has been giving me a few commercial leads, and it's awesome . . ."

"But?"

"But I don't know if I want to do *just* commercial policies." I sigh. "And I think that's the direction Martha wants me to go in."

"And Martha's your boss?"

"Right."

"What do you want?"

"Honestly?" I ask, and he nods. "I want to be Martha one day."

"So, do it. What does it take to be Martha?" He pours the wine into two cups.

"Well, I guess the first step would be to open my own agency."

"OK. Well, do that. Then what?"

"Well, it's harder than it seems. It's kind of like buying into a franchise, but there's a lot of politics. I'd need Martha's endorsement, then corporate approval. It's not that easy."

"Nothing worthwhile ever is, but you can do it."

"How do you know? You don't know me." My shoulders slump.

"I'm getting to know you." He hands me a cup. "I know this is one of your favorite wines."

I give him a sideways smile, then take a sip. "How was your day?"

He leans over the counter and says, "It was good."

"That's it? It was *good*?"

"It was like any other day. I've been doing it for years. I met with some doctors. I told them about our new drugs. Answered some emails. Then before I knew it, it was time to go home."

"And now you're here."

He lets out a chuckle. "Yup." He takes another sip and says, "You didn't finish telling me yesterday about Thanksgiving. How did your stuffing turn out?"

"A little dry, but everyone ate it anyway." I shrug. "What about you? How was yours?"

"It was good." He clears his throat. "My mom asked about you."

My eyes widen, and I lift my brows. "I didn't know your mom knew I existed."

"Well, she didn't . . . at first. She asked if I was seeing anyone, and so I told her."

I swallow the lump in my throat, then take a long drink of wine. Then stare down at the island counter. The grout between the white tiles is grayish beige, the result of three men being left to care for it. *Just a little bleach would do it.*

"Don't sweat it. You don't have to meet her or anything. She asked and so I told her." He looks down at the floor, then reaches down and picks Emmy up. "I gotta feed her. I'll be right back. Help yourself to more wine." He eyes my cup, then opens the pantry and pulls out a can of food. He carries Emmy off toward the dining room.

I finish the wine in my cup, then pour from the bottle until my cup is half-full. Then stare out the kitchen window. *Am I his girlfriend now? Is this a thing?* I look down at the sink. It's empty and wiped down. Beside the sink a rack is full of clean dishes set to dry. *Do I want it to be a thing?* I take another sip of wine. Matthew steps back into the kitchen and asks, "Are you hungry?" He opens the fridge. "I could make a little pasta. Or I could order Thai food. What sounds good to you?"

He's my boyfriend. Marry him. Have his children. I press my lips together, then draw them up at an angle and chew on the inside of my cheek. He says, "Or you could eat the inside of your face, and we'll skip an appetizer." He shuts the fridge and scrolls on his phone. "How about instead of your cheek, we get some egg rolls?"

Pump the brakes! I nod. "I don't know if I'm super hungry, though."

"It won't get here for another forty minutes. You'll be hungry by then. What else? Do you like pad Thai? What about curry?" He looks up at me. A photo of a dish with thick yellow sauce illuminates the screen of his phone.

"What did you tell your mom about me?" I say, staring at the screen in his hand.

He takes a step back, and his hand drops to his side. "You want me to tell you?" I pinch my lips together, then nod. He says, "I told her I just started seeing you and that I liked you." I lift my brows, my lips still pinched shut. He sets his phone down on the counter and says, "I told her you were beautiful and smart . . . and a little *off*."

"Uh-uh." I smack his arm and laugh. "You did not say that!"

"All right. All right." He lifts his hands and ducks sideways dramatically. "I didn't say that last part." He straightens his posture and takes a sip of wine. "What'd you tell your mom?"

My shoulders slump, and I shake my head slowly.

"That bad, huh?" he says.

I grimace. "I didn't tell her *anything*."

He lowers his head, then finishes the rest of his wine and pours himself some more, filling the cup nearly to the rim. "That's cool," he says.

My brows draw together. "Well, she didn't ask. . . . Not like your mom did, anyway. I didn't think there was anything to tell. It's only been a few weeks, and . . ."

"No. You're right. It's fine. Don't sweat it." He takes a drink and sets his cup down. He lifts up his phone. "Do you want red curry or yellow."

"Red." I bite my lip. "Unless you want yellow," I blurt. "I like yellow too."

"No. Red is fine. Whatever you want is fine."

"I don't know what I want. I told you I wasn't that hungry. You decide."

"I'm ordering red. It's what you want and I'm fine with it."

"If you say 'fine' one more time I'll scream."

"Fine." He crosses his arms and I let out an exasperated sigh. "I like you and I like yellow curry. But I'm ok with getting red tonight. We'll get yellow next time. I don't let stuff like that bother me. And I'm not bothered by you not telling your mom about me. My mom's nosey. Yours isn't."

"Well she is but . . ."

"It's different when she lives with you. I only see my mom maybe once a month, and she crams everything she can into it."

"She sounds like a good mom."

"The best. Maybe you'll meet her one day."

"Yeah. I think I'd like that."

17

WISHING FOR A MARRIED CHRISTMAS

I blink rapidly. It's morning. I smile. Then I throw back the covers, and Teddy flops out onto the floor. I pick him up and place him back on the bed, tucking him under the covers. I open a dresser drawer and pull out pajama pants. They match the gingerbread thermal shirt I wore to bed. I tug them on, slam the drawer shut, and throw open my bedroom door.

Outside Mom's bedroom I knock three times. "Come in," her voice calls out from inside. I push open the door and bound toward her bed. Then pounce onto the empty space beside her, where I writhe like a slippery fish on a boat deck.

"Merry Christmas. Merry Christmas." I shake the mattress.

"It's not Christmas." Mom yawns and grabs her glasses off the nightstand. "What are you doing up so early?" She pushes them onto her face.

"I don't know. I couldn't sleep anymore. I'm too excited."

"Well, I can see that. I didn't expect you to be up for at least another hour."

"Who can sleep on Christmas?"

"It's not Christmas. It's Christmas Eve. Christmas is tomorrow. Go back to bed." She picks up her phone and looks at the time.

"Tomayto, tomahto. And no way."

"Since you're up, do you want to open the gift I got you?"

"No." I sit up. "OK. You're right. It's too early."

"Can I give you a hint anyway?"

I shrug. "If you insist."

"What's something you told me you really wanted but haven't gotten yourself?"

"A husband?" I lift a brow and smirk.

"If I could get you one, I would." She sets her phone down. "What about the *friend* you keep sneaking off to see?"

I feel my face flush, and I press my lips together. Then say, "I don't know what you're talking about. You mean Sam?"

"No. I mean whoever you've been *secretly* seeing for the last few months."

I let out a loud sigh. *She's just as nosey as his mom.* "It's not a secret. And it hasn't been that long. That's why I didn't tell you about it." She crosses her arms and makes a face as if to say, *Continue.* "His name is Matthew and he's nice. I think I really like him. But I'm trying not to do what I always do."

"And what's that?"

"You know." My shoulders slump. "Stuff a round peg in a square hole."

"I think it's stuff a *square* peg in a *round* hole."

"Whatever. You know what I mean. I just don't want to do *that* anymore. But it's like if I'm not busy obsessing about a guy, I'm busy obsessing about being alone. I don't know how to stop it."

Mom nods slowly. Her eyebrows draw together. She opens her mouth. Then seems to catch herself and presses her lips together.

"What? What were you going to say?"

"Nothing." She shakes her head.

"You were going to say something." Jaw clenched, I stare hard into her eyes. "Just say it."

She lets out a long loud breath. "I don't know. I guess I'm proud of you for recognizing it. You've had more boyfriends than I can keep track of."

"Mom!"

"What? It's true. Ruthie, since your dad died—"

I frown and cross my arms.

"Don't make that face. Ruth, I need to be honest with you. Since your dad died, I've felt like you've been trying to fill his place. And it only got worse once Renée got married."

"That's not true." I stand and back away from the bed. "That's not true. It's been longer." Tears fill my eyes, and I bite down on my lip. "I've wanted to get married since you and Dad divorced. I want a family again."

"You have a family. You have me and your sister."

"It's not the same. I want my *own* family. My own husband. My own kids. And I'm never getting divorced. I don't want to end up sad and lonely like you. Or die alone like Dad." Mom's face seems to freeze, only her eyes grow wider as she sits staring at me. *Why did I say that?* "Mom, I'm sorry. I didn't mean it." Tears run down my face.

She takes off her glasses and looks down at the bed. My body trembles. "I'm so sorry," I say and wipe my face.

She shakes her head slowly. "Sometimes I am sad, and sometimes I'm lonely. But I know plenty of people that are married and still feel lonely and sad sometimes. And everyone dies alone. That's nothing to be afraid of. Marriage is not going to magically solve all your problems."

"But it'll help." I slouch against the bed beside her feet.

Mom puts her glasses back on. "No, it won't. You know that. That's why you didn't marry Tom." I look down at my lap and pinch my lips together. She says, "I wish I was as wise as you and didn't marry your father."

"But then we wouldn't have Renée. And we both know she's your favorite."

"I love the two of you equally."

"That's too bad because she's *my* favorite." I let out an uncomfortable laugh. "What time is she coming over?"

"Your sister said she'd be over around five."

"So, she'll be here at six."

"She's got two kids. Cut her some slack."

"Can you imagine if she had a third? She'd never get out the house."

The sound of feet plodding up the stairs makes me jump in my seat. I pause *Home Alone* and listen. Then smile at the loud, rapid knock on the middle of the door. *They're here!* I spring to my feet, straighten my sweater dress, and sprint toward the entryway. The knocking continues, then stops abruptly at the sound of Renée's low, muffled voice.

"I got it, Mom!" I shout before opening the door.

"Can you hold Rebecca?" Renée hands her to me as Jacob squeezes past me through the door. "I need to help Joe bring the kids' presents up from the trunk."

"Sure." I smile and smooth Rebecca's dress. The hem of her red plaid dress hangs over my arm. She sneezes, misting me with a fine layer of baby saliva, then sniffles.

"Sorry." Renée's brows draw together. "She's getting over a cold. She's not contagious. I'll be right back." She whips around and hurries down the stairs.

I close the door softly and head back into the living room. Jacob's kneeling on the floor beside the Christmas tree, rifling through the gifts, the seat of his pants covered in red and gold glitter. The whole tree shakes when he lifts his head and brushes against a low branch.

"What are you up to, dude?" I ask.

"Counting how many presents are for me and Becca."

"How many are there?"

"A lot." He flashes a gap-toothed smile. "A bunch are from you." He sits down beside the tree, picks up a thin box, and shakes it. "This sounds like clothes."

"That's from Grandma," I whisper. "Don't worry. I got you guys lots of good stuff."

Rebecca sneezes again just as there's another knock at the door. "I'll get it this time," Mom says as she emerges from her bedroom to the hallway and opens the door. Renée and Joe rush in toward the tree to set down the armfuls of glittery packages. *That explains Jacob's pants.*

"I have something for you," Renée says as she reaches into a bag full of gifts and pulls out a small gold-wrapped box.

"Oh, I got you something too. But I thought we were going to wait to exchange gifts until after dinner?" I pull Rebecca off my hip and set her on my lap as I sit down on one of the sofas.

"This is something special that I want you to open now. Mom, I got you one too," Renée says.

Renée hands her a similar silver-wrapped box, and Joe takes Rebecca from me. I untie the ribbon on my box, unwrap it, and pull off the lid. Inside is a gold and white ornament encased in tissue. "It's beautiful. Thank you, Sister." I pull it out of the box and read the back side: "Best Aunt Ever" is scrolled in cursive letters. Tucked into the tissue is a blurry black-and-white photo. My eyes water as I pull out the ultrasound image.

"You're having another baby?" Mom asks, smiling, her eyes wet with tears.

"Yes," Renée says with a tearful laugh.

"Excuse me." I set down the box and get up. I walk straight toward the open doorway of my bedroom. Then shut and lock the door behind me. *Stop it. Be happy.* I slump onto the edge of the bed and wipe my face. *Take a deep breath.* I inhale deeply through my nose and breathe out slowly through my mouth. *Again.* I inhale deeply again. A soft knock on my bedroom door interrupts my exhale.

"Sister, can I come in?" Renée asks, and tugs on the door handle. I stand and open the door just wide enough for her to enter. Then shut it behind her. "Are you OK?" Her face scrunches up as she tilts her head and stares into my eyes.

"I'm great. Thank you for the ornament. That's awesome news." I straighten my posture and force a smile.

Renée grabs my hand and sits on the bed, tugging me down to sit beside her. "I knew those ornaments were a stupid idea. I should have told you sooner. I thought you might be a little sad."

"I'm not sad. I'm happy."

"You don't have to lie to me. I'm not Mom. I know you. And I know you're happy for me. But I also know you're a little sad." She squeezes my hand.

"I don't want to be sad." A tear falls and I rub my lips together. "I just want to have a baby too."

"I know."

"I can't help it. It's *that* time of the month. I'm extra awful lately. Did Mom tell you we fought this morning?"

"No. What about?"

"The usual." I shrug. "I'm a jerk and said mean stuff." I throw my hands up. "See, that's why you're her favorite."

"She does not have favorites," Renée says, and I shoot her a sideways look. "She doesn't. Anyway, I always thought you were Dad's favorite."

"I wish." I shake my head slowly. "I miss him so much, I can't stand to think about him." A dull ache starts up in my chest.

Renée nods. "Even when I think of the annoying stuff he used to do I still miss him. Remember how mad he used to get when we were running late for church?"

"Ugh. I remember how he would pull on my fingers to crack them while he held my hand. I hated it." I sigh. "And somehow loved it."

"Me too," Renée says, and sighs also. I take her hand and pull on her fingers interlocked in mine. "Stop it," she squeals, then laughs. The sound of Rebecca crying in the living room stops our laughter. "It was only a matter of time." Renée offers a crooked, wistful smile. "Are you coming?" She stands and tugs on my hand.

"I'll be right out."

When the door shuts, I stand and grab my phone off the nightstand. Then type out a new message: "Merry Christmas. I miss you."

After dinner I pick up the dishes from the table and help load them into the dishwasher, scraping the remnants of green beans and chicken skin off the plates into the trash can before giving them a quick rinse. Renée washes the pots and pans while Mom entertains Jacob and Rebecca with a tattered copy of *The Night Before Christmas.* Beside the tree Joe wrestles with the never-before-lit fancy Italian marble gas fireplace.

"Can we open our presents now?" Jacob whines.

"When your aunt and I are done, yes, you can open presents," Renée says.

I stick the last fork in the dishwasher and shut the metal door while Renée washes a final casserole dish. I pick my phone up off the counter and illuminate the screen. No new alerts. I frown, then set the phone back down.

"Hey, what is it?" Renée looks at me and sets the casserole dish on the rack to dry.

"Nothing. It's present time." I lift both pointer fingers in the air and dance. Then refill my empty glass from the uncorked bottle of cabernet.

"Got it." Joe stands, chest puffed and shoulders squared, beside the mantel as the fire roars to life. The scene in the living room feels like it's been ripped straight from a Christmas movie. The kids, in coordinating holiday outfits, sit beside the tree smiling up at Renée's iPhone. When they finish taking photos, Mom sits on a sofa with iPhone in hand, poised for more pictures, while Renée sits on the floor beside the kids. I slouch onto the sofa beside Mom and take a long sip of wine.

"Ruthie, would you mind collecting the trash?" Renée asks as Jacob tears the red paper off a gift.

"Nope."

I take another sip of wine, then stand and head back to the kitchen to grab a garbage bag. I shake the bag up and down. It makes a loud slapping sound as it cuts through the air and finally opens. I pour the rest of the wine into my glass. Then throw the bottle into the bag. My phone lights up atop the counter. A new message from Matthew: "Come outside."

"Ruthie, can you hurry with the bag? The trash is piling up," Mom says with her iPhone held up to her face. Renée pushes the paper out of the camera's view.

I set down my wineglass, then hand the bag to Joe. "I just remembered I left something in my car. I gotta run down. I'll be right back."

"Did you forget your—" Mom shouts as I slam the door behind me. I run down the stairs and finally stop when I reach the last step. The streetlights illuminate the pavement. I walk down the sidewalk. The neighbors' windows are lit up, but the blinds and curtains are drawn shut. *I should have grabbed a jacket.* I rub my arms.

Finally, I see him as he turns the corner and walks toward me. Hands stuffed into his jean pockets, he looks up to see me. We pace toward each other, meeting under the light of a sidewalk lantern. "Hi," he says. His smile makes the fine lines under his eyes stand out. Like well-worn paths to a beloved place.

"Hi." I smile, then bite my lip. "What are you doing here?"

"I missed you too." He steps toward me, then presses his warm hands to my cheeks, holding my face as he gives me a brief kiss. "I can't stay long, but I brought you something." He pulls a slightly crumpled small brown paper bag from his jacket pocket.

"What is it?" I ask.

"Open it." He smiles. I open the bag and peer in at the small bundled green leaves inside. "It's mistletoe," he says.

"Really? I don't recognize it."

"Here, try it out. Test to see if it works." He takes the mistletoe out of the bag and places it in my hand. Then gently lifts my hand over my head. "All right, now close your eyes."

I furrow my brow. Then give a tight-lipped smile and finally shut my eyes. I hold my left hand over my head, dangling the mistletoe. *This is ridiculous.* I squeeze my eyelids tighter. *This is taking forever. I'm just going to open my—* Suddenly his arm wraps around my waist, and he pulls me against him. He kisses my forehead, then my nose, and finally my lips. I feel my hands clench momentarily, then release and wrap around his back. My knees seem to loosen as my whole body grows warm. Like he's poured a bowl full of warm honey over my head and it's dripping deliciously down from my crown to my toes.

When he releases me, I stagger back and clear my throat. "Yeah, I guess you're right. It must be mistletoe. Thank you." My throat feels dry.

"You're welcome." He smiles again. "I'll text you later."

I look down at the ground and nod. He lifts my chin and gives me a chaste kiss. Then drops his hand, takes a step back, and turns around. I watch his figure retreat in the darkness. "Where are you going?" I shout.

He yells back, "I parked outside your gate!" He waves, then turns the corner, and he's gone. I rub my arms again, then hold myself in a tight self-embrace. I clutch the paper bag as I pace back home.

"Everything OK? Did you find what you were looking for?" Mom asks as I shut the door behind me.

"Uh . . . yeah, thanks, Mom." I put the paper bag inside a drawer in the kitchen. Then grab my wineglass off the counter and slump onto the long sofa opposite her. Renée gets up off the floor and brushes the glitter and pine needles off her bottom before sitting down beside me.

"Where'd you go?" she whispers, and lifts a brow, smiling mischievously.

"To my car." I shrug.

"Really?" She tilts her head. "Because you left your keys right there on the counter." She points toward the kitchen.

"Crap." I drop my chin. "Did Mom notice?"

"Yeah. But she's not going to say anything. Quit sneaking around. If you like this guy, *you like this guy.* I know what Sam told you and maybe she's right. But what if she's not?"

I nod and take a long sip of wine.

"This'll cheer you up," Mom says as she hands me a brightly wrapped gift box. I smile hesitantly and shake the box.

"It's not your first choice," Renée laughs.

"Very funny." I roll my eyes. As soon as I tear the paper, the shade of orange of the gift box makes my smile widen. "It's not a husband." I force a chuckle. "But Louis will do."

18

NEW YEAR'S IRRITATION

The back seat of this Prius is gray and dingy. The fabric of the seats is matted in patches, and the floor mat's missing. The dark-complected driver looks straight ahead at the road while I look out the window. He says nothing and I can't decide if it's due to a lack of conversation skills or a language barrier. Either way I'm thankful. Once we drive over the Santa Ana River, my hands grow clammy. *We're almost there.* I look down at the Lyft app and watch the little white car move down PCH on the screen.

When we turn into his neighborhood, I hold my breath as my stomach flutters. The driver slows down when he sees the kid-shaped yellow sign. The street is filled with cars. And cars are double-parked in front of his driveway. I point out the window and tell the driver to stop in front of the house with the blue porch swing. He shifts into park and looks straight ahead. I stare out the window at the cars parked in front of Matthew's house.

"Everything OK, miss?" the driver finally asks with a thick unrecognizable accent.

My brow furrows and I take a deep breath. "Yeah." I reach for the handle, and the driver turns around to face me. "I'm going. Sorry." I push open the door and step out. Then slam the door behind me. As the Prius drives away, I stand on the sidewalk and press four stars for the review.

I tug my turtleneck up higher on my neck, then rub my arms. *Just go.* I shuffle around on the sidewalk, then finally force myself to pace up his driveway to the door. The porch light is bright, and I squint at the door handle, the sound of voices and muffled country music audible through the shut door. I reach for the handle and tap my thumb against the lever, then retract my hand and step back.

I knock three times, then tuck my hair behind my ear and tuck the hem of my sweater into the front of my jeans. I knock twice more. *Maybe they can't hear me?* I bite my lip. Then reach for the handle and press down on the lever. It goes down easily, and I stumble forward as the door swings open.

"Oops. Watch your step," a slender brunette girl says as she holds the door open. "Come on in. Welcome."

"Thank you." I force a smile and step into the entryway. It's too warm inside, and I tug down on my turtleneck, then push my sleeves up.

"Would you mind taking off your shoes?" she says, flashing a game-show-model-perfect smile "Uh, yeah. Of course." I bend over and unzip my boots, then untuck my hair when I think she isn't looking. I tug off the left boot and set it alongside the rack in a pile of unfamiliar shoes.

While I'm still bent over, she says, "So are you a friend of Matty, Billy, or Chris?"

I stand up, my right boot unzipped and sagging around my ankle. "Matty—M-Matthew," I stutter. Then bend back over. "I'm Ruthie. Nice to meet you." I stare down as I tug off my boot.

"Ruthie?" Her voice is overbright. Then in an almost accusatory tone, she says, "So, *you're* Matthew's girlfriend! *So* nice to meet you. I'm Therese."

Eyes wide, I stand up straight to face her just as Matthew comes down the stairs behind her. His face looks flushed. *Did he hear that? Did he tell her I'm his girlfriend?* He clears his throat and Therese turns around. I smile awkwardly and offer him a weak wave. "I forgot something upstairs," he says, then turns around and runs back up.

Therese looks back to face me, and I feel my cheeks burn. "Excuse me. I need to use the restroom," I say.

"It's through the kitchen to the—"

"I know where it is. Thank you." I pinch my lips together and walk past her.

The music grows louder as I enter the kitchen. I ignore the people standing around the counter and hurry into the bathroom. I shut the door behind me and lean against it, staring at the flushed, frowning reflection in the mirror. Then lock the door and run the tap. The hand towel looks wet and sad wrinkled into a heap on the counter. I wash my hands, then dry them on my jeans. There's a knock at the door. "Just a minute!" I shout.

When I open the door, there's no one waiting. I straighten my posture and pace back into the kitchen. It reeks of cheap, greasy pizza. Large cardboard pizza boxes are stacked one on top of another on the kitchen island. The lid of the top box hangs open revealing a single remaining slice of pineapple and ham. Beside the pizza are bottles of alcohol. Kirkland vodka, Fireball whiskey, Bacardí, and bottles of cheap-looking wine cover the counter. Along with a tall stack of red cups. Surrounding the island are strangers. I bite the inside of my cheek, force an awkward smile, and reach my hand between two bodies to grab a bottle of wine. *Crap. Should I reach back in for a cup or grab a glass from the cupboard?*

"Do you need a cup?" Matthew asks as he walks up from behind.

I flinch, then smile. "Yeah, that would be great. Thank you."

"Everything OK?"

"Everything's great."

He nods, then opens a cabinet and pulls out a stemless glass. He takes the bottle from me and pours the glass full. The glass is heavy, but I force a thin closed-mouth smile, then take a long drink. "Sorry about Therese," he says as he reopens the cabinet and pulls out a second glass.

"She seems nice." I take another long drink, looking into my cup.

He pours his glass full and drinks nearly half of it before saying, "She's been a family friend for a long time. She works at the vet office we take Emmy to. You would like her."

"I'm sure." I nod dismissively and toss my hair behind my shoulder. As I set my glass down on the counter, I see Therese approaching, her red lipstick nearly the same hue as her snug, low-cut sweater. *God, she has a big mouth.*

"There you are!" she says. "I was waiting for you to come out of the bathroom. I've been asking Matty about you, but you know how tight-lipped he is."

"Mm." I offer a crooked smile and nod before taking a drink of my wine.

"You're not drinking wine, are you? You have to try the drink I made." She turns around and reaches between two of the people huddled around the island. "Sorry, Tim." She apologizes after she bumps one of them with her plastic pitcher. "Tim, would you mind?" The tall stranger named Tim pulls two red cups off the stack and hands them to her. "Thank you," she says. She's still smiling brightly as she turns back around to face us. *I already hate her.*

She pours from the pitcher into both red cups and hands one to me. "Here. I insist," she says, then holds up her cup for me to tap mine against it. She sets down the pitcher, and I put my glass down. Then tap my plastic cup against hers and take a sip of the sickly sweet peppermint drink. It smells like a bottle of rubbing alcohol.

"Mm. Mm-hmm." I purse my lips and nod at her.

"Be careful." She leans in. "It's strong. Matty and Billy love it. I make it every Christmas and New Year."

"I'm sorry. Who's Billy?" I ask.

"My brother," Matthew answers.

"Of course." I shake my head. "I'm sorry. I don't know where my head's at. And your name is Theresa?"

"Therese. No *a*. Just Therese." She exaggerates the "ese."

"What exactly is in this drink?" I lift my cup. *Lighter fluid?*

"Oh no, I never tell. It's my little secret. If I give it away, they won't have to invite me back every year." She giggles and playfully slaps Matthew's shoulder.

"Therese, why don't you see if Billy or Chris needs a refill?" Matthew says.

"Sure thing." She grabs the pitcher off the counter, reaching between Matthew and me, and saunters toward the living room.

"Don't look at me like that," Matthew says, then shifts his weight. I relax my brows. I didn't realize they had scrunched together in a glare at him. "She's just a friend," he says.

"I didn't say anything."

He lifts his brows and tilts his head.

"I didn't say anything," I repeat and take a gulp from the red cup.

"You don't have to drink that. We don't actually like it, but no one has the heart to tell her."

"You know, it's actually not that bad." I drink the last of it and cough. "It's just too bad she took the pitcher."

"You're not going to make it to midnight if you don't slow down."

"I'm fine." I pick up my wineglass and take a sip.

"Have a slice of pizza. I'll be right back."

He sets down his glass and walks toward the bathroom. My stomach lurches. *I should eat something.* I set down my drink. "Excuse me. Tim, could I squeeze just past you?" Tim shuffles aside and I lift the top box to look at the pizza underneath. *Meat lover's. Yuck.* I lift the lid of the third box. It has peppers and mushrooms. I grab a slice and close the box.

There are no plates in sight. I grab a paper towel from beside the sink and eat standing. There are dozens of people standing around. Hovering around the kitchen island. Standing in front of the TV in the family room. Sitting on the eighties furniture in the great room. And there are still more people outside in the backyard.

I lean over the sink and look out the kitchen window watching six guys huddled over a plastic table playing beer pong. One wearing a backward cap sinks a white ball into a red cup opposite him. Then stands back, throws his fists up, and shouts. Two girls standing nearby cheer. Then the guy in front of the red cup sulks. The carbonated liquid spills out the sides of the cup and down his shirt as he drinks. It reminds me of college. *I don't belong here.*

"How are you doing?" Matthew places a damp hand on mine. I recoil from his touch. "Sorry, I just washed my hands," he says.

"It's OK." I put my hand over his. "I was just surprised."

"Do you want to go outside and play?" He motions at the window with his wineglass.

"No, thank you."

"Come on. It'll be fun. I'll introduce you to my brother and Chris." He grabs my hand and tugs me toward the door.

As we step outside, I search for Therese's red sweater. She's nowhere in sight. *Maybe she's still in the living room looking for them.* I smile and take a sip of wine. Out on the grass, a couple people stand smoking beside the fence. Everyone else is huddled near the plastic pong table in the dim light of the patio lantern. I search their faces, trying to decide which one of them might be the adult version of the photo I've seen of little Billy. I don't recognize anyone. Matthew taps on the shoulder of backward-cap guy. He turns around to face me and smiles. His eyes, though hazel, are warm like Matthew's.

"Billy, I want you to meet Ruthie." Matthew claps his shoulder. "Ruthie, this is my brother, Billy."

I smile and lift my wineglass. "Nice to meet you."

"So, you're the mysterious girlfriend," Billy says.

Billy grins broadly, then grabs a red cup off the pong table and takes a long drink. I feel my face burn bright red. My lips curl into an awkward, toothy smile. Matthew claps his shoulder again, this time harder.

"Come on. You know it's not like that." Matthew lets out a nervous chuckle.

Billy shrugs and says, "Nice to meet you."

He lifts his red cup. Then turns around to face the table again. I tug my turtleneck up and look into my glass as I finish the last of my wine.

"Let's head back inside. I don't know where Chris is," Matthew says and starts toward the sliding glass door. I pinch my lips and follow him back inside. In the kitchen I set my glass down on the counter. My shoulders slump and I hold my left elbow as I stare down at the ground. "Do you want more wine? Or should I find Therese and get you more of that candy cane drink?" he asks.

I shake my head. "No, thank you. I think I'm done drinking tonight." My stomach turns, and I clutch my belly. "I think I should go home."

"Do you want to lie down? You can take a nap in my room. I'll wake you up for the countdown." He sets his glass down and places his hand on my lower back.

"Excuse me, guys. I need to get behind you into that cupboard." A stranger reaches behind my head to open a cabinet and pulls out a large beer stein.

"Hey, Chris, this is Ruthie," Matthew says.

"Hey, what's up, Ruthie? I'm Chris. Nice to meet you."

He leans in to hug me. Chris's too-tight black T-shirt is damp under his muscular arms. He smells like sweat and overly masculine body spray. I lift one arm to hug him and hold my breath to keep from gagging. "Nice to meet you," I choke out.

"Hey, Matt, where'd you put the bong we used last weekend?" Chris asks.

"I don't know. Ask Billy."

"All right," Chris says, then walks outside.

I look up at Matthew. "I need to go home."

"Now?"

I nod. "It's loud in here, and I don't feel good." I put my hand over my mouth. Then grab his hand and tug him toward the entryway. I order a ride. Then lean against the wall beside the shoe rack and tug on my boots. As I zip them up, Therese stumbles into the entryway.

"Aw. Are you leaving?" she asks, lipstick on her teeth.

"She's not feeling well," Matthew answers.

"Well, I hope you feel better." She puts her arm around my shoulder.

I press my lips together, then pat her hand and step out of her embrace. "I'm gonna wait outside for my Lyft. I need the fresh air," I say to Matthew. Then turn to Therese and say, "It was nice to meet you."

"It was great meeting you," she says and waves dismissively. Then looks at Matthew. "Matty, we need you to tap the keg outside."

"I'll be right out," he says. She pouts, then turns around and walks toward the kitchen.

"You can go," I say once she's gone. "My ride will be here soon."

"Are you sure?" he asks. I nod, and he says, "Get home safe."

At home the lights are off. I stumble through the dark living room back to my room. It's just after ten, and the house is quiet. *Mom's probably asleep.* I take off my boots and lie back on the bed. Despite how much I drank, I don't feel drunk so much as nauseated. My limbs feel heavy. I put my hand over my heart, where there's a weight in my chest. *"It's not like that."* I close my eyes. *I'm not his girlfriend.*

I let out a deep breath, then reach into my purse and pull out my phone. My thumb hovers over the image of Sam. *Don't call her. It's New Year's Eve. She's busy with Niko.* I set the phone down on the bed, then stare up at the ceiling. The slight buzz of my phone vibrating startles me, and I sit up reflexively. An incoming call from Matthew.

"Hello?" My voice shakes.

"Did you get home all right?" he asks. It's silent in the background.

"Yeah. Where are you?"

"In my room," he says. I tuck my hair behind my ear and bite at the cuticle of my thumb. "I'm sorry about what happened," he says finally.

"What are you talking about? There's no reason for you to apologize." I pull at a newly formed hangnail, tugging at the strip of dead skin with my pointer nail. My heart pounds loudly inside my chest.

"Yes, there is. I'm sorry for what I said to Billy. I—" He lets out a noisy exhale. "I don't know why I said that. I guess I don't really like labels."

"It's not a big deal." I bite at the hangnail, then taste blood on my lip. I use my pointer finger to apply pressure to my thumb, then hold it over my head to stop the bleeding.

"I don't want you to be upset. I thought maybe that's why you left."

"I left because I'm not feeling well." My stomach churns as if on cue.

"You and Emmy both."

"What's wrong with Emmy?"

"She threw up downstairs. She probably ate something off the floor she shouldn't have."

"Poor Emmy."

"It's all right. Therese said I could take her into the vet tomorrow, and they'll see her first thing."

"That's great." I lower my hand to my mouth and bite at the cuticle again. It stings.

"There's another reason I called you."

"OK."

"My company is sending me on a weekend retreat to Palm Springs in a couple weeks. I was hoping that you would come with me."

I swallow hard. "All right." My body aches from the emotional whiplash.

"So, you'll come?"

"Yeah. That sounds like fun," I hear myself say.

"Great. Well, happy New Year."

"Happy New Year," I say, then press the red phone on my screen to end the call.

I set my phone on the nightstand, then flip off my light and get up. I walk down the hall to Mom's room and knock on her door. "Come in," she answers sleepily. Her room is dark, illuminated only by the muted television. On the screen two bundled-up hosts mouth into microphones while the time ticks down on a digital clock beneath them. Mom yawns and reaches for her glasses. She puts them on and looks at me, then at the time on the screen.

"What are you doing home so early? Is everything OK?" She sits up and straightens the collar of her pajamas.

"Everything's fine. I didn't feel good, so I left early. Can I lie down with you?"

Mom's brows draw together, but she nods and pulls back the covers on the empty side of the bed. "Are you going to be hot wearing that turtleneck?"

"I'm fine. I feel comfortable."

I get in under the covers. My jeans swish against the sheets. Mom lies back against her pillow. Then unmutes the television. The volume is just loud enough to make out what the announcers are saying. The crowd in the background is inaudible, though they are visibly screaming. Minutes tick down on the digital clock.

"Did you get into an argument with Matthew?" Mom asks, looking straight ahead.

"He's not my boyfriend."

"I didn't say he was. I just asked if you were arguing with him."

"No." My stomach hardens. "Actually, he invited me to Palm Springs." I cross my arms.

"Well, that'll be fun."

"Yeah." I tug the covers up to my neck. "Thank you for letting me watch the countdown with you. I didn't want to be alone."

"Of course." She stifles a yawn. "I'm glad you're here."

"Me too. . . . Hey, Mom?"

"Yeah?"

"I love you."

"I love you too."

19.

IT'S A
DOG'S LIFE

The drugstore by Matthew's house has a different layout then the Rite Aid I'm used to. But it's as bright and cold as expected. I grab a bag of Oreos, then wander down the pet care aisle. Beyond the bags and cans of pet food, an entire section of a wall display is dedicated to treats. I pick up a bag with a picture of a cartoon dog licking its lips. "Tastes Like Real Bacon," the package reads. I toss it in my basket.

I grab a Cherry Coke from the minifridge by the cashier and get in line. There are three people ahead of me. The cashier scans a bag of beef jerky, then adjusts her glasses and leans over her keypad. I watch her punch some buttons, then scan again. She lifts her brows and readjusts her glasses before picking up the store phone. Her smoker voice is loud over the speaker as she requests a price check. I tap my foot, then check the time on my phone.

There's no one standing by the pharmacy. I turn around and walk to the pickup counter at the rear of the store. Then set down my basket.

"Name on the prescription you're picking up?" the pharmacist says.

"I'm not picking up anything. I just want to buy this stuff." I tap the basket.

She narrows her eyes, then says something under her breath to one of the other pharmacists. It feels like I'm at a nail salon and they're criticizing me in a language they know I don't understand. I pinch my lips together, then stare down at the counter. "Actually, I do have a prescription I need to drop off."

"This is the pickup counter." She scans the cookies, then looks sideways at the other pharmacist.

"OK."

She lets out a noisy exhale, then says, "I can take the prescription from you once you pay. It won't be ready for two hours." I nod, then give her my debit card.

At Matthew's house I push open the door and yell, "I'm here!" as I step out of my Vans. Emmy is first to greet me. The sound of her snort comes loudly from the family room, followed by her scratchy, shuffling steps. "I brought treats." I put my shoes beside the rack and carry the plastic bag into the kitchen.

"What'd you bring?" he says as he sits up on the couch and rubs his hands through his messy hair.

"Oreos for us and bacon treats for Emmy." I force a weak smile as I take the packages out of the shopping bag and place them on the island counter. Emmy hobbles over to my feet, then stops and slowly lowers her rear to the floor. Her wrinkled face looks even whiter than I remember.

"Thank you," he says as he staggers from the family room into the kitchen. He kisses me, then picks up the Cherry Coke from the counter. "What's this?"

"An impulse buy." I shrug.

He picks up the bag of dog treats and flips it over to look at the ingredients. "She really shouldn't be eating this stuff," he says, then lets out a long sigh. "But I guess it doesn't really matter now."

"May I?" I ask, and he nods slowly. I tear the plastic strip off the top and pull open the package. The meaty imitation bacon aroma is overwhelming, and I turn my face away from the bag. Emmy doesn't move.

"She can't smell it. Or if she can, she doesn't care." His voice is flat. Matthew leans over the counter and rubs his forehead.

I pull a treat out and lower it to her face. She sniffs it. Then licks it and lowers her head. I sink down to sit beside her. When I pet her back, she turns her head to look at me as if confused. "It's gonna be OK, girl," I whisper to her. I can feel her bones through her thinning coat. She rests her head on her front paws, then closes her eyes. A tear rolls down my cheek. I wipe at it, then sniffle loudly, but she doesn't flinch.

"How's she been?" I finally ask. Then stand and slap the dust off my rear.

"She's dying." He runs his hands aggressively through his hair. "She's been terrible." His shoulders droop and he puts his hands over his face. He sucks in a loud breath, then lowers his hands. The wrinkles around his eyes have deepened, the lids red and wet. "Therese thinks we should put her down."

"Well, what did the vet say?"

"He wouldn't advise us one way or another."

"What do you think?"

He shakes his head, then lets out a strained laugh that becomes a cry. A tear runs down his face as he says, "I think we should put her down." He stoops down and lifts her up, cradling her like an infant. Emmy blinks her watery eyes open. They're gray from cataracts. She yawns, then moves her paw as if to pat and comfort Matthew, *There, there.*

I rip open the bag of Oreos, pull one out, and bite into it. I hold my left elbow, then tap the bitten cookie against my lips as I chew. "Is there anything we can do?" I finally ask.

"Nothing. There's nothing anyone can do for her. Her quality of life is going to keep declining." He wipes his face, then walks over to the fridge. He pulls out a beer and pops the top single handedly. He takes a long drink, then asks, "Do you want one?"

I shake my head and grab another cookie. Then squint at the clock in the family room. *Will the pharmacy still be open when I leave?* I twist the cap off the Cherry Coke and take a long sip. The carbonated liquid goes down too quickly, and it burns through my chest. I cough and it startles Emmy. Her eyes shoot open, and she lifts her head from Matthew's arm. "Sorry," I choke out, then pet her.

"Will you please stay with me tonight?"

"I really shouldn't. I need to be at my office super early tomorrow."

"I'm taking her to the vet in the morning." He lets out a noisy exhale. "I don't think I'll sleep at all tonight. I could really use some company."

I pinch my lips together and look down at Emmy. Bundled in his arms, she looks like a weathered, long-loved toy. As if her arm might just fall off from loose stitching. I look up at Matthew's tired, unshaved face, then nod slowly.

Emmy's bed is tucked beside his mattress. The queen mattress, pushed against the wall, is supported by a visible metal frame. The only other pieces of furniture in his room are more late-eighties glossy wood pieces: a pair of walnut nightstands and an oversize matching dresser with an attached vanity mirror. His laundry bin is always full, the lid propped open by the overflowing mass of clothing inside. Beside the bin more clothes are littered on the floor. It smells like a gym bag and Curve for Men.

I wondered what the smell was for weeks until I stumbled on the cologne bottle while looking for aspirin in his medicine cabinet. I want to tell him to stop wearing it or, better yet, to buy him another fragrance. But without him putting a label on our relationship, it feels premature to buy him such a personal gift.

He sets Emmy down gently on her bed, then covers her with her pink fleece blanket. I message Mom that I'm not coming home, then shrug off my clothes. He hands me a fresh white T-shirt, and I tug it on. It fits like a dress. I've never slept over during the week. *I wish I'd packed pajamas or even just my toothbrush.* I can't leave anything behind here. Once when I accidentally left my deodorant in the bathroom, I came back a week later to find a body hair on it. His roommate had helped himself.

When Matthew turns out the lights, I stare up at his darkened ceiling. Emmy snores softly in an erratic pattern. *No wonder he can't sleep.* I squeeze my eyes shut, then roll over to face his back. I stroke his shoulder, and he turns over toward me.

"I don't want to do it," he whispers as though keeping it secret from Emmy.

"I know."

"I love her." His voice cracks.

"That's why you have to do what's right. Even if it hurts you, it's what's best for her. You have to let her go."

He rolls onto his back. Then puts the crook of his elbow over his face, covering his eyes. After a long while, he finally says, "Yeah." Then all I hear is the sound of his labored breathing and Emmy's snores.

* * *

I wake before my alarm is set to sound. Both Emmy and Matthew are snoring. Gray light sneaks in through the blinds. It's just enough that I can avoid flipping on the lights and waking them. I pull off the T-shirt he lent me and fold it before placing it on the lid of his laundry hamper. After getting dressed I kneel beside Emmy and stroke the length of her back. She looks so small and fragile tucked under her pink blankie. She stirs, then blinks her eyes open. Her sad gray eyes are wet and sleepy. I whisper softly, "Goodbye, Emmy." Then leave.

I rush home to get ready for work. The office is loud with the sounds of keyboard clicks, documents printing, and people chatting by the coffee maker. I walk straight back to my office and shut the door. Then sit at my desk and stare at the black reflection in the monitor. My hair is frizzy and my face sullen. Matthew's tossing and turning kept me up all night. It wasn't until he started snoring late this morning that the shuffling stopped. Whenever I started to drift into a dream, it was of Emmy. Her huge glossy eyes staring back at me pleading as a thick shiny needle came closer and closer. Then she'd shut her eyes and she'd be gone. Every time I woke and heard her snoring, I was relieved. "I'm so sorry I had to leave this morning," I message Matthew. Then I turn on my computer. As I type in my password, there's a knock on my door.

"Come in," I say without looking up from my monitor.

"Good morning." Tammy swings the door open. "Ooh, you don't look so good. What's wrong?" she asks and shuts the door behind her. I shake my head. "Are you upset because of the transfer?" She stares at me. "Because I found out that the transfer is only to the Irvine office. So, it's not far at all." She sits down.

"What are you talking about?"

"The commercial team opening. I found out the transfer details yesterday from a *friend*." She wiggles her brows.

I swivel in my chair to look at her. "I'm not up for promotion. I'm not transferring. I didn't bother to submit a letter of interest."

"Why not?"

"Because I don't want to do strictly commercial." I feel my brows gather, then straighten them and press my lips together.

"But the money is good." She shakes her head, scrunching up her face as though thinking, *What an idiot.*

"It's more than just the money." I let out a long sigh.

"OK." Tammy lifts her brows, then looks sideways. "Well, if the transfer isn't what's bothering you, what is it?" She tosses her long blond kinky hair over her shoulder.

"I've just got a lot on my mind."

"Like?" She tilts her chin down, her expression full of sass.

"Like Matthew's dog is being put to sleep this morning."

"And you came to work?" Her brows shoot back up.

She really should have been a soap opera actress. I slump against my chair. "I had to. My workload is insane. You know that."

"Ruthie, he needs you. His dog is dying. You should be there for him." She stands.

"I don't even know where his vet is. I can't just leave."

"You could call him and find out." She puts both hands on my desk and stares down at me with a look that says, *Do it.* Then turns around abruptly, her hair whipping behind her as she takes a step to the door, pulls it open, and steps out. Somehow her shutting the door softly feels even more theatrical than a slam. *She's such a drama queen.*

I grab my phone and call Matthew. The phone rings five times. I clear my throat to leave a voice mail. The sixth ring is cut short by a forced-sounding "Hello."

"How are you?"

"I'm OK. Just sitting here at home with Emmy."

"How's she doing?"

"She's terrible. She looks miserable. It's like she knows."

"I'm so sorry." I suck in a deep breath. "What time are you taking her in?"

"Her appointment is at eleven thirty a.m."

"Can I come with you to the vet?"

"No, it's all right. Therese is here with me. She's off today and offered to drive us."

"That was awfully nice of her." I pinch my lips together and stare down at my desk.

"Yeah. Well, I gotta go. I want to spend time with Emmy before her appointment."

"OK—" The phone beeps in my ear before I can say, "Goodbye."

I open the cabinet under my desk and shove my phone into my purse. At 1:00 p.m. when I pull out my lunch cooler, I reach back into my purse and check my phone. I have no new messages. *Did he cry? Did Therese hold his hand?* I send him a message: "Hope it went ok. Call me if you need anything." I eat kale salad alone at my desk. I forgot it's Friday, the one time a week I usually take a proper lunch break.

After work I check my phone again. Only the floral wallpaper greets me. I send him another message: "I'm going to stop by after work. Text me if you want me to pick anything up." Then stuff my phone back into my purse and drive to his house. The blinds in his window are open, but the lights are off. At his door I push down on the handle, but it doesn't budge. *Is he home?* I knock, then step back. Hold my breath as I wait. Finally, I knock again. *Is he ignoring me?* When no one answers, I turn and leave.

I stop at the drugstore by his house. Passing the cookie and cracker aisle, I walk straight back to the freezer case. Then grab two cartons of Breyers Oreo cookies and cream and set them on the pharmacy pickup counter. The same surly pharmacist approaches. I give her my name and push the cartons toward her.

"You really like Oreos, huh?" she says as she scans the cartons.

"Not as much as I like Xanax." I flash a toothy smile and hand her my card.

At home I swallow a pill and eat half a carton of ice cream for dinner. When he texts, "Sorry. I'm taking it harder than I thought. I'll call you when I'm ready," I clutch my phone to my chest but don't respond. I wait to message him until Sunday, but he doesn't answer. *Is he ghosting me?*

Monday night I buy more ice cream and a bag of Oreos. I don't need to worry about gaining weight, but when I did worry, I'd skip lunch and take a Xanax instead, saving my calories for an ice cream and cookie dinner in my bedroom with the door locked. By Friday I'm down to my last carton of ice cream. I haven't heard from him. I sent him messages Tuesday and yesterday. *He's probably banging Therese.*

I peel off the lid and stick my spoon in before turning on Netflix. I cross my legs with my knees out as I lean against my pillow. My phone chimes and I ignore it. I feel numb. As I click through the romantic comedy titles, they all seem to run together. *It's all the same.* I lick the spoon and set the remote down. Then finally grab my phone off the nightstand and drop the spoon into the carton when I read, "Come over."

I stare at the screen and reread his message. *Come over? You don't call me for a week, and you want me to come over?* I pick up the spoon and take another mouthful. Then look up at the Netflix screen. The images seem clearer. It's all couples smiling, sitting side by side or standing back-to-back. *Tammy warned me about "being benched," as if dating were some sort of sport.* I press Play on a random movie I've never heard of. When the opening credits music starts playing, I toss my head back and press Pause. I put the lid back on the carton.

At his door I knock softly, then stand back on his porch. I tug down on my pullover hoodie. *I should have changed into something cuter.* I look down at my ripped-up jeans and my jaw clenches. He opens the door. The weak smile on his lips doesn't reach his eyes. "Come in." He steps aside. I step out of my sandals, then follow him into the family room. It smells like weed and pet odor. He sinks into the huge old gray couch and leans against the cushion. Wadded up beside him is Emmy's pink flannel blanket.

I take a seat beside him, my posture rigid. "How are you?"

"I'm good," he says mechanically, staring ahead at the big-screen TV.

"No. I mean it. How are you really?"

He looks at me, then lowers his chin. "Not great. I know it was time for her to go but I miss her. I wasn't ready to lose her yet."

"I'm so sorry." I swallow hard. "How was the procedure?"

He turns his face to glare at me. As if to say, *How could you ask that? What's wrong with you?* Then looks back at the television. He grabs a beer off the coffee table and takes a sip. A three-foot smoke-stained bong is set on the floor beside the table. When he catches me staring at it, he asks, "Do you want a hit?"

I shake my head. "No, thank you. I don't smoke."

"Do you want a beer then?"

I shake my head again. "I had a Xanax earlier. I'm not supposed to mix it with alcohol."

"Do you have any more?"

"I left the bottle at home. I'm only supposed to take it as needed. I didn't think I would need any more."

He takes a long drink of his beer, then turns his face back to the TV. "I'm sorry."

He looks down at the blanket beside him, then tugs it onto his lap. "Well, at least I won't have to worry about her when I'm gone next weekend." He smiles ironically and shakes his head.

"Do you still want me to come with you?"

"To Palm Springs? Yeah, of course."

"I just thought that maybe with everything that's happened . . ." My voice trails off, and I look at the TV.

"I could use the distraction." He sets the blanket down on the couch. Crushes his beer can, then gets up and walks into the kitchen. "Are you sure you don't want a beer?"

"I guess one won't hurt."

20

NOT SUITABLE FOR WORK

Outside the hotel I hand my keys to the valet attendant. Then grab my jacket and weekender out of the trunk and slam the lid shut. It's warm outside but I tug the jacket on anyway. As soon as I step through the automatic glass doors of the hotel, I'm blasted with cold air. I pull the collar of my jacket up, then walk through the lobby. On the red-velvet-papered walls, there are full-size glass cases displaying costumes. A black-studded Gene Simmons suit hangs opposite a sparkly Britney Spears concert ensemble.

I set my weekender atop a purple velveteen sofa, then slump against it. I drove almost three hours in Friday rush-hour traffic to get here. My butt cheeks are sore from sitting for so long, but I'm too tired to stand. I reach into my purse and pull out my phone to message Matthew. "I'm here in the lobby." I toss my head back against the cushion and stare at the ceiling covered in vintage records. Then close my eyes. The lids feel heavy and hot. He drove out yesterday with his boss. I was supposed to meet him forty minutes ago.

My phone chimes and I pry my lids open. "Great. We'll be right over to meet u," his reply reads. *Who's we?* I glare at the screen. Then pick at the cuticle of my left thumb while my teeth busy themselves against my cheek. I flatten the collar of my jacket, then bounce my knee. Watching people rolling their luggage behind them as they walk up to the front desk.

I miss Matthew, surrounded by strangers and wearing an aloha shirt, when he enters the lobby. I don't recognize him until he's standing over me. His eyes glassy and his hair disheveled, he stinks of cheap whiskey. He looks down smiling, and I rise to my feet, forcing a smile through clenched teeth. *Who are these people?*

Six strangers stand around Matthew, smiling back at me. Their eyes all glassed over. There's a punch stain on one of the women's dress. And one of the men has sweat through his American flag tank top. When he leans in for a hug, I take a step back, offer an awkward smile, and extend my hand. "Nice to meet you." I shake each of their hands. Then wipe my palm against my jeans when I think no one's looking.

"We're gonna have dinner with these guys tonight. Do you wanna head to the bar to grab a drink before we go?" Matthew asks, his smile exposing too many teeth.

I pinch my lips. "I—"

"Yeah! Come have a drink. We're going to walk over to La Copa," the woman in the stained dress says, then eyes Matthew.

"I'd really like to freshen up." I point toward my jeans. The rest of them are wearing shorts and dresses. "We'll catch up with you at dinner." I grab Matthew's hand.

"Come on. You're fine. Just take off your jacket," tank-top guy slurs, and smiles. "Have one little drink with us. Then we're all going to go up and change." Matthew looks at me, his brows drawn together. His face like that of a puppy dog pleading for a treat.

I shake my head. "No thanks, guys. I really need a break." I look down at the carpet. Matthew presses his lips together, and his shoulders droop slightly as he picks up my weekender off the sofa.

Inside our room he drops my bag on the floor, then flops facedown on the king-size bed. I pick up my bag and set it on the dresser. Then sit down beside his feet.

"Is something wrong?" I ask.

"Nothing's wrong. I mean, I did want to go to the bar before dinner. But this is fine too." His voice is muffled, his face pressed into the fluffy white comforter.

"I'm sorry. It was just a really long drive, and I had a super long day at the office." I lie down beside him, resting my weight on my elbow. He turns his face away, and I let out a noisy exhale. "You're not upset, are you?" I watch him lie there, then run my fingers through his hair. Moments tick by, and finally I sit up. His eyes are shut, and I lean over him. *He passed out.*

I groan, then throw myself back against the bed. The odor of alcohol and sweat seems to pour out of him. I roll onto my side and shut my eyes. Then he lets out a loud snort, makes a slight choking sound, coughs, and starts snoring loudly. I put my hands over my ears. Then put a pillow over my head. But the sound of his phlegmy gasps and nasal droning makes napping impossible.

I grunt, then slam the pillow down on the bed. He rustles around for a moment, then sniffs noisily and resumes snoring. I get up and unzip my weekender. Then grab my toiletry bag and walk into the bathroom. I dig through toothpaste and facewash, then realize what I'm looking for is in another bag. I pull out a pink bag full of period supplies from my weekender and search beneath panty liners until I find my earplugs.

I stick them in my ears, and everything outside of myself goes silent. The sound of my breathing is noisy as I stare into my pink period bag. My breath catches in my throat as my eyes widen. *Am I late?* My heart accelerates and my breathing grows louder. I pull out a tampon and zip the bag shut. *Why did I pull this out? I'm not bleeding.* I drop the tampon into the weekender and grab my phone from my purse. Then thumb open the calendar app and count back the days to my last period. I'm two days late. *It's only two days. It'll probably start tonight.* Matthews stirs, then rolls over onto his back. I set my phone down, then lie on the bed beside him. *Everything's fine.* I bite my lip, then squeeze my eyes shut.

My stomach twists in knots as we walk into the restaurant. Lola is stark white. It would be almost sterile looking if it weren't for the pops of color throughout. Neon green, pink, and blue chairs encircle the tables. Above, a bright electric-colored art deco installation hangs high. I follow Matthew past the hostess stand through the dining room to a large corner table. Though they've changed clothing, the six strangers I met in the lobby are wearing the same glassy-eyed, inebriated expressions.

Matthew pulls out a chair and I quickly sit. He then pulls out the chair beside me and asks me to move over. To my left are the three women and to the right Matthew and his three colleagues. The woman who wore the stained dress earlier is now wearing a low-cut hot-pink blouse. She matches the restaurant. All three women are blond, but her hair is the lightest, nearly platinum, and she has the biggest engagement ring. The other two, wheat blond and maple, seem to hang on to her every word.

I tuck my hair behind my ear, then look down at its mousy brownness draped over my shoulder. I brush it behind my back, then look at Matthew. He's leaning over the table talking loudly to sweaty-tank-top guy, who is now wearing a blue aloha shirt. He nods and gestures broadly at the other two men. *Sweaty Guy must be Matthew's boss.* I grimace. *I need a drink.* I look up as a tall girl with jet-black hair walks by the next table with a tray full of candy-colored martinis.

I lift my hand, and Matthew squeezes my knee under the table. Then I drop my hand to my lap when I see Sweaty Guy lift his. The server approaches our table, and Sweaty Guy reaches onto her tray and takes two martinis off. I watch her face change from scrunched-brow shock to pursed-lip anger. This doesn't stop him from taking the last two drinks off her tray. She stands slack jawed and empty trayed as he passes out the drinks. He hands one to Platinum Blonde, then one to me, then one to Matthew and holds on to the last one. I look down at my lap until she walks away. Then finally grab the glass and take a drink. Matthew leans into my ear. "Steve's going to say something. Don't drink yet." I swallow hard, then nod and set down my glass.

"To Matt." Sweaty Guy Steve lifts his glass. "May this promotion make you rich and may your wife raise your kids." *What the hell kinda toast is that?*

Matthew lifts his glass and squeezes my knee again. I lift my glass but don't clink anyone else's drink. Instead I retract my arm and down half of the too-strong pink cocktail. I cough, then set the glass down. "I'm sorry," Matthew mouths. Then whispers, "He's drunk. He doesn't mean anything." He puts his arm around my shoulder, then turns back to Steve.

Steve looks past Matthew and narrows his eyes at me. My shoulders droop as I pinch my lips together. "So, Ruthie, what is it that you do?" Steve asks. Everyone at the table turns to look at me, and I feel my cheeks burn, the knots in my stomach now replaced with fluttering and acid.

"I—I work in insurance," I stammer. Then lift my glass, take a drink, and look away. *Someone else, please say something.*

"Yeah, Matt told us that," Steve says. "But what specifically do *you* do?"

I clear my throat. "I'm a sales agent. Property and casualty mostly."

"What does that pay?"

I feel my jaw drop as my brows shoot up. *What's wrong with this guy?* He lets out a chuckle but keeps his eyes on me. It feels like we're in a stand-off. I straighten my posture and say, "It's commission based." Then swallow down the rest of my drink.

"You don't need to keep doing that with the raise Matt here just got." Steve gives Matthew a "good ol' boy" slap on the back. I search Matthew's face. His eyes are tight and his lips pressed into a hard line, but he looks straight ahead as though somewhere else. *Say something. Stop him.* Steve continues, "Nikki, my wife, is a stay-at-home mom, as is Doug's wife, Christine, and, Jen, remind me what you do."

"I'm a part-time home health aide, Steve," snaps Jen.

"Ooh, sorry, Jen," he says condescendingly, then laughs. "Jen's just mad because she has a master's degree, and her husband, my buddy Ted here, makes three times what she makes."

He takes another drink of his cocktail and slaps the table. "Come on, Ted. Tell Jen to lighten up. I'm just messing around. You know what this table needs? Another round of drinks." Steve looks around, then waves down a lean red-haired server. When she ignores his wave, he shouts at her, "Excuse me! We need drinks over here." I cringe as the red-haired server clenches her jaw, squares her shoulders, then paces toward him. "We'll take another round of drinks," he says and hands her a black card.

"I'll tell your server." Her tone is gruff as she takes his card and walks away.

Steve finally turns his attention to Ted. I let out a long breath. Then take a sip of water. When the tall black-haired server returns with drinks, I'm tempted to reach onto the tray like Steve. But instead tug at a hangnail in my lap. Her brows are lifted the entire time she's setting down drinks and taking our order. As though she's waiting for someone to say something stupid so she can slap one of us.

When the check arrives, Matthew, Doug, and Ted reach into their pants pockets. Steve smiles and dismisses them with a wave. He'd already paid. He signs the receipt inside the bill holder, stands, and gulps down the last of his drink. Then shakes his head and makes a loud grumbling sound. Ted and Doug do the same. Matthew's glass is already empty, but he picks it up anyway and shakes an ice cube into his mouth. Then grabs my hand, and we follow the group out. His palm is sweaty against mine.

At the entryway of the hotel, Steve and Nikki turn away from the glass doors of the lobby. Nikki's platinum-blond hair shines in the dim light of the moon. She tugs Steve's hand, leading him toward the security guard by the open side door. Loud electronic dance music escapes into the night air. There's a line of people standing along the building waiting to show their IDs. Steve leans into the security guard's ear, then hands him a folded bill. He gestures at the rest of us, and the security guard nods. Then lifts the retractable belt from the stanchion.

I lean into Matthew's ear and whisper, "Where's everyone going?"

"We're going to the club for a little bit."

"Do we have to?" I whine and look up at him. My brow furrows. I rub my glossy lips together, then ask, "Wouldn't you rather go up to the room so that we can be *alone*?"

"I promise we won't stay long. Come on, Ruthie. It'll be fun."

I sulk.

Walking inside, I feel my pupils dilate. Then put my hands over my ears as I follow Matthew. The music is loud. It feels like all my internal organs are vibrating with the beat. On the dance floor, girls twerk in tight sweaty circles while guys stand around watching them as they sip their drinks. A few silver-haired couples stand around the cocktail tables. Cuban shirts and fedoras are intermingled with miniskirts and tube tops. *Palm Springs is weird.*

Matthew leaves me with the wives beside the dance floor. He and his colleagues push through the crowd up to the bar. I clutch my elbow and stare down at my feet. I put on chunky leather wedges to go with my floral-print dress. Nikki, Christine, and Jen are wearing bright-colored stilettos.

"Try to have fun!" Nikki shouts over the music.

"What?" I shout back and shake my head.

She leans into my ear, close enough that I feel her lips brush against my skin. Then repeats, "Try to have fun." She stands back and smiles at me. Her hooded-eye, pouty-lip expression makes me draw back as a prickle creeps over my scalp.

"OK!" I shout back, then clutch my arms tight against myself. I look up as Matthew approaches holding two drinks. When I grab a drink out of his hand, his eyes seem to bulge. I take a long sip. It tastes like nail-polish remover smells and lemon.

"Are you having fun?" Matthew asks.

"Not really." I slurp down the rest of the drink. Then cough into my fist.

"Do you want to dance?" He grabs my hand. His is cold and wet. He tugs me onto the dance floor. Then stops when he reaches a clearing between two older couples. *I want to go home.* He pulls my hand onto his shoulder and shuffles his feet in time with the music. As he smiles down at me, the small wrinkles around his eyes make up for the glassiness of his pupils. My grimace curls into a grin.

I shuffle my feet too, following his lead. Smiling like an idiot with his hands wrapped around my waist. *The nail-polish-remover drink is finally working.* The space around us shrinks as Matthew's colleagues and their wives dance their way into the gaps. When I feel a tap on my shoulder, I ignore it and shake my hair out. The second tap is more forceful. I look back as Nikki rests her hand on my shoulder. Her warm fingers pull against me. Nikki's hooded gaze moves from me to Matthew. "I'm cutting in." She squeezes in front of me, wedging her body between us.

Matthew raises his eyebrows at me. Then he shrugs and continues dancing, though with seemingly less enthusiasm now. She puts her arms around his neck, tosses her head back, and thrusts out her chest. Her long blond hair dances over her shoulders and sticks to her sweat-glistening cleavage. I stand beside Steve watching Matthew and Nikki gyrate, feeling paralyzed.

Steve can barely keep his eyes open. The people dancing behind him seem to prop up his sagging and swaying figure. My muscles tighten as my jaw clenches. *What a slut!* My breathing speeds up and grows coarser as my stomach hardens. I reach out and grab Matthew's arm, then violently pull him away from her.

"Let's go!" I shout, my face hot.

"All right!" he shouts back.

He blinks rapidly as if I've just woken him from a dream, his expression groggy and confused. I grab his hand and drag him off the dance floor. I don't look back, pulling harder when I feel resistance. *To hell with those people.*

The lobby is cold and bright. My head is cloudy as I pull him into the elevator and stare at the silver buttons. I put my hand over my forehead. It's damp. Then I squint at the numbers. "We're on four," Matthew slurs, then presses the button. He stumbles back, then leans against the wall of the elevator. I clutch my belly. *I need to pee and throw up.*

The elevator doors open, and we stumble down the hall to our room. I run into the bathroom and swing the door shut as I hurry to sit. *Still no period.* I vomit in the trash can. Then finally flush, stand, and look at my pale sweaty face in the mirror. *What am I doing?* I splash cold water on my face. Then rest both palms on the counter and lean into my reflection. *This isn't me.* My heart aches inside my chest. I reach into my purse and pull out the orange vial. As I twist off the cap, the white pill powder swirls out in a little chemical puff. *What if I am pregnant?* My chin drops and I twist the lid back on. Then rub my hands over my face. I shove the bottle back into my purse. *Everything is fine.*

21.

WHEN ONE DOOR CLOSES . . .

The sound of Matthew's choked snores wakes me up. The blackout curtains are drawn shut, and the room is dark. I rub my eyes and feel greasy flakes of mascara smear across my knuckles. Then sit up and look at the digital clock. The boxy red numbers are the only light in the room. It's almost seven. My skin feels chafed where my bra rubbed against my back all night. And my face is creased from where I lay against the sleeve of my jacket.

I unbuckle the leather straps of my wedges. My ankles are swollen, red, and indented where the leather squeezed. I take off the shoes and drop them on the floor beside my weekender. Then drag myself to the bathroom and check my panties. *Nothing.* I bite my lip. *I'm three days late.* My shoulders droop.

I force myself to wash my hands, then my face. I rub off all the mascara and blotchy foundation, then stare at my reflection in the mirror. The wrinkles around my eyes and forehead seem to have grown deeper. Beneath my eyes the skin is a few shades darker than the rest of my face. I look tired. I lean in. *I am tired.*

With my face nearly pressed into the mirror, I stare hard into my eyes. The irises, a bright brown, form halos around the pupils. Reflecting the lights around the mirror. It feels like I haven't really *seen* myself in a long time. Most of the time I spend at the mirror I'm looking for all the things that are wrong with me. Putting on bronzer or slathering on wrinkle cream. The tears in my eyes make them seem to glitter. I take a deep breath, then smile. *I have me. I am fine alone. Baby or no baby. Husband or no husband. I don't need anyone else. And I need to clean up my act.* I grab my makeup off the counter and toss it in my bag, then pull my hair back into a ponytail.

Back in the room I push open the curtains. The sky is still dark, but the rising sun promises to bring blue with it. I look down at Matthew, his eyes shut, his wavy brown hair splayed over the pillow. The comforter is bunched and sagging onto the floor on his side of the bed. Tucked under the covers, he has one arm draped over them, pushing them down to expose his bare chest. His clothes lie in a crumpled heap beside the bed. It smells like morning breath and alcohol, his snores the only sound in the room.

I unzip my weekender and pull out clothes. Tug on a pair of jeans under my dress. When the snoring pauses, I look over at Matthew. He rolls over, scratches his head, then resumes snoring. I pull off my jacket and dress, then shrug on a pullover hoodie. Then pack the rest of my stuff and tug on the zipper. The bag is half-shut when Matthew stirs.

"Good morning," he says, then yawns as he rolls over onto his back. "What are you doing?" He smiles as he rubs his eyes.

I finish zipping my bag shut, then stand up straight. "I'm leaving."

His smile melts into a frown. "Why? Is something wrong?" He sits up and rubs his hands through his hair, then over his face.

I cross my arms over my chest, where a fluttery feeling has bloomed. "Nothing's wrong. I'm just ready to go home." I pinch my lips together.

"What? Why? Is it because of last night?" He rubs his hand over his face again, then pinches the bridge of his nose. "Everybody was drunk. Come on. You can't be that upset."

I shake my head. "Last night wasn't great, but it's not the reason I'm leaving." I sit down at the foot of the bed and look at him. "I'm sorry." I rub my hand over my forehead. "I don't want to say, 'It's not you. It's me,' but seriously, it is." I let out a sigh. "I can't drink like that anymore. And I don't want to get married, then end my career to raise kids."

"Steve was kidding around. You know it's not like that."

"I know. And I know he was kidding. But I have been obsessed with getting married and having kids for as long as I can remember. I've been afraid of being alone. I don't want to be afraid anymore. So, I have to let you go."

"That's it? It's over? You're just gonna leave?" He throws his hands up, then lets them drop onto the comforter with an anticlimactic splat. "*This* isn't that serious. I think you're overreacting." He lifts his brows, and half his mouth pulls up into a smile. Like he's confident that I'm going to come crawling back. "You're going to get lonely."

I nod and pinch my lips together. "You're right. I probably will." I stand. "Which is why this is the right thing to do." I grab my weekender off the dresser. "I'm sorry. Thank you, Matthew."

"I guess." He shakes his head slowly. "Bye, Ruthie."

The moment I step outside the hotel the cold of the desert surprises me with a slap of bitter air. I pull the drawstrings of my hoodie tight around my neck, then hand the valet my ticket. When my car pulls up, I throw my weekender into the passenger seat. Then repeatedly press my finger against the Heat button until it's on full blast, fogging the windshield. I press the Defrost button and run the wipers. My car still smells like perfume from yesterday, now mixed with the musty smell of recirculated air from the heating vents. The gear in park, I stare at the pavement ahead waiting for the windshield to clear up. *I can't believe I just did that.* I bite at the inside of my cheek. When the car behind me honks, I turn off the wipers and go.

I focus my eyes on the road. Noting the beige mountains and brown brush that blurs by as I drive past. Monitoring my speed for an extra thing to pay attention to. *Don't think about it.* I turn the volume up. It's been the same playlist for weeks. I mouth along with the lyrics, but it feels like there's a disconnect. Like my body is functioning without my brain, my performance perfunctory. I don't even know what song is playing. The music stops and I'm left open mouthed waiting for the next lyric.

I pick up my phone and glance down at the screen. A gray wheel in the middle of the app screen turns. There's no service. I tap the screen repeatedly. *Come on.* My heart sinks. There's nothing to look at. Nothing else to think about. My eyes water and I feel the tingling start in the tips of my fingers. *Stop it. Don't think about it.*

It's silent.

The sound of the road beneath my tires is quiet compared to the volume of my uneven breathing. *I need this.* My thumb prickles as I continue to tap the screen. The wheel continues to turn. "Buffering." I shake the phone violently, then throw it onto the passenger-side floor. *It's hot in here.* I smack the Heat button off. Then stare at the road ahead. My eyes widen when I see the sign for the 60 come and go. *I missed my exit.*

My face flushes and I look down at my phone on the floor. It's too far to reach. I flip on my turn signal, then press on my hazard lights. *I need to pull over.* My chest constricts and my breathing begins to feel choked. *Breathe.* The gravel crunches against my tires as I pull off the freeway onto the shoulder. I inhale through my nose, then squeeze my eyes shut and clench my hands around the steering wheel. *Breathe.* My exhale is stunted. I struggle to catch a breath. My muscles tighten as sweat beads on my forehead. *It's happening.* Tears roll down my face, but I can't move. *It's happening again.* My whole body is tingling and immovable. *I want my pills so bad.* I let out a scream, and it turns into a cry. *I can't have them.* My body trembles with each sob that tears through my chest. Stomach acid rises in my throat, and I feel my mouth watering. My eyes shoot open. *I'm gonna be sick.* I pry a hand off the steering wheel and pull the handle on my door. Opening it just in time. My stomach lurches and green liquid spews from my throat onto the asphalt. I cough until the liquid runs into a clear dribble. Then wipe my mouth with the back of my hand and with all my strength slam the door shut. *Am I hungover or pregnant?*

I lean against my headrest and stare out the windshield. The sky is now a pale blue streaked with smudgy white clouds. I suck in a deep inhale, ignoring the sour taste in my mouth, then blow it out slowly. *What am I doing?* I shut my eyes. *I should have told him.* I slump over the steering wheel. A car whirs past me, and my car shakes. I grip the wheel, then bang my head against the horn. It lets out a low brief honk. *God, tell me what to do.*

I sit up straight and open my eyes. *Be certain.* Fresh tears bead at the corners of my eyes, then run down the sides of my face. I swallow hard, then grab my phone off the floor. *Don't call him.* I thumb open my phone, let out a breath, then open the map. "Rerouting." The jagged route line across the screen lights up blue with patches of red. I shift into drive.

* * *

I drive slowly through the neighborhood of Spanish-tile-roofed stucco tract homes. Jacob's bike lies sideways across the lawn, the rear wheel on the driveway. I park in the street. Then stare at my phone screen. I bite my lip, then finally dial her number. "Hello?" Renée's voice is soft and sleepy.

"Can I come over?"

"Yeah." She breathes deeply, then rustles against the phone. "Joe just took the kids to get breakfast. How long before you're here?"

"I'm outside your house."

"I'll come downstairs."

I listen to her shuffle, then pace down the stairs as I get out of my car and walk up to her entryway. When she opens the door, she finally says, "Bye" into the receiver and ends the call. She's wearing one of Joe's T-shirts over a pair of Christmassy leggings. Her hair is sticking up out of a messy bun. *Bedhead.* I smile at her for a moment before my lips pinch together and my face scrunches up.

"What's wrong?" Her eyebrows gather and her eyes water as though she too might cry.

"My period's late." My shoulders shake as my eyes fill with tears.

"Come in. Come in." She puts her arm around my shoulder and leads me up the stairs. Morning light fills her otherwise, sleepy house. In her bedroom she shuts then locks the door behind me. "In case they get home early," she says. Her covers are disheveled. *I woke her up.* Joe's slippers are neatly tucked under the bed. On her nightstand are picture frames with photos of their wedding day, both of them smiling brightly as they look into each other's eyes. Beside her alarm clock, a baby monitor emits white noise.

"Can I turn this off?" I ask.

She nods. "I tune it out. I don't even notice it anymore." She shrugs. "Not unless she's crying or screaming." She shuffles into the bathroom. Her slippers make a soft scraping sound against the floor. They're a smaller version of Joe's. I flip off the monitor. Without him or the kids home, the house is quiet.

She yawns, then opens the cabinet under the sink and bends over to look inside. I stand in the doorway watching as she pulls out a bag of cotton balls and bottles of lotion. Then finally she reaches in and pulls out a box. "I bought a three pack." She smiles, holding up an open box of home pregnancy tests. "The first one I peed on was positive, so I have two left." She hands me the box.

"What am I supposed to do?"

"Pee on it."

My eyes widen as I lift a brow at her. "Right now?" I rub the back of my neck.

"Yeah. That's why I locked the door."

My shoulders droop and I look inside the box. Inside are two individually plastic-wrapped tests. I clear my throat. "Are there instructions in here?"

"Just pee on it window side up for five seconds. Then put the cap on, and lay it on the floor," she says, matter-of-factly.

"How long will it take?" My stomach flutters.

"Three minutes." She grabs my shoulders and pushes me toward the toilet. "Now go. I'll turn around while you pee."

I sit down and stare ahead at her back. Her posture stiff and arms crossed like she's supervising my time-out. I hold the plastic stick—window side up—in place and try to breathe. There's an empty feeling in the pit of my stomach. When I don't immediately pee, Renée taps her toes. "I'm trying," I whine. Then finally pee. I wait five seconds, then put the cap on and place the test on the floor as instructed. Renée turns to face me as I'm zipping up my pants. "Now what?"

"Now we wait," she says, and sits down at the edge of her bed, then pats the space next to her. "And you tell me what happened."

My eyebrows gather. "What do you mean 'what happened'? You know how a baby is made." She tilts her head and I groan. "I don't know what happened. We always used a condom, but my period is late this month."

"What else is wrong?"

What are you, some kind of psychic? I stare down at the floor, but I can feel her eyes on me. I sniffle loudly. "I broke up with Matthew."

"I thought he wasn't your boyfriend."

"He wasn't. But I ended it anyway. How much time is left?" My mouth feels dry.

She looks down at her phone. "Two minutes. Continue."

My shoulders slump. "I guess this whole late period thing was kind of a wake-up call. I mean, there I was, hours from home drunk and trapped in Palm Springs, with a guy I wasn't sure about. I realized if I'm pregnant, I'll be tethered to him the rest of my life. You can't give a baby back the way you can a ring."

"I thought you wanted a baby."

"I did." I sigh. "I do. . . . But not like this. I mean, if I'm pregnant, I'll make it work. But if I'm not, Renée, I have to stop. I can't keep jumping into relationships just to run away from being alone. You know? Maybe I haven't found Mr. Right, because I keep settling for Mr. Right Now." I wipe a stray hair away from my face. "I don't know. . . . I just need to be alone for a while." I shake my head.

She nods. "It's time."

We both stand and walk into the bathroom. Then look down at the plastic-capped stick on the floor. There's a single blue line in each of the test windows. It's negative. I squat down and pick it up. Hold it in my hands before I drop to my knees. *It's negative.* I smile, then cover my mouth with my hand as a tear rolls down my cheek. She puts her hand on my shoulder and pats me.

"Everything's going to be OK, Ruthie." Her eyes are watery, and her brow is furrowed. She lowers to her knees beside me and puts her arm over my shoulder. She wore the same expression the day our parents' divorce was finalized. We knelt at the church pew and prayed. Then again when Dad died years later. That was the last time I knelt at a Catholic church, the last time I knelt beside my sister. I sniffle, then wipe my face with a wad of toilet tissue and nod.

"I don't know what's wrong with me." My legs wobbly, I lower my rear to the floor and sit on the cold tile.

"Nothing's wrong with you." Renée rolls the toilet paper downward then tears it. She hands me a long strip of squares. "Everyone makes mistakes."

I blow my nose. "Not you. You got everything right." My head droops and I lift my hand. "This beautiful house. Jakey and Becca." I look down at her feet. "Matching slippers." I let out a snuffling, shaky laugh.

"I bought these slippers. I can buy you a pair too. Then we'll all match." She squeezes my arm and sits on the floor next to me. "And I have not gotten everything right."

I snap my head up and glare at her.

Her eyes water. "Do you remember my boyfriend from high school?"

"Vaguely." I shrug.

"I never told you this." She shakes her head. "I never told anyone, but he got me pregnant."

"What?" My voice comes out strained, and my mouth falls open.

"Keep your voice down. Joe'll be back soon." She waves her hand dismissively, her brow furrowed. "I miscarried."

I draw my head back quickly. "Oh my God. I'm sorry, Sister. I had no idea."

"No one did. I wasn't that far along when it happened. When I found out I was pregnant, I was so scared. I thought about getting an abortion. I didn't know what to do and so I prayed."

"Then what happened?"

"Then one morning I woke up, and it was gone. My period started and didn't stop for nine days. I felt so guilty. I felt like I *made* it happen somehow." Her shoulders slump. "So, I promised myself I'd never let something like that happen again." She rubs her belly. "It took me a long time to forgive myself."

I stare at the ground and shake my head.

"My point is, it's OK if you've screwed up, but you have to learn from it. Otherwise, they're not mistakes. They're choices." She scoots back, then grabs the top of the counter and pulls herself up. Then dusts off her bottom and offers me her hand. "*Choose* to learn from this."

I nod, then take her hand, and she lifts me up. I throw my arms around her and hug her. Her firm pregnant belly presses against my empty stomach. "I will." I sniffle loudly, biting my lip to hold back the tears. She pats my back, then gives me a crooked smile.

"Now put on your aunt hat because it's about to get loud in here."

I step back and lift a brow.

"They're home. I just heard the garage door open."

"Are you sure? I didn't hear anything."

"Trust me." She points at her ear. "I have supersonic mom ears."

A door slams downstairs, and immediately the sound of voices echoes through the house. Joe shouts, "We're home!" while Rebecca screams, "Mama" repeatedly. There's the sound of little hurried footsteps I recognize as Jacob's coming up the stairs.

"I'll give you a minute," Renée says. Then opens the door. The volume immediately increases. "I'm coming!" she shouts as she pulls the door shut behind her.

I press the lock button and lean against the door. *I'm not pregnant.* My stomach cramps and I drop my hand to my belly. *Seriously?* My lips curl into a weak smile.

22

IT'S MY PARTY AND I'LL CRY IF I WANT TO

stare at the date at the bottom corner of my computer screen. June 15, 2017. Another year older. *Another year wiser?* I bite my lower lip and open my email. Wedged between gray rows of policy question and change emails are subject lines that read, "Happy Birthday." I click to open an email from Tammy. Her e-card explodes confetti onto the screen with a GIF of five shirtless men dancing. I can't help but laugh. Tammy walks into my office.

"Did you open my card?" Wide-eyed, she smiles at me. "Tell me that's why you're laughing."

"That's why I'm laughing."

"Shut up. Don't lie to me." She smiles brightly.

"I'm serious." I turn my monitor to face her.

"Isn't that hilarious?" she asks and lifts her mug to her lips. Her engagement ring sparkles brightly under the fluorescent light of my office. Tammy got engaged last month to someone she met on Bumble. "You're next, girl," she says when she catches me staring.

"I'm really not. You know I don't have a boyfriend."

"Not yet." She wiggles her brows.

I shake my head. "I don't want one."

She sets her mug on my desk and narrows her eyes at me. I stare back smirking. Unblinking.

"Damn. I guess you really don't," she says finally. "I came in here for another reason."

"Oh yeah? What's that?" I lift my mug and take a sip of coffee.

"Susan is retiring."

"OK?" I shake my head and shrug.

"She's selling her agency." She presses her lips together and lifts a brow.

I set my mug down hard on my desk, and coffee splashes out onto my hand. "I thought her son was taking over."

"I guess not." She flashes a toothy grin and stares at me.

"So, it's for sale?" I ask wide eyed as I wipe my hand with a tissue.

"Not yet. No one knows about it."

I lift a brow and tilt my head. *How do you know about it?* She puts a hand on her hip and looks down at me as if to say, *You don't want to know.* I ask, "Should I go for it?"

"That's a stupid question. Yes." She grabs her mug off my desk. "Happy birthday."

At home my keys jingle in my left hand as I walk up the stairs. As I step closer to the door, I hear the sound of muffled chatter. Then I put my key in and it goes silent. I smile, then open the door. Inside it's dark. Before I can flip on the light, Jacob shouts, "Happy birthday!"

Then a chorus of voices erupts, "Surprise!"

My eyes widen and the smile on my face spreads into a broad open-mouth grin. I pick up Rebecca as she stumbles up to me. Then thank and hug everyone. "How'd you beat me here?" I ask Tammy as she leans for a hug.

"It was easy. You're always last to leave the office," she says.

On the dining table, a frosted white cake has the numbers three and four stuck into it. Sam lights them with a match, then shakes it to put it out. I lean into the cake and take a deep breath, then close my eyes. "Make a wish," says Mom. I blow the candles out.

"What did you wish for?" asks Jacob.

"The same thing she wishes for every year." Sam laughs nervously.

"Not this year." I smile.

"What *did* you wish for?" Renée's voice rises as she takes Rebecca from me.

"If I tell then it won't come true." I pull the candles out of the cake and lick the frosting off the bottoms.

"Honestly, I'm just glad you're not freaking out like you did last year," Sam says, then passes me a slice of cake.

"What happened last year?" asks Joe as he takes a piece.

"She threw out the numbers and said she was thirty again." Sam laughs again and continues cutting the cake.

"Yet you still bought me numbers again this year." I lift a brow and put the candles I licked clean on her plate. She pinches the wicks together, then throws them in the trash.

Renée laughs. "I thought you were going to say something crazy. That's no big deal. She did the same thing when she turned thirty-two. Only they weren't candles. They were balloons. She finished a bottle of champagne by herself, then popped them."

"Haha, super funny, guys." I pause. "This year is different. I've embraced my age." Sam stops cutting cake and lifts her head to glare at me. "I'm serious," I say, then shove a forkful of cake into my mouth. Everyone seems to stare at me. I chew slowly, then finally set my plate down. "Could I have some wine?" I ask, and Mom fills a glass and hands it to me. I lift my glass. "To thirty-four."

"To thirty-four," everyone echoes as they clink my glass.

"The year I freeze my eggs." I lift my glass again. This time only Jacob lifts his cup.

"What?" Mom exclaims, her eyes bulging.

I take a long drink, then nod slowly. Tammy and Sam stare down at their cake plates, then at each other. My stomach hardens and suddenly the air in the room feels taut. Like one wrong move might tear the familial scene apart.

Renée passes Rebecca to Joe, then leans into Mom. "It's fine, Mom. Let it go."

"But we're Catholic," Mom says.

"Ruthie's not," Renée answers.

"Well, doesn't your church agree it's a sin," Mom says, and stares at me.

I shrug. "I'm not sure. But even if it is . . . I need this." I look down at the table. The remaining slab of cake is smeared and sad looking.

"Let's talk about it later." Mom forces a thin smile and pats my back, then nods and smiles at Tammy and Sam.

When the party's over, I walk back to my room and shut the door. A red bow Sam stuck on my head earlier crunches against my pillow when I lie down. I take it off and look at it. She bought me a wine-saving device. The bow is glittery and roughly the size of a tangerine. The bottom is still sticky, so I place it on my belly. *The gift of more time. Happy birthday.* I smile at the bow and close my eyes. Then open them when there's a knock at the door.

"Yeah?" I shout.

"Can I come in?" Mom asks as she opens the door slightly.

"Sure." I sit up and rip the bow off my shirt. I set it on my nightstand and cross my arms over my chest.

"I'm sorry about how I reacted." She sits down on the foot of the bed. Her eyes full of regret as if she gave me a spanking I didn't deserve.

"It's fine. There's drama for my birthday every year. You heard Sam and Renée." I shrug. "I'm used to it."

"I want you to know that I support you. Even if I don't agree with you."

"Thanks, Mom."

"I mean it." Her eyes narrow. "And I want to put my money where my mouth is. I was going to buy you another purse, but if you're going to freeze your eggs, I want to help."

"You really don't have to. I've been saving money—"

"Would you rather have a new handbag?" She lifts her brows, and I sag against my pillow. "I didn't think so. I know it's expensive, so let me help."

I let out a deep breath. "Thank you, Mom. It means a lot."

She nods. "When is your appointment?"

"Not until December."

"That's a long time from now. Why then?"

"Honestly?" I sit up, and she makes a face as if to say, *Yeah, duh.* "There's still a small dumb part of me that's hoping for a happily ever after.

But the bigger smarter part of me that booked the appointment knows that I'm my own happy ending." I let out a chuckle. "I'm, like, really good at being a spinster."

"You're not a spinster." Mom frowns.

"We're talking about freezing my eggs." I tilt my head. "This is for sure spinster territory. Anyway, it's for the best because there's something else that I really want to do." I grit my teeth and smile at her.

"What's that?"

"Tammy told me today that there's going to be an agency for sale in Newport." I clench my teeth again. "I think I wanna go for it. What do you think?"

She smiles broadly. Her eyes seem to sparkle. "Yes. Absolutely. You should definitely go for it."

"Yeah?" I let out a breath, and my shoulders drop. "I mean, I would have to take out a giant loan, but I feel like it would be worth it."

"It *is* worth it. This is something you've been wanting for a long time." Mom puts her hand on my shoulder. "Happy birthday. I hope you get everything you wished for." She grabs the bow off my nightstand and sticks it back on my head. Smiles again, then leaves.

My phone chimes on my nightstand. All day I'd received birthday messages from friends and family. Grandma left a voice mail singing "Las Mañanitas." I pick up the phone and stare wide eyed at the screen. A new message from "Do Not Answer." I thumb-open my phone and read, "Happy Birthday." I roll my eyes, slump against my pillow, and set the phone down.

* * *

I press Start on the Keurig. The machine buzzes, then makes a mechanical belching sound before it releases a stream of coffee. I watch it fill my mug, then shake the creamer and pour it in. I put the creamer back in the fridge, turn around, and let out a gasp.

"Holy sh—" I close my eyes and clutch my chest. "You scared me."

"You're in an office full of people and *I* scared you?" Tammy smiles and scoots past me to the coffee maker. She pulls a hot-pink mug that says "Bride" from the cabinet overhead.

"I guess I'm just jumpy." I lift my brows and take a sip of coffee.

"I would be too after the night you had. What was up with your mom? She seemed really intense about *your* eggs." The coffee maker whirs behind her.

I shrug. "After everyone left she apologized. She just worries about me. My love life, my eggs, my eternal soul—it's all one big worry for her." I laugh.

She opens the fridge and shakes the creamer before pouring. "Your love life I can fix. I told you Travis has a cute friend, right?" She lifts her mug and takes a sip holding it with her ring hand. *She's so extra.*

"Only a dozen times." I lean against the counter. "I don't want to meet your fiancé's friend. I'm still shaking off my last guy."

She sets her mug down. "What happened with Matthew?"

I shrug and look down into my coffee. "He texted me 'Happy Birthday' last night."

"Ew." She curls her lip. "That's almost as bad as 'Hey, stranger.' "

"I know. Anyway, I'm good alone." I point at my pelvis with my coffee mug. "Once I put these babies on ice, I won't have to worry about marriage or men for at least another decade." I'm lifting my mug to take another sip when Martha walks into the break room.

"Good morning, Martha," Tammy says, then walks out faster than I can react.

"Good morning," Martha says to her retreating figure, then walks up to the coffee maker. "Good morning, Ruthie," she says, and smiles.

"Hmm. Morning." I pinch my lips together in an awkward smile, then look up at the clock over the microwave. *Crap.* Martha puts in a new pod and presses Start on the machine. I inch toward the break-room door.

"Ruthie."

"Yeah?" I pause in the doorway.

"Would you stop by my office after lunch? There's something I wanted to talk to you about."

"OK."

I snap the lid onto my plastic bowl. Inside, soggy bits of oily kale remain stuck to the bottom of the container. I toss the container into the cabinet under my desk, then open the camera app on my phone to check my teeth. I run my fingers through my hair, then apply a fresh coat of lipstick. Tug at my blouse and the hem of my skirt before letting out a long breath.

I square my shoulders and pace down the hallway beside the row of cubicles to her office. I stand in her doorway and shift my weight watching as she reads a document at her desk. *Should I knock?* She flips the page she's reading and continues looking down, her reading glasses perched on the edge of her nose. I lift my fist to her doorframe. Before I can knock, she finally looks up. "Come in. Close the door," she says.

I step into her office, press my lips together, and slowly close the door behind me. When she motions for me to take a seat, I sit down and cross my legs. Then shift in the chair, uncross my legs, and cross my ankles instead. My stomach flutters.

"How was your lunch?"

"It was ... *good.*" My voice rises and my response sounds more like a question than an answer. "How was yours?" I say in a knee-jerk follow-up.

"Great. Anyway, the reason I called you into my office is because I have an opportunity I think you would be perfect for."

"Really?" My voice is now nearly a screech. My heart races. *This is it!*

"Now, what I'm about to tell you can't leave this office, because no one knows about it yet. There's an agent in Newport retiring and selling her agency."

"Wow, what an incredible opportunity." I nod and smile. "I had no idea." I lower my eyes and bite my lip.

"It really is. Her office is in a great location, and she has a diversified business of loyal customers. I think Jared is the perfect agent to take it over. I haven't spoken with him yet, because he is going to need a strong support agent to help him. And I thought, who better than you?"

"Wait. . . . What?" I shake my head, my eyes blinking rapidly.

"You would be perfect in that office. You're great with customers. You understand the Newport demographic. And these past few months you've consistently been a top producer."

"Thank you, Martha. . . . I. . . . Well . . . it's just not really what I had in mind." I furrow my brow as I feel heat rising from my chest to my face, flushing my cheeks a bright red.

"I know you have had some personal issues lately." She presses her lips together. "But you can't let that stop you from growing in your career. Besides, this is more of a small side step. I knew you weren't ready for that commercial promotion in Irvine. When Bill asked why you didn't submit for consideration, I told him the timing wasn't right. You've had a lot on your plate, but I think now is the time, and working with Jared is the opportunity you need."

"Bill wanted me for that promotion?" I ask, wide eyed. *Bill knows who I am?*

"Yes, but I knew you weren't interested. So, they promoted someone out of the Santa Ana office."

"Wow." I shake my head. My muscles grow rigid. I draw a breath in and release it. "Thank you, Martha. But I don't want to work for Jared." I stand, keeping my eyes fixed on her. "I'm a better agent than he is, and I want to buy that agency. I didn't submit for that promotion because I've been waiting for an opportunity like this one."

She looks down at her desk, then shuffles the documents she was reading into a manila folder. She lets out a loud breath as though annoyed with me. "Ruthie, that's a lot of responsibility, and on top of that, the seller has a steep asking price. I don't think you know what you're asking for."

"I'm ready, Martha. And I'm *asking* for your help." I sit down and lean forward.

She shakes her head slowly, then sighs deeply. "Why don't you think about it? I just sprung this on you today."

"I have thought about it. I want this."

She presses her lips into a thin line. Then stands. "I'll give you until the end of next week to show me your business plan."

Yes! "OK." I nod and offer a thin smile. Holding back the toothy, wide-mouthed grin I feel.

"It needs to be flawless for me to consider it."

"Of course." I stand and nod again.

"I expect you to keep this conversation to yourself. The sale of the agency has not been officially announced." Her lips curl up slightly, and I can see the smile in her eyes as she nods for me to leave. She sits back down behind her desk, and I grab the handle of her door.

My heart leaps and I turn around. "Thank you, Martha." I open the door and pace out. Then pick up speed as I hurry past the cubicles to my office. I shut the door behind me and lean over my desk panting. *I can't believe I just did that.* Slowly a smile stretches across my face. A knock at my door snaps me up straight.

I walk around the desk and sit down behind it. I shake the mouse and brighten the screen of my monitor. "Come in."

"What happened?" Tammy asks as she opens the door, her eyes bulging.

My posture sags and I release the mouse. "Shut the door," I whisper and motion for her to come in. She shuts the door softly then sets a paper bag atop my desk.

"What's that?" I ask.

"My lunch." She smiles. The aroma of french fries wafts out of her bag, filling up my office.

"I thought you were on a diet." I tilt my head with a sideways smile.

"I am. It's a cheat day."

"It's Thursday."

"Don't try to distract me. What did Martha say?"

"She told me about the agency for sale in Newport. She also told me that it was confidential, and *no one* knew about it yet." I raise a brow.

"Don't give me that look. You know I have my ways." She juts out her hip.

"Mmmm-hmmm."

"Well, did she talk to you about buying it?"

"Mmmm, not really. She thought Jared should buy it and suggested I work for *him.*"

"What?" She reaches into the paper bag, pulls out a waffle fry, and waves it around as she talks. "Why Jared? He's awful. She probably just wants to get him out of her office and out of her hair." She bites the fry and crosses her arms over her chest. "I know he's got the money to buy it. Maybe that's why she's offering it to him and sticking you in there to do the *actual* work."

"I don't know. But I told her I want to buy it, and she gave me until next Friday to give her an actionable business plan."

I point at the bag. She nods, and I reach in. We chew silently, neither of us looking at the other. I reach for another fry, the bag now half-empty. She sets a bitten fry down on my desk and says, "So, you're going to do it?"

I eye the greasy spot on my desk under the fry. "Yeah, I have until next Friday." I repeat and brush my hands together as if dusting them off.

"No. I mean, are you going to buy Susan's agency?"

I nod slowly. "I don't know how I'm going to do it yet, but yeah. I feel like I have to. Like I need to do it. For myself. You know?"

"Yeah." She dusts the salt off her hands and grabs me by the shoulders. "You got this. You *will* buy that agency, and you *will* be successful." She smiles maniacally as she shakes me.

"Thank you. I needed that."

23

MINE FOR
THE TAKING

stare at my laptop screen and tap my pencil against my forehead. My entire backside is achy from hours spent hunched over the keyboard. My glass of water ran out long ago, but the thought of taking precious time away from work to get something as trivial as a drink feels wasteful. *I'm so close.* The kitchen table is covered in Post-it notes, stacks of documents, folders, and blackened pink eraser shavings. Half the table and the floor around it has become my home office. The other half, when not in immediate use, Mom has forced me to clear off for breakfast and dinner.

I read the last page aloud, then smile and hit the floppy disk image to save. *I'm finished.* I raise both fists in the air and lean against the dining chair to stretch my back. I rub my eyes and finally stand. My legs feel like jelly. I let out a deep breath, then finally grab my glass off the table and walk into the kitchen to refill it. Standing over the kitchen sink, I take a long drink.

"Did you finish?" Mom asks as she comes into the kitchen and opens the fridge.

I smile into my glass, finish the last of the water, nod, then refill the glass. An expression flits across her face, too quick for me to register its meaning.

"What was that look?" I ask.

"What look?" she says.

"That look you just had. The one you're trying to suppress now."

"It was nothing. I'm just glad you're following through."

As soon as the words leave her lips, her face morphs into an expression of regret. But it's too late. She's said it. *It's what she's been thinking all along.* The words seem to hang in the air. I set down my glass and stare into the sink.

"That's not what I meant," she says.

"I know what you meant." I nod slowly without lifting my gaze. "I don't blame you. I know I'm a fuckup." I sigh. "But I'm trying, Mom. I know you don't want me here—"

"Of course, I want you here."

"No, you don't. Not like this. And I don't want to be here either. That's why I need this to work." I gesture at the dining table littered with documents. "I need this agency so I can afford to move out. So I can feel like a grown-up again."

The fridge dings an alert. It's been open too long. Mom shuts the fridge door. Her hand drops to her side. She looks exasperated. *Tired of me.* Finally, she says, "You are not a 'fuckup.' " She straightens her posture. "I just never know what to expect from you." Her eyes seem to water. "And I'm proud of you just as you are."

* * *

Nervous, I lick my lips. *I'm not wearing lipstick.* I reach into the cabinet under my desk for my purse. I don't bother to pull it out but instead fumble blindly inside. I'm feeling for the thin tube when my hand grips the rattling thick bottle of my pills. *I forgot I had these.* The vial's rattling had become white noise in my purse. The bottle was something that got shuffled with tampons and keys every time I changed purses.

I pull the bottle out and look at the clock. Ten till four. *They take at least twenty minutes to metabolize.* I grip the bottle and shake it softly. The sound of the tiny pills knocking around inside makes my mouth salivate. *What am I doing?* I haven't taken one in months. My hand drops to my lap, and I look down at the presentation folder on my desk. *I need this meeting to be perfect.* My grip around the bottle grows sweaty. I let out a breath, then shake my head. *I have to be focused.* I bite my lip and throw the pills back in my purse, then shut the cabinet door.

I need to do this on my own. I stand and smooth down my blouse and grab the folder off my desk. I wipe a fingerprint off the cover with my sleeve. Then grab my binder-clipped copy, square my shoulders, suck in a deep inhale, and pace out of my office.

My heart beats loudly in my chest, and her office is so quiet. *There's no way she can't hear it.* I clear my throat. I remove the binder clip from my copy and turn to the first page. "As you can see—"

She waves her hand dismissively. "I don't need you to present it. I want to read it for myself. Do you mind?" She lifts her reading glasses to her face.

"Not at all." My voice squeaks and I clear my throat again. "Would you like me to . . ." I point toward the shut door. Then start to stand.

"Please sit. I want to be able to ask questions."

"Of course." I sit up straight and rest my palms on my thighs.

I press my lips together as she looks down and reads. I look at her, then over her shoulder at the picture of her cats. Lining the walls of her office are gold plaques and bulky acrylic awards from almost two decades. "Top Production," "District Manager of The Year," "Presidents Council." *She is one badass cat lady.* I smile at her as she continues to read, admiring her perfectly tailored Chanel jacket.

When she pauses and lifts the folder closer to her face, I flip open my copy and try to guess what she's looking at. *Is it a chart? My profit and loss?* Sweat beads on my forehead, and I bite at the inside of my cheek. Finally, she takes off her reading glasses and sets them atop the folder. She clasps her hands together. Her shiny red nail polish glistens under the fluorescent lights. I hold my breath. Then she looks up at me and smiles. I exhale noisily.

"I can see that you spent a great deal of time putting this together," she says. "May I ask you something?"

"Of course." I nod.

"Why do you want to be an independent agent? Why not just stay here? From your proposal I can clearly see what you plan to do and how you plan to do it. But I want to know *why*."

"So that I can expand my earning potential and have the freedom of being a business owner."

"Hmmm." She purses her lips.

"So I. . . . So. . . . I need to see if I can do it. I'm scared. I mean I'm literally terrified. I don't know how I'm going to come up with all the money yet. I don't know if I'll make it on my own. . . . But I *need* to do it. I have to, Martha. I need to believe that I have what it takes. I know that sounds stupid. And that I should probably stay here where it's safe, but I just can't anymore. I believe I can make it on my own, and I need to try." It takes everything in me to keep from crying.

Suddenly I feel light-headed and drained. Like if she blew on me, I would fall over. I force a smile knowing that my face is bright red and frightened looking. I rub my palms against the thighs of my slacks, thankful I wore black, then shake out my hands. She says nothing. Then slowly her pursed lips curl into a slight smile. Her eyes never straying from mine, she finally stands. Then presses her hands on her desk and leans forward. "OK."

"OK?" My eyebrows gather and I bite my lip. *Now what?*

She nods and smiles broadly. "I'm approving your business plan. I'm going to pass it up to Bill on Monday for his review."

"Oh my God. Seriously?" I can't hold back the shock in my voice.

She nods again. "Seriously." She lets out a chuckle.

"Thank you, Martha. You don't know what this means to me."

She shakes her head. "I know exactly what this means to you. I sat in your seat once." Her eyes seem to twinkle. "Before you leave, I suggest you talk to Geraldine. She has a loan officer nephew who can help you get a small-business loan." She looks at her watch to check the time. "Never mind. It's after five. She's already left for the day. You'll have to ask her next week."

"Ok. I will." I stand. The smile across my face stretched so wide my cheeks hurt.

"Have a great weekend." She sits down. "And congratulations."

Tears prick my eyes, and I nod, then quickly turn to leave. It feels like I'm floating as I walk back to my office. With my head held high, I don't even feel the floor against my feet. Once I press the door shut behind me, I feel tears escape my eyes and roll down my smiling face. *I did it.* I pinch my lips together. *I really did it.*

I back away from the door. I jump up and down, then run in place, shaking my hands in the air to suppress the scream in my chest. *I freakin' did it.*

"Go home, Ruthie," Martha calls out playfully from the hallway.

"OK!" I shout back. Once the door slams shut behind her, I finally let out the trapped scream. "Yeessss!"

* * *

I park my car and look up at the dark window of suite B. *My new office.* Susan gave me the keys yesterday. It took three months for the sale to be finalized and thirty minutes for me to pack up my old office. The two-story building is small, its windows covered with blue awnings, the ones on the first floor with planter boxes. It looks like one big flower shop.

Her name has already been removed from the door sign. I smile knowing that a new sign with my name on it is coming. I take a deep breath, put the key in the lock, and open the door. It smells like fresh paint and the fibrous aroma of new carpet. *It smells like my new home.* I flip on the light and my smile broadens. It's so quiet. I pace slowly to the middle of the empty room. Arms outstretched I toss my head back and turn in a circle, like I'm in a movie. I half expect it to snow. *This is mine.*

I lower myself to the floor and sit on the fuzzy new carpet. Running my hand over the soft, tight loops of fiber. The window stretches from the floor to the ceiling. Outside the leaves in the planters sway gently with the breeze. A bare curtain rod is mounted to the ceiling in front of the window. *Who wants curtains with a view like this?* I stretch my legs out in front of me, then recline on my elbows and shut my eyes.

I open them when I hear a knock on the door. *My first visitor.* I stand and open the door. Sweating, the UPS man taps at his scanner, then looks up at me and smiles.

"You the new tenant?" He taps at the screen again. "Um, Ruth? I can't pronounce the last name."

I nod and smile. "That's me. I'm Ruthie."

"Great, I have a delivery."

"Really? I wasn't expecting anything until Friday."

"Well, it's a good thing you're here. Otherwise, all your packages would have been returned to the warehouse for you to pick up."

"All my packages?" My eyes widen. "Is there a lot?" I bite my lip, remembering all the furniture I ordered.

"Oh yeah."

Once he's brought in the final package, he asks me to sign and returns to his truck, leaving me crowded by boxes. *It's like Christmas.* I use the back of the office key to cut into the largest box. Then pull the white packaging inside off and reveal the dark wood of the desk I ordered. I cut open another box and it's a printer. Another box and it's a chair. I'm tempted to throw the packing peanuts in the air like confetti but instead take a photo and post it to Instagram: "I bought myself presents #Adulting."

A moment later my screen lights up. Sam liked my photo. I smile as the phone lights up again with an incoming call from Sam. "I'm coming over," she says. "Text me the address."

"Right now?" I look around at the cut-open boxes. "There's nowhere to sit yet." I eye the boxes with chairs. "I guess I could assemble something."

"It's fine. I'm not coming over to sit. I'm coming to celebrate."

I watch through the window as Sam parks her car and walks up to my office. Under her arm she carries a tall budding orchid in a pink vase. She smiles and waves at me through the window. Then raps a shave-and-a-haircut knock against the door. I get up off my desk box and open the door. My cheeks ache from all the smiling I've been doing.

"Aw, Sam. You shouldn't have." I grin and take the orchid. "It's beautiful. Thank you." I place it on the desk box.

"You're welcome." She smiles again, looking around the single, empty room. "So, show me around."

"Well, it's not much now." I take a few steps back. "But this is where I'm going to put my desk." I bend my knees and pretend to sit. "And that's where I'm going to put an employee desk." I point to the left wall. Then stand up straight and walk toward the front of the office, near the window.

"And here is where I'm going to put a bookcase so I have somewhere to put awards once I earn them."

"It looks great." She nods. "I can totally picture it." She puts her hands up and mimes that she's looking through a picture frame. "The only thing you're missing is a bathroom."

"Oh. It's down the hall. Here. Just reach into my purse. The keys are in there."

She reaches into my purse, and the sound of the vial rattling immediately makes my heart sink. She pulls out the keys and looks at me. I know that face. *She's disappointed.*

"It's not what you think."

"I didn't think anything." She shakes her head and looks at the ground. "Well, I guess . . . I did think you stopped taking them." Her shoulders drop.

"I did. I did stop taking them! Sam, it's been months since I've taken a single pill. I should have thrown them away." I shake my head slowly. "I mean it. I promise."

"It's fine. You don't have to convince me."

"I'm serious. Pull it out and look at it. Look at the fill date. They're old."

She pulls it out and looks at it, then nods as she reads the label. "See. Old," I say as I walk toward her then take my keys. "I'm going to show you where the bathroom is."

I throw open my office door, and she follows me out. I lead her down the hall to the bathroom and unlock it. The light automatically flips on and I step inside. It's small, a single-person restroom with a slatted door hiding the toilet. I push open the slatted door. "Hand me the vial." I stare into the toilet and hold out my hand. She hesitates. "Come on, Sam."

"I don't think—"

"I have to do this," I interrupt her, and she hands me the bottle. I twist off the cap, then drop the pills into the toilet and flush. I smile as they swirl down with the water. Then look up at Sam's grimace.

"I don't think you're supposed to flush pills." Her grimace curls into a smirk.

"Crap." I let out a nervous chuckle. "I think you're right."

She laughs, then reaches out her arm. "I'm proud of you, dude."

"Thank you, Sam." I give her a weak smile and she hugs me.

"I mean it. I'm really proud of you."

I pull back, tilt my head, and smirk at her. "For throwing those away or for the agency?"

"Both. I know neither was easy."

I nod slowly. "You know . . . I realized I didn't need them anymore the day I pitched. I wanted this opportunity so bad, I was panicked." I wrap the empty bottle in toilet paper and throw it in the trash. "I wanted to do it on my own, for *myself*." I look up at her and she nods. "I used to panic every time I thought about marriage or kids. It felt almost good to be anxious about something else. And as anxious as I felt, the feeling I got when Martha congratulated me was so worth it. I know if I had been on those pills, I wouldn't have felt as high as I did sober."

24.

WEDDING DATE

The sound of scraping hangers on the rack grates on my ears. They're all the same—blush-colored dresses of different lengths. One with sleeves, another strapless. The one with a cowl-neck makes me grimace. I grab the hanger for a spaghetti-strap dress and drape it over my arm before walking over to the blue section.

"Are you finding anything?" Renée asks without looking up from the rack of gold and silver gowns.

"Not really." I groan. "You're so lucky you already have a dress and don't have to do this."

"Oh yeah, real lucky. Because we all know how attractive bridesmaids dresses are."

"Yours isn't that bad."

"Would you want to wear it?"

I pinch my lips together. "Anyway, thank you for coming with me. I hate doing this kind of stuff."

"No problem. Anything that gets me out of the house and gives me a break from the kids, I'm into." She lifts a floor-length gold gown. "What about this one?"

"Get outta here. That looks like something Mom would wear." I laugh.

"You're right. You have to look good for your date." She lifts her brows. "Lauren told me you RSVP'd with a plus-one. Why didn't you tell me you were seeing someone?" She lowers her eyes to the rack.

I scrape a hanger loudly. "Because I'm not."

"Who's your plus-one then?"

I stop scooting hangers and look her in the eyes. "Mom."

"Mom's your date?" She smirks.

"Yeah. And I'm actually pretty pumped about it. Thank you very much."

She nods and continues scooting hangers. When the salesgirl approaches, I hand her the blush dress for the fitting room and continue searching. I pull a blue dress off the rack and hold it up, then realize Renée's staring at me. "What?" I say.

She makes a face, drawing her lips to one side, then says, "Well . . . since you're not seeing anyone . . ."

I tilt my head and shoot her a look. "I'm not seeing anyone, because I don't want to."

"Why don't you want to? It's been for-ev-ver."

"It's only been a few months. And I haven't met anyone worth giving up my spinsterhood for." I smirk. "I gotta tell you, being an old maid is the jam." I hold up the low-cut blue gown again. "How about this one?"

"That's too sexy for Lauren's wedding. Her family will flip their wigs." She narrows her eyes. "And it's been closer to a year. . . . Can't you just meet this guy? It's the engineer I tried to tell you about last year. He would be perfect for you. He's smart. He's nice, a little shy maybe. But, really, you would love him."

"Mm." I shake my head. "Not interested." I stare at the blue dress. "I'm going to try this on."

"That looks like something Sam would wear."

"Perfect."

"Fine. Whatever." She shakes her head at the dress. "Come on, Ruthie. Will you at least think about it? I'm not trying to arrange your marriage here. I'm just asking you to meet the guy."

"OK." I shrug. "I'll think about it."

She smiles mischievously and stares at the dress in my hand. "You're right. That dress is perfect."

I look at her and my brows gather. "He's going to be at the wedding, isn't he?"

"Who?" Renée furrows her brow. Then lets out a nervous chuckle. "What?"

I hang the dress back on the rack.

"No. Try it." She grabs the dress and shoves it at me. "He happens to be friends with Lauren and Andrew. We all went to school together. What do you want me to do? Call Lauren and tell her to uninvite her friend because you don't want to meet him?"

"No. It's just embarrassing. I don't want to go and have some stranger thinking everyone is intervening to fix us up."

"Nobody thinks that. He doesn't even know. Lauren doesn't think you'll like him. It's only *me* trying to fix you up."

"That's somehow worse."

"What?"

"Yeah. If Lauren doesn't think I'll like him, what makes *you* think I will?"

"I know you better. You're my sister. I'm telling you, this is *the* guy. I won't force you to meet him. But we'll all be at the same place at the same time. If you want to avoid him like the plague, that's on you."

* * *

The chapel is filled with flowers. Bunched at the end of every pew are bouquets of white roses and pink peonies. The floral aroma fills the church. At the altar more flowers arch around the priest. The same priest who baptized Lauren three decades ago. Light pours in through the stained-glass windows, shining down on the smiling groom and the men beside him. I close my eyes, listening to the piano melody of the bridal chorus. Mom gently squeezes my hand.

I blink my eyes open as Renée walks up the aisle. Her face smiling and serene. Behind her a little girl with flowers in her hair sprinkles petals from a tiny white basket. When the melody changes, we rise to our feet. On her father's arm, Lauren seems to float up the aisle. Her beaded, glittering veil flows behind her. I bite my lip. *She looks so happy.* Tears wet my eyes.

When we sit I dab at the tears on my cheeks, and Mom hands me a tissue. "Are you OK?" she whispers. I nod and she gives my hand another gentle squeeze. *I am OK.* I let out a deep breath. If this were a year ago, I would have been crying hysterically in the bathroom, missing the ceremony. I'd have been panicking about not being married. Jealous that this beautiful wedding wasn't for me. But today, I'm happy. I smile looking up at Lauren as her groom lifts the veil from her smiling face. *I'm happy that she's happy.*

I feel eyes on me, and I look from the altar toward the pews ahead, catching his profile before his face turns forward. *Who's that?* I stare at the stranger's back, searching his frame for something familiar. Joe nudges me with his elbow, looking straight ahead at the arch of flowers. There's a smirk on his face. I shift in my seat and straighten the hem of my blue dress before looking ahead at the bride and groom. We cheer as they kiss, then clap when they walk hand in hand down the aisle. I feel a tingle at the back of my neck as Lauren and Andrew walk through the bright open doors of the church. My posture grows rigid. *Someone's watching me.*

Outside the church Mom, Joe, and I wait for Renée. We watch as she smiles standing beside Lauren for the wedding photos.

"You have confetti in your hair." I pick at the small pink pieces of paper on Joe's head.

"You have an admirer." Joe smiles and lifts his brows.

"Don't be annoying." I punch his arm playfully.

"Ruthie, don't hit Joe." Mom shoots me a look. "He's right. I saw someone looking at you during the ceremony too." She turns to Joe. "Do you know who that was?"

"That's Henry. That's who Renée is trying to hook Ruthie up with." Joe chuckles.

"So *that's* Henry," Mom says in a way that tells me she's been colluding with Renée. "Handsome guy," she says, her tone too casual. She looks away.

"Stop," I say. "I already told Renée I'd *think* about it."

"Think about what?" Renée asks as she walks up behind me.

"Henry likes your sister," Joe tells her.

"He does?" Renée's brows shoot up and she claps. "This is perfect."

"Uh . . . hello?" I scrunch my brows together. "I didn't say I like him back. I haven't even met the guy, and already I feel like all of you are in cahoots to marry me off."

"Don't you want to get married?" Mom asks, her brows drawn together, her expression worried, like I'll surely shrivel up and die if I don't.

"Maybe." I shrug. "Maybe not. I'm not really worried about it. If I meet someone, awesome. And if I don't, awesome." I shake my head. "You guys need to calm down. I'll meet you at the reception."

"Come on, Ruthie. Don't leave," Renée says.

"I came with you," says Mom.

"I'm ready to go. I'll see you guys at the reception." I walk toward my car in the parking lot.

The hotel ballroom looks like it's been taken straight from the page of a bridal magazine. Overhead, a grand crystal chandelier hangs, softly illuminating the champagne-colored walls. More flowers. Flowers and leaves spill over the top of glass and gold vases at every table and on columns throughout. Illuminated on the sparkling white dance floor are the couple's initials surrounded by cocktail tables. Tuna tartare and tiny shrimp cocktails are passed on silver trays as Nat King Cole coos in the background, just audible over the chatter. It smells like a fancy restaurant and flowers.

At the bar, I'm next in line when I feel the tingle at the back of my neck again. I ignore it and step forward as the man in front of me walks away with his beer. I order a glass of merlot and bite at my lip. *I'm being chary. It's nothing.* I rub at the back of my neck, then slowly turn my head to look behind me. He looks up with a crooked smile. Biting at the corner of his lip. His dark brown eyes intense. My breath catches in my throat and my face flushes. I whip my head back around just as the bartender finishes pouring. "Thank you." I grab the glass and hurry toward the place card table.

I find my name at table five, then find myself continuing to stare at the name cards. *Where's Henry sitting?* I search for his name. *Henry, what's your last name?*

"Did you find your seat?" he asks, his voice low and smooth.

I bite my lip and feel goose bumps tickle my forearms. I turn around slowly to face him. His skin is a rich, deep gingerbread color. His dark eyes sparkle despite their intensity.

"Uh, yeah. Mm-hmm." I nod.

"What table are you at?"

"Five." I hold my card up.

"Ruth?" He squints slightly as he reads my name.

"Ruthie." I smile weakly.

"Nice to meet you. I'm Henry." He holds up his card. "Table six." His silvery-gray suit fits him perfectly. Tailored to his broad shoulders and muscular arms.

"Well, very nice to meet you, Henry." I look down. "I'm going to go find the rest of my party."

I turn and walk away. Outside, the air is crisp and I inhale deeply. The sun has begun to set, and the sky is orangey pink. Joe's car pulls up to the valet stand, and I straighten my posture. Then smile and lift my wineglass as they all step out of the car.

"Finally. You made it," I say as Mom approaches.

"You know how Joe drives." Mom rolls her eyes and lets out a chuckle.

"I have three kids," Joe says as he slams the passenger door behind Renée.

"But they're not with us tonight." Renée laughs.

"Where are we sitting?" Mom asks.

"Table five." I hand her my place card. "The rest of your cards are inside. I'm sorry I didn't grab them." I shake my head. "I got distracted."

Inside, I follow them back up to the place card table. I take a sip of wine as they search. Clutching at my elbow, I shift my weight and take another sip, watching as Renée turns around holding their three cards.

"Got 'em. Do you wanna go sit?" Renée asks.

"I'm gonna head to the bar," Joe answers.

"I'll come with you," says Renée.

"Get me a glass of wine," Mom says to Renée, then turns to me. "I'm gonna go sit." She winks. *What are you winking about?*

"Hey, Joe . . . Renée. Wait up." Henry's voice comes from behind me.

"Hey, man." Joe looks at him, then smirks at me with a knowing expression. *He's dead. I have to kill my brother-in-law now.* I pinch my lips together.

"Hi, Henry." Renée flashes a toothy grin over my shoulder. Then her eyes dart from him to mine. "Have you met my sister, Ruthie?" She grabs my shoulder and turns me around to face him.

"I did. Just briefly." He clears his throat. "I didn't know you had a sister."

"I do." Renée's voice is overenthusiastic. "And she's single."

I jab my elbow into her ribs, but she doesn't flinch. *I did it too softly.* My jaw clenches. "She's kidding." I feel my face turn bright red.

"About you being her sister? Or about being single?" Joe chortles.

I laugh nervously. "Both." I narrow my eyes at him, then Renée.

Joe shrugs it off, then turns to Henry again. "We're gonna head up to the bar to get drinks. Do you wanna come?" Joe asks, then looks down at the full drink in Henry's hand.

"I'm good." Henry lifts his glass.

"Great. You can keep Ruthie company," Renée says, then grabs Joe's hand and tugs him toward the bar.

My heart skips and I bite my lip. Renée smiles at him, then stretches her mouth into an even wider grin at me. As if to say, *Haha, sucker. I knew you'd like him.* I imagine her singing in her head, *Ruthie and Henry sitting in a tree . . .*

"So, uh." Henry shoves his free hand into his pocket and lowers his eyes. "Do you know the bride or the groom?"

"The bride."

"I should have guessed that since Renée's a bridesmaid." His cheeks seem to flush.

Is he nervous? I take a sip of wine, then ask, "Who do you know?"

"I'm friends with both." He shrugs.

"So, you're an engineer too?"

"Uh, yeah. Civil." He smiles shyly.

"Mm." I nod and swallow.

"What do you do?" He lifts his eyes and gazes into mine.

"I own an insurance agency in Newport." I lift my chin and flip my hair back.

"Really?" He lifts his brows and nods slowly. "That's impressive. What kind of insurance?"

"Home, auto, commercial, you name it." I smile.

"Do you have a card? I've been thinking about changing carriers."

"Uh, yeah." I nod, then dig through my clutch and hand him a card.

He takes it and places it in the breast pocket of his jacket. Then pats his chest over where the card is, as if to reassure himself. The music fades and the sound of the DJ's voice comes loud over the speakers calling us to our tables for dinner service. I offer Henry a thin smile, then walk to my seat.

The lights dim and a spotlight shines on the glossy wood floor in front of the double doors. Everyone stands. The sound of cheers is so loud that the DJ is barely audible as he announces the bride and groom's grand entrance. As they promenade onto the sparkling dance floor, the roar of cheers and applause recedes. Giving way to hushed "ohs" and "aws." I smile watching as Andrew twirls and dips Lauren. Her dress shimmers under the spotlight.

Mom leans sideways and whispers into my ear, "If you don't get married, can I throw you a birthday party here?"

I lift a brow and dip my chin. "Like a fake wedding?" I shake my head. "No thanks, Mom." The light turns pink, and a mirrored ball spins overhead, bathing the room in glittering light. *But I would look good in a puffy princess dress.* I lean into Mom's ear. "Never mind. Let's do it. . . . It'll be like a quinceañera."

Mom nods and laughs, then Renée elbows me.

"What's so funny?" Renée asks, seeing Mom laughing.

"Mom's throwing me a quinceañera since I'm not getting married."

Renée's face scrunches up. "What about Henry?"

"What *about* Henry?" I repeat.

"I thought you liked him."

"And?"

"Well, if you like him, then . . ."

"Then *what*? I have to marry him?" I smile at her, her face still scrunched up, perplexed. "I'm happy, Renée. I have everything I need." I put my arm around her shoulder and squeeze her.

When the bride and groom walk off the dance floor, the lights grow brighter. As we sit down, a server approaches our table with a bottle of champagne. I put my hand up and shake my head to stop my glass from being filled.

"You don't want champagne?" Renée's brows dart up. "And you've hardly touched your wine. What's wrong?"

"I told you." My lips curl into another smile. "I'm really happy. I just don't feel like drinking that much these days." I shrug.

"I guess I haven't seen you happy in so long I forgot what it looked like," Renée says, and stares into my face. "Your skin looks great. You can hardly see your wrinkles." She laughs.

"Rude!" I slap her thigh, then straighten my posture and toss my hair over my shoulder playfully. "But thank you for the backhanded compliment." I nod. "My skin does look good."

By the end of the night, my feet ache from the tall strappy sandals I wore with my new blue dress. *Sam would be proud.* I stand, then look around the ballroom one last time. I watch as other tired-looking guests yawn and stretch. The flower girl is asleep, draped over her mother's chest, shoeless. I smile, then grab my clutch off the table and follow Mom out through the double doors of the exit.

"Hey!" Henry's voice comes from behind, and I turn around to see him jogging toward me. Mom and I both stop.

"You forgot your wedding favor." He hands me a mini bottle of champagne with Lauren and Andrew's wedding date scrolled on a ribbon tied around it.

"Thank you." I smile and nod. Then Mom winks at me and walks away toward the valet.

"You were going to leave without saying goodbye?" Henry asks with a sideways smile.

"I . . . I didn't see you. I figured you had left."

He shakes his head. "I was helping Andrew's dad load gifts into their car."

"Oh. Well, it was nice meeting you."

He stuffs his hands into his pockets and leans forward. "It was nice meeting you too. Can I give you a call?" He pulls one hand out of his pants pocket and pats at his chest.

"Yeah." I nod and bite at my lip.

He smiles broadly and I smile back. Then turn and walk toward the valet as the attendant opens the driver's-side door of my car. As soon as the door slams shut, Mom turns to me and grins. Wide eyed, she asks, "So how did it go?"

"We said goodbye." I buckle my seat belt.

"I know he likes you. I could tell. A mother knows."

"I like him too. But the important thing is, *I* like me." I shift into drive.